THE
Dragon's
DILEMMA

(Lochguard Highland Dragons #1)

Jessie Donovan

The Dragon's Dilemma
Copyright © 2015 Laura Hoak-Kagey
Mythical Lake Press, LLC
First Edition

Cover Art by Clarissa Yeo of Yocla Designs.

ISBN 13: 978-1942211310

Other Books by Jessie Donovan

Stonefire Dragons
Sacrificed to the Dragon
Seducing the Dragon
Revealing the Dragons
Healed by the Dragon
Reawakening the Dragon
Loved by the Dragon
Surrendering to the Dragon
Cured by the Dragon
Aiding the Dragon (May 2017)

Lochguard Highland Dragons
The Dragon's Dilemma
The Dragon Guardian
The Dragon's Heart
The Dragon Warrior

Kelderan Runic Warriors
The Conquest
The Barren (Aug 2017)

Asylums for Magical Threats
Blaze of Secrets
Frozen Desires
Shadow of Temptation
Flare of Promise

Cascade Shifters
Convincing the Cougar
Reclaiming the Wolf
Cougar's First Christmas
Resisting the Cougar

CHAPTER ONE

Holly Anderson paid the taxi driver and turned toward the large stone and metal gates behind her. Looking up, she saw "Lochguard" spelled out in twisting metal, as well as some words written in a language she couldn't read.

The strange words only reminded her of where she was standing—at the entrance to the Scottish dragon-shifter clan lands.

Taking a deep breath, Holly willed her stomach to settle. She'd signed up for this. In exchange for trying to conceive a dragon-shifter's child, Clan Lochguard had given her a vial of dragon's blood. The money from the sale of that dragon's blood was funding her father's experimental cancer treatments.

All she had to do was spend the next six months sleeping with a dragon-shifter. If she didn't conceive, she could go home. If she did, then she would stay until the baby was born.

What was a minimum of six months of her life if it meant her father could live?

That's if you don't die giving birth to a half-dragon-shifter baby.

Readjusting the grip on her suitcase, Holly pushed aside the possibility. From everything she'd read, great scientific strides were being made when it came to the role dragon hormones played on a human's body. If she were lucky, there might even be a way to prevent her from dying in nine to fifteen months' time, depending on the date of conception.

This isn't work. Stop thinking about conception dates and birthing babies. After all, she might luck out and never conceive at all.

Holly moved toward the front entrance and took in the view of the loch off to the side. The dull color of the lake's surface was calm, with rugged hills and mountains framing it. Considering she was in the Scottish Highlands in November, she was just grateful that it wasn't raining.

She wondered if it was raining back in Aberdeen.

Thinking of home and her father brought tears to her eyes. He was recovering well from his first course of cancer treatments, but her father's health could decline at any moment. If only dragon's blood could cure cancer, then she wouldn't have to worry.

But since cancer was one of the illnesses dragon's blood couldn't cure, surely the Department of Dragon Affairs would grant her another few weeks to help take care of her father if she asked.

As the taxi backed down the drive, Holly turned around and flagged for the driver to come back. However, before she could barely raise a hand, a voice boomed from the right. "Lass, over here."

She turned toward the voice and a tall, blond man waved her over with a smile.

Between his wind-tousled hair, twinkling eyes, and his grin, the man was gorgeous.

Not only that, he'd distracted her from doing something daft. If Holly ran away before finishing her contract, she'd end up in jail. And then who would take care of her father?

The man motioned again. "Come, lass. I won't bite."

When he winked, some of Holly's nervousness faded. Despite the rumors of dragon-shifters being monsters, she'd followed the news stories over the last year and knew Lochguard was one of the good dragon clans. Rumors even said the Lochguard dragons and the local humans had once set up their own sacrifice system long before the British government had implemented one nationwide.

It was time to experience the dragon-shifters firsthand and learn the truth.

Pushing her shoulders back, Holly put on her take no-crap nurse expression and walked over to the dragonman. When she was close enough, she asked, "Who are you?"

The man grinned wider. "I'm glad to see you're not afraid of me, lass. That makes all of this a lot easier."

Before she could stop herself, Holly blurted, "Are you really a dragon-shifter?"

The dragonman laughed. "Aye, I am. I'm the clan leader, in fact. The name's Finn. What's yours?"

The easygoing man didn't match the gruff picture she'd conjured up inside her head over the past few weeks.

Still, dragons liked strength, or so her Department of Dragon Affairs counselor had advised her. Her past decade spent as a maternity nurse would serve her well—if she could handle frantic fathers and mothers during labor, she could handle anything. "You're not a very good clan leader if you don't know my name."

Finn chuckled. "I was trying to be polite, Holly." He lowered his voice to a whisper. "Some say we're monsters that eat bairns for breakfast. I was just trying to assure you we can be friendly."

Confident the smiling man wouldn't hurt her for questioning him, she stated, "You could be acting."

"I think my mate is going to like you."

At the mention of the word "mate," Holly's confidence slipped a fraction. After all, she'd soon be having sex with a dragon-shifter to try to conceive a child. That was the price all sacrifices had to pay.

And there was always a small chance she turned out to be the dragon-shifter's true mate. If that happened, she might never be able to see her father again. Dragons were notoriously possessive. She didn't think they'd let a mate go once they found one.

Finn's voice interrupted her thoughts. "Let me take that suitcase, Holly. The sooner we get you to my place, the sooner we can settle you in and answer some of your questions."

Finn put out a hand and she passed the case over. She murmured, "Thank you."

"Considering that you're helping my clan more than you know, the least I can do is carry a bag."

She eyed the tall dragonman. "You don't have to comfort me. I know what I volunteered to do."

Finn raised a blond eyebrow. "You looked about ready to bolt or cry a few minutes ago. I think a little kindness wouldn't hurt."

He was right, not that she would admit to it. After all, she was supposed to be strong.

Holly motioned toward the gates. "How about we go so you can give me the spiel and then let me meet my dragonman?"

The dragonman's smile faded. "So you're giving orders to me now, aye?"

Even though Holly was human, she still sensed the dominance and strength in his voice. She could apologize and try to hide her true self, but that would be too tiring to keep up long term. Instead, she tilted her head. "I'm used to giving orders. In my experience, as soon as a woman goes into labor, her other half goes crazy. If I don't take charge, it could put the mother's life as well as the child's in danger. I'm sure you've read my file and should know what to expect."

The corner of Finn's mouth ticked up. "Aye, I have. But I like to test the waters with potential clan members."

"I'm not—"

Finn cut her off. "Give it time, lass. You may well become one in the long run."

Without another word, Finn started walking. Since he was at least eight inches taller than her, she had to half-jog to catch up to him. However, before she could reply, another tall, muscled dragonman approached. He still had the soft face of late adolescence and couldn't be more than twenty.

The younger dragon-shifter motioned a thumb behind him. "Archie and Cal are at it again. If you don't break it up, they might shift and start dropping each other's cattle for the second time this week."

Finn sighed. "I should assign them a full-time babysitter."

The younger man grinned. "You tried that, but my grandfather escaped, as you'll remember."

"That's because he's a sneaky bastard." Finn looked to Holly. "This is Jamie MacAllister. He'll take you to my mate, Arabella. She can help you get settled before you meet Fergus."

"Who's Fergus?" Holly asked, even though she had a feeling she knew.

Finn answered, "Fergus MacKenzie is my cousin, but he's also your assigned dragonman."

Of course she'd be given the cousin of the clan leader. After all, Holly was the first human sacrifice on Lochguard in over a decade. They'd want to keep tabs on her.

Holly didn't like it, but since she had yet to meet this Fergus, she wouldn't judge him beforehand. For all she knew, Fergus MacKenzie might be a shy, quiet copy of his cousin.

Maybe.

Not sure what else to do, Holly nodded. After giving a few more orders, Finn left to address the problem and Jamie smiled down at her. "There's never a dull moment here, lass. Welcome to Lochguard."

Holly wasn't sure if that was a warning or a welcome.

~ ~ ~

Fraser MacKenzie watched his twin brother from the kitchen. His brother, Fergus, was due to meet his human sacrifice in the next few hours and instead of celebrating his last hours of freedom, Fergus was doing paperwork.

Sometimes, Fraser wondered how they were related at all.

Taking aim, he lobbed an ice cube across the room. It bounced off his brother's cheek and Fraser shouted, "Goal."

Frowning, Fergus glanced over. "Don't you have a hole to dig? Or, maybe, some nails to pound?"

Fraser shrugged a shoulder and inched his fingers toward another ice cube. "I finished work early. After all, it's not every day your twin meets the possible mother of his child."

As Fraser picked up his second ice cube, his mother's voice boomed from behind him. "Put it down, Fraser Moore MacKenzie. I won't have you breaking something if you miss."

He looked at his mother and raised his brows. "I never miss."

Clicking her tongue, his mother, Lorna, moved toward the refrigerator. "Stop lying to me, lad. You missed a step and now have the scar near your eye to prove it."

Fraser resisted the urge to touch his scar. "That was because my sister distracted me." He placed a hand over his heart. "I was just looking out for the wee lass."

Lorna rolled her eyes. "Faye was sixteen at the time and you were too busy glaring at one of the males."

"He was trouble. Faye deserved better," Fraser replied.

Fergus looked up from his paperwork. "Where is Faye?"

Lorna waved a hand. "The same as every day. She leaves early in the morning and I don't see her again until evening."

Fraser sobered up. "I wish she'd let us help her. Does anyone know if she can fly again yet?"

His younger sister, Faye, had been shot out of the sky by an electrical blast nearly two months earlier while in dragon form and her wing had been severely damaged. While she was no longer in a wheelchair, the doctors weren't sure if Faye would ever fly again.

His mother turned toward him. "I trust Arabella to help her. Faye will come to us when she's ready."

Jumping on the chance to lighten the mood again, Fraser tossed the ice cube into the sink and added, "I'm more worried about Fergus right now anyway. Who spends their last few hours of freedom cooped up inside? Even if he doesn't want to go drinking, he could at least go for a flight."

Fergus lifted the papers in his hand. "For your information, this is all of the new procedures and suggestions from the Department of Dragon Affairs. Finn worked hard to make Lochguard one of the trial clans for these new rules, and I'm not about to fuck it up." Lorna clicked her tongue and Fergus added, "Sorry, Mum."

Lorna leaned against the kitchen counter. "I still applaud you for what you're doing, Fergus. After the last fifteen years of near-isolation, the clan desperately needs some new blood."

Fergus shrugged a shoulder. "It's not a guarantee. Besides, how could I pass up the chance to help our cousin?"

Fraser rolled his eyes. "Right, you're being all noble when I know for a fact you just want to, er," he looked to his mum and back to Fergus, "sleep with a human lass."

"No one around here has stirred a mate-claim frenzy and I'm not about to look in the other clans. I'm needed here," Fergus replied. "A human sacrifice is my only other chance."

"And what if she's not your true mate, brother? Then what?" Fraser asked.

"I'll still try to win her over. If she gives me a child, I want to try to convince the human to stay."

Lorna spoke up. "Her father's ill, Fergus. Let's see how things go before you start planning the human's future." Lorna looked to Fraser. "Let's just hope she has spirit. I can handle anything but fear."

Fraser answered, "If Finn picked her out, then we should trust that he chose a good one."

"You're right, son," Lorna answered. She waved toward the living room. "Now, go get that ice cube."

"Fergus is closer. He could just toss it over."

Fergus looked back at his stack of papers. "Get it yourself."

With a sigh, Fraser moved toward the living room. "You were always a lazy sod."

Fergus looked up. "Takes one to know one. But at least this lazy sod is about to get his own cottage."

THE DRAGON'S DILEMMA

Lorna's voice drifted into the living room. "It's about time. One down, two more to go."

Fraser scooped up the ice cube and faced his mother. "Don't worry, Mum. You'll always have me. If I'm lucky, I won't have a mate until I'm fifty."

Fergus chimed in. "She'll kick you out on your arse before then."

"I'm feeling the love, brother."

Fergus looked up with a grin. "Someone has to love you, you unlovable bastard."

Tossing the ice cube into the sink, Fraser dried his hands. "You know you'll miss me, Fergus. I give it a week and then you'll be begging for my company."

"We'll see, Fraser. If I'm lucky, I'll be spending a week in my sacrifice's bed."

The thought of not seeing his twin every day did something strange to his heart. Brushing past it, Fraser headed toward the door. "As much as I'd love to stay and watch you read boring protocol, I'm going to watch some paint dry instead."

Fergus raised an auburn eyebrow. "What happened to spending time with your brother?"

"I never said anything about spending time with you. I wanted to show you a good time. The offer's still open if you're interested."

Shaking his head, Fergus answered, "Your good times always result in us waking up in strange places and not remembering the night before. I think I'll stay here."

Fraser shrugged. "Your loss." He looked to his mum. "I'll be home for dinner, don't worry."

Lorna answered. "You'd better be. Finn wants us to have a quiet dinner with Holly and help ease her into her new life here."

"Quiet is a bit of a stretch."

Lorna picked up an apple and tossed it at his head. Once he caught it, she answered, "Just get your arse home on time."

Fraser winked. "I'll try my best, but you know how the lasses love me."

Not wanting to hear his mother's lecture about settling down for the hundredth time, Fraser ducked out the front door.

While the human wouldn't be over to their house until dinnertime, she was due to arrive on Lochguard at any moment. He had known that Fergus wouldn't want to go out, but asking gave Fraser the perfect cover and no one would suspect what he was about to do.

It was time to spy on his brother's future female and make sure she was worthy of a MacKenzie.

~~~

Holly kept her thoughts to herself for the duration of the walk to Finn's cottage. Not like she'd had a chance to say anything anyway.

Jamie MacAllister liked to talk. A lot.

Jamie gestured to the left. "Over there is the training area for the wee ones. I wouldn't go there until you've been presented to the clan." He glanced at her. "Dragon-shifter parents are a bit protective, you see."

She nodded and opened her mouth, but Jamie beat her to it. "This here is the main living area. Finn's cottage is straight ahead. You can tell it's his by the overgrown flowers and shrubs in the front." He lowered his voice. "Neither Finn nor his mate like gardening. To be honest, the wildness suits them."

"If you say so," she murmured.

18

Jamie carried on as if she hadn't spoken. "Most of these cottages have been here for over two hundred years." He glanced down at her. "Unlike the Scottish clan near Stirling, we survived the Jacobite rising of the 18th century just fine."

Since she'd had a history lesson during her DDA counseling sessions, Holly already knew there had once been two Scottish dragon clans. But she decided it was easier to let Jamie keep talking so she wouldn't have to try and be social or polite.

Jamie opened his mouth to say something else when the door to Finn's cottage opened. A tall dragonwoman with dark hair stood there. The scar across her face and the healed burn on one side of the woman's neck told Holly it was Arabella MacLeod. Like most of Great Britain, Holly had watched the dragonwoman's interview on the BBC several months earlier.

Arabella frowned. "Jamie, stop talking the poor human's ear off. She doesn't care about the Jacobite rising or how old the cottages are."

Jamie straightened his shoulders. "She might."

Arabella looked to Holly. "Do you care?"

The dragonwoman's voice threaded with dominance. While Holly had thought Arabella brave for recounting her story on national television, she had even more strength in person. "Not really." Jamie's face fell so she added, "But I did like learning where the different areas were situated. I now know not to stray toward the children's area until I'm more settled."

Jamie beamed, but Arabella rolled her eyes. "Please don't feed his ego. If there's one thing you'll learn quickly, it's that dragon-shifter males think they are able to move the sun if they merely try hard enough."

Jamie replied, "That's not fair, Ara. Your mate is the worst out of us all."

Arabella waved a hand. "Let's not argue about Finn." Arabella looked back to Holly. "I know what it's like to come to the clan as an outsider. I bet you could use some tea and cake."

Holly blinked. "Dragon-shifters eat tea and cake?"

The corner of Arabella's mouth ticked up. "Of course. It's the best way to serve ground-up human babies."

Holly laughed. "Nice try, but the DDA staff assured me at least twenty times that dragon-shifters don't eat humans. At least, not since the middle ages."

Even from a few feet away, Holly saw Arabella's pupils flash to slits and back. *She must be talking with her dragon. I wonder what that's like.*

But Holly was the stranger here and didn't know how things operated on Lochguard. So far, everyone seemed friendly, yet it could all be an act. There were stories about sacrifices being treated poorly and sometimes even abused. As far as Holly knew, Lochguard didn't do that, but she wanted more time to draw her own conclusions.

Arabella looked to Jamie. "You can go, Jamie."

With a nod, the young dragonman smiled at Holly and went back the way they'd come.

Arabella stepped to the side. "Come. There's a lot to do before you meet Fergus."

Holly sobered at the name of the unknown dragonman she'd soon be sleeping with. "When will that be?"

Arabella studied her a second before replying, "In a few hours. Finn has some things to go over with you first." The dragonwoman paused and then added, "Fergus can sometimes be irritating, especially when he's paired with his twin brother, but he's a good male. You shouldn't be afraid of him."

"That's good to know."

20

Arabella raised an eyebrow. "So you had been a little afraid?"

Holly shrugged. "Of course. A few paragraphs on his history and occupation as an analyst hardly tells me much about him."

"You're honest. I like that." Arabella motioned inside. "Now, come in before the whole clan comes out to gawk at you."

She frowned. "Why would they gawk at me?"

Arabella met her eyes. "Because you're the first human sacrifice to set foot on Lochguard in over fifteen years."

CHAPTER TWO

Fraser peeked around one of the cottage's walls just as a short, dark-haired female disappear into Finn and Arabella's home. When the door shut behind her, he cursed. He'd just missed her.

His dragon spoke up. *We can spy on her from one of the windows. Arabella won't be happy if she finds us spying.*

Then make sure she doesn't find out. I want to see this human meant for our brother.

Okay, but if Arabella notices us, we're shifting. Maybe your innocent dragon eyes can sway her.

His beast snorted. *Maybe if we were a wee one. Just don't get caught.*

We almost never get caught.

Before his dragon could reply, Fraser scanned the area. The best way to spy on his cousin-in-law and the human was to climb the rear wall and hide in the overgrown garden.

Fraser moved from one cottage to another, grateful it was the middle of the day. Almost everyone would be at work and that meant fewer witnesses.

He reached the seven-foot tall wall at the rear of Finn's place. His cousin only turned on surveillance cameras in the evening or when no one was home, so Fraser gripped the top of the wall, pulled himself up, and hopped down the other side.

Keeping crouched low, he spotted the rear kitchen window. Through the tall grass he saw Arabella's dark hair and scarred face talking whilst doing something over the sink.

Fraser remained still until Arabella turned away.

Slinking through the grass and wild rosebushes, he was a foot from the window before a thorn on one of the rosebushes snagged his arm. Despite the sting, Fraser crept to the window. Inching up until he could peek inside, he noticed both Arabella and the unknown female sitting at the kitchen table.

Unfortunately, all he could see was the back of the female's head. Her hair was pinned into a bun at the base of her neck and she wore a dark red jumper.

His dragon growled. *That's not enough. I want to see her face. Why do you care?*

I like females. I want to see her face.

It was a bit of an odd request, but Fraser pushed the doubt aside. He was as anxious to see his brother's new sacrifice as his dragon was.

Arabella stood up from the table and Fraser ducked down. Plastering himself against the wall, no one should be able to see him even if they looked at the garden. After all, no one had a reason to look below the window.

The click of the kettle told him Arabella would move to the other counter, away from the window. Fraser peeked inside again, but Arabella was nowhere to be seen.

The rear glass sliding door opened and Fraser looked over. Arabella stood with her arms crossed over her chest and her brows raised. "Just wait until I tell Finn you've been spying on me."

Fraser stood up and shrugged. "I wasn't spying on you. I'm curious about the sacrifice. After all, there hasn't been one on Lochguard since I was a teenager."

Arabella shrugged. "That's still spying."

He straightened his shoulders. "I just want to protect my brother."

Arabella studied him a second and then uncrossed her arms. "Promise me you'll clean up the garden and I'll introduce you."

Fraser eyed the garden, with its knee-high grass and impressive collection of weeds. "That is going to take me days."

Arabella smiled. "Exactly."

He sighed. "I don't really have a choice, do I?"

"No, not really."

His dragon spoke up again. *Do it. You enjoy working with your hands anyway. Besides, we can plant some giant hogweed. Finn and Ara won't recognize it and might touch it. Then they'll get a rash.*

Fraser laughed inside his head. *You're bloody devious, dragon.*

I know.

Fraser nodded. "Fine, it's a deal. Now, introduce me to the lass."

"Then come on."

Arabella went back inside the cottage and Fraser followed.

The instant he stepped foot into the kitchen, the human turned her head.

Despite her hair being pulled back from her face and the lack of a smile, she was pretty with a round face and small nose. Her eyes were curious yet intelligent. Their light brown color made him think of a jar of dark-colored honey.

Fraser had always had a thing for brunettes, but when combined with the color of her eyes, Holly was one of the most beautiful lasses he'd ever seen.

Before he could wonder where that thought had come from, his beast growled. *Say something. I want to hear her voice.*

24

Fraser was careful to keep his confusion from showing on his face. *Since when do you care about voices?*

Just do it. We need to question her for Fergus anyway.

Fraser grinned and put out a hand. "What's your name, bonny lass?"

Arabella rolled her eyes. "Excuse my mate's cousin. He's incorrigible."

"I'm just trying to welcome our guest." He looked back to the human. "All I want is your name, or I'll just have to refer to you as honey."

A flicker of amusement danced in the human's eyes. "And why is that?"

"Because your eyes remind me of dark-colored honey. I bet you're secretly sweet as well."

Arabella opened her mouth, but the human beat her to it. "More like I use honey to lure you in and then kick you in the bollocks."

"A lass with fire. I can appreciate that." Fraser leaned closer. "So, what's your name, honey?"

"Call me that again, *ruadh*. I dare you."

Fraser lightly brushed his hair. "It's more auburn than red, honey."

Holly smiled. "And here I thought dragon-shifters weren't self-conscious."

"Who said I was?" Fraser rustled his hair and tossed his head. "Many a lass envies these luscious locks."

Before the lass could make a reply, Arabella stepped between them. "I'm not sure how much more I can take of this. Fraser, this is Holly. Holly, this is Fraser MacKenzie, twin brother to your assigned dragonman, Fergus."

Fraser winked. "At least I was close, guessing your name started with an H."

Instead of a witty reply, Holly's face and eyes turned neutral. "Mr. MacKenzie."

He barely resisted frowning at the change in her demeanor. "There's no need to go formal on me, lass. Fraser is fine."

Holly looked to Arabella. "I've changed my mind about the tea. Is it all right if I unpack and freshen up before Finn returns?"

Arabella gave her a puzzled look. "Sure. You'll be staying with us for the first few nights, so I'll show you to your room." Arabella moved her gaze to Fraser. "I held up my end of the deal. Go start on the garden."

Fraser did frown at that. "Today?"

Arabella raised an eyebrow. "If you have time to spy on us, then you clearly have time to clean up the garden."

His dragon chimed in. *I want to do the work.*

Why?

I'll explain later, when Arabella isn't watching us.

Fraser and his dragon had always been open with one another. Between Holly's and his dragon's behavior, Fraser wondered what the hell was going on.

Keeping a smile pasted on his face so as to not stir Arabella's curiosity, Fraser nodded. "Aye, I'll do it. But you can't complain about what I do with it."

Arabella waved a hand. "Fine. Go make yourself useful."

He sighed. "I miss the days when we were conspiring on how to get back at Finn."

Arabella cracked a smile. "Oh, we'll have plenty of time for that in the future. Right now, I'm just trying to keep my food down. Finn's hellspawn likes to make my life uncomfortable. So far, being pregnant is one of my least favorite things in the world."

"Said with such love, cousin."

Arabella swatted his arm. "Go outside before I decide to kick your arse."

Fraser winked. "Anything for my cousin." He looked back to Holly and nodded. "I'll see you tonight at dinner, Holly. Just know that I'm the more mature one in the family, so be prepared. It will be an interesting night for sure."

Arabella rolled her eyes, but before she could castigate him, Fraser fled out the back door. As he surveyed the wildness, he decided to do the work but in his own special way, complete with inappropriate hedge sculptures and the ugliest garden gnomes he could find.

Fraser began pulling out some weeds when his dragon spoke up. *Maybe we should spy on the human some more.*

I don't think so. Cleaning up the garden is going to take us a few days. I don't need any more extra work. We'll never have the chance to sneak away and have fun if the chores pile up.

But I want to know why she stopped flirting.

I hardly call that flirting, dragon.

She shouldn't be cold with us.

Fraser stopped pulling a weed and stilled. *And why is that?*

She should always smile with us. She will be ours soon.

Fraser's heart skipped a beat. *No, she's Fergus's sacrifice, not ours. I thought neither you nor I wanted to settle down.*

That was before Holly and her honey-colored eyes.

Bloody hell, it couldn't be true. *Tell me you're joking. She can never be ours.*

His beast growled. *She will be. Get used to the idea. I will allow her some time to settle in. But after that, I'm going after her.*

Fraser tossed aside the weed in his hand and fell back on his bum. Looking up at the window for the spare bedroom Holly would most likely use, a sense of panic came over him. As much as he enjoyed teasing the lass, his dragon had just stolen Fraser's future from him.

Apparently, if his dragon was correct, Holly was his true mate.

He resisted telling his dragon to stuff it. As long as Fraser didn't kiss Holly, he could keep away from her. Fergus could have his sacrifice and all could be well with the clan.

Fraser might not have studied the new protocols and guidelines like his brother, but there was one thing that hadn't changed—if Holly violated the terms of the sacrifice contract, she would go to prison.

And who the hell knew what Finn would do to him.

Standing up, Fraser made a decision. No matter what his dragon threw at him, he would resist the human female. The only way to do that was to keep his distance. He'd just have to think of a good excuse to get out of dinner with his family.

His beast roared inside his head, but Fraser stuffed him into a mental maze. For once, Fraser would deny his dragon.

After all, the last time Fraser had stolen a lass from Fergus, his brother had stopped talking to him for five weeks. If he did it again, Fraser had no idea what would happen. Not to mention there would be hell to pay with Finn. Screwing up Holly's term on Lochguard might endanger the possibility of future sacrifices.

And Lochguard desperately needed the new blood. Unlike Stonefire, they hadn't won over any special privileges to mate any human female they wished.

Right, then. As Fraser went back to work pulling weeds, he thought of every reason why he didn't want a mate.

He'd lose his freedom, for one. And the thought of being a father in less than a year scared the living shit out of him. He might work as an architect and help out with construction, but he was the farthest thing from a responsible adult. He wasn't about to change for a bloody female, no matter how sweet her eyes.

Yes, all of those reasons would help him stay away from the lass. On top of that, his special closeness with his twin was far more important than having a true mate.

Or, at least, that was what Fraser tried to convince himself as he went back to pulling weeds.

~~~

The instant Fraser stepped outside, Arabella looked at Holly. "I know I give him a hard time, but all of the MacKenzies are wonderful. It's a good first step that you ignored his flirting, though. He's nearly as bad as my mate."

Holly couldn't remember the last time she'd had the urge to flirt with a man. For a brief second, she'd thought she was lucky and Fraser had been her assigned dragonman. Not just because he was handsome with auburn hair and dark blue eyes, but talking to him was easier than it was with most men.

It was just her luck that it was the twin of her assigned dragonman.

Forget about him, Holly. You can't have him.

Focusing on Arabella, Holly shrugged. "I wouldn't really call it flirting. He was being ridiculous, so I decided to follow suit."

Arabella's brown eyes studied hers and Holly resisted the urge to fidget. Ever since she'd stepped foot on Lochguard, everyone seemed to be watching her.

Arabella motioned toward the door on the far side of the kitchen. "Come, I'll settle you into your room. Finn texted me earlier and should be home within the hour, provided the two old coots don't throw tantrums this time and start destroying other people's property."

As she followed Arabella, Holly jumped on the distraction. "Finn mentioned something about Archie and Cal dropping cattle. What was he talking about?"

Arabella shrugged. "It's no big secret. The two dragonmen are in their seventies and have been accusing one another of stealing for over forty years. They have neighboring farms, so they're always yelling at each other. Sometimes, they shift into dragons, snatch their rival's cattle, and drop it into their yard."

"Why don't they just move farther apart from one another?"

The corner of Arabella's mouth ticked up. "Finn's been proposing it every day for more than a year. But the two stubborn males each claim their families have had their land for centuries and suggest the other should be the one to move."

As they ascended the stairs, Arabella paused a second to close her eyes and cover her mouth. Holly laid her suitcase down and went to the same step as the dragonwoman. "You look pale. Maybe you should sit down and I'll find something to help with the nausea."

Arabella took a few deep breaths and then removed her hand. "Nothing has worked so far. I've tried everything. The best I can do is push on until the baby is born."

Holly turned Arabella around and guided her down the stairs to the living room. The dragonwoman's pregnancy was just the distraction she needed. "You haven't let me have a go. Give me a chance."

Arabella sat down on the couch and rested her feet on an ottoman. "Why? You seem nice, but I don't know you."

Holly stood up tall. "I'm a trained and experienced midwife. I may not have worked with dragon-shifters, but I often handled some of the worst cases of morning sickness and difficult pregnancies during my time. I can help." Arabella remained silent, so Holly added, "I have no reason to poison you or harm you. If I don't serve out my time as a sacrifice, I'll be imprisoned and I won't be able to help my dad. He's ill, but recovering. I'm the only family he has. I can't risk leaving him alone."

Arabella's pupils flashed to slits and back. "I hear the truth in your words." She placed a hand over her still flat belly. "If you can help me tame the little beastie, then you'll have my gratitude and I'll owe you. And believe me, having the good graces of the clan leader's mate could come in handy."

Holly had glimpsed the wild garden out back, but she still asked, "Do you have anything useful growing out there? I noticed a small greenhouse in the back."

"You're observant." Arabella adjusted her position on the sofa. "There might be. But I couldn't tell a tea leaf from a strawberry leaf." Arabella paused, then added, "But just a warning—Fraser is out there and he flirts with almost anything female. If he bothers you, just send him in to me."

That certainly explained Fraser's behavior earlier. She wouldn't think twice about it again.

Holly motioned with her hands. "You stay there. I'll see what I can find in the kitchen first. If there's nothing there, then I'll check the greenhouse."

"You're ace, Holly Anderson. Once you're settled in, the surgery could use your help, provided the doctors approve of you. If you feel up to it, of course."

Arabella was referring to Holly's possible pregnancy.

Pushing aside that thought, she focused on the positive. "I've been reading up on the effects of dragon-shifter hormones on human women as well as some of the latest research. I'd love more than anything to work with the doctors and nurses here."

Arabella smiled. "Here a few hours and you've already got a grand plan. You remind me a bit of some of the humans back home."

"On Stonefire."

"Yes. But enough about me. I can't believe I'm being this chatty. It must be the midwife in you. Go see what you can cook up for me because the second I stand up again, I'm going to have to rush to the toilet. And considering I have a million things to do today, I'd rather not."

With a nod, Holly went into the kitchen and started looking through the cupboards.

For the first time since learning she'd been approved as a sacrifice, Holly wasn't dreading her time on Lochguard. Between crazy old men dropping cattle, to flirty redheads, to working in a dragon-shifter surgery, everything pointed to a decent stay.

Well, except for the fact she hadn't met Fergus yet.

Holly looked out of the kitchen window. Fraser had his hands on his lean hips as he surveyed the jungle that passed for a garden. Just looking at his broad shoulders and slightly wavy hair made her wonder what it'd be like to have him hold her close.

Blinking, Holly reminded herself she was assigned to Fergus, not Fraser.

Besides, they were twins. If she found one attractive, surely she'd find the other one attractive as well.

Yet their personalities could be vastly different for all she knew.

The Dragon's Dilemma

Rather than think about just how different Fergus could be from his brother, Holly went back to searching the cupboards. If she were lucky, she would find something in the kitchen to help Arabella. Otherwise, Holly would have to go outside and ignore Fraser, no matter how nice he might be.

Because if she talked with him again, she might start to like him. And a woman in her position didn't have that option.

Chapter Three

Fraser had just finished clearing a six-foot square patch of weeds when the glass sliding door opened. Glancing over his shoulder, he watched Holly march from the door to the wee greenhouse in the far corner. She didn't so much as look in his direction.

His dragon growled and forced his way out of the mental maze. *Why is she ignoring us? Follow her.*

No. I have work to do.

Fraser turned back around and moved to a new patch of weeds, but his beast roared so loudly that Fraser clapped his dirt-and-grass-covered hands over his ears. *What the hell are you doing, dragon? Stop throwing a fit.*

You won't win. I want to talk to Holly. Otherwise, I will do this all day long until you do.

His beast went back to roaring and snarling. It was the closest thing to what he'd call a dragon temper tantrum.

With a grunt, Fraser turned toward the greenhouse. The door was open, but because of his dragon's ruckus, he couldn't hear what Holly was doing. Fraser yelled inside his head, *Shut it, dragon. I'm going.*

His beast went silent before replying, *Good. Now, hurry.*

THE DRAGON'S DILEMMA

Muttering under his breath, Fraser took his time walking to the greenhouse. He might be doing what his dragon asked, but Fraser would do it on his own terms.

Before his beast could go into another tantrum, Fraser peeked his head inside the greenhouse. Holly was bent over a collection of peppermint.

The greenhouse covering was dirty, which made the light streaming inside dim, but dragon-shifters had keen eyesight. He could see every tendril of dark hair that had escaped her bun. One curved against her cheek while another cascaded down the soft skin of her neck.

Holly's hair went all the way down her back.

Studying her plain dark red jumper and black trousers, combined with her bun, he wondered what Holly looked like when she was carefree. He didn't like her reserved appearance. He bet underneath there was a wild, adventurous spirit dying to get out.

His dragon chimed in. *We will find out soon enough.*

His beast's words was like a slap in the face. *No, we won't. Fergus is the one who will bring her out of her shell.*

Fergus is too reserved around strange females. It will take him too long. We should do it.

Before he could reply, Holly's voice echoed inside the greenhouse. "Are you just going to stare at me or do you have something to say?"

Fraser cleared his throat and took a step inside the greenhouse. "I was just wondering if you needed any help, lass. That's all."

Holly met his gaze and raised an eyebrow. "I'm quite good with medicinal herbs and plants. You can go now."

His dragon growled. *She shouldn't be brusque with us.*

As Holly tucked one of the long, dark tendrils of hair on her cheek to behind her ear, Fraser closed his mouth to admire her ears. There were wee, dainty, and she had a single silver stud in her earlobe.

Holly's voice interrupted the study of her ear. "I know my hair is a mess, but it never stays put, especially when it's humid." She gestured toward his head. "Besides, you're not one to judge."

Fraser blinked. "Pardon?"

As she walked toward him, Fraser caught the scent of female and peppermint, which made his dragon hum. *She smells good. I bet she'll taste good, too.*

No tasting. Hush.

Holly raised a hand and plucked something from his hair. Lowering her find, she twirled a blade of grass between her fingers. "What happened? Did you dive headfirst into a grass pile?"

Fraser should grunt and walk away. The female was meant for his brother. He couldn't afford to flirt with her.

Yet before he could think twice about it, he smiled and murmured, "There's more than one way to get grass in your hair." He leaned closer and whispered, "Have you never tumbled in a field with a bloke before?"

~ ~ ~

Holly had tried her best to ignore Fraser MacKenzie, but after a full minute of him watching her, she had confronted him.

It didn't help that he looked handsome despite the dirt on his cheek or the grass in his hair. When he smiled at her, her heart rate kicked up.

THE DRAGON'S DILEMMA

The bloody dragonman was too attractive and charming for his own good.

Yet with his mouth mere inches from her face, it took everything she had to keep her gaze on his eyes instead of his lips.

Then he whispered, with his breath hot against her cheek, "Have you never tumbled in a field with a bloke before?" and images of her and Fraser rolling around in a field during the height of summer flooded her mind. Despite his auburn hair, she imagined his chest being as tan and toned as his forearms.

Maybe even his bum, since dragon-shifters didn't care about nakedness.

Fraser's pupils changed to slits and back before she could make her voice work again. "Honey, you need to be careful around dragon-shifters. Our senses tell us heaps about you."

Heat surged through Holly's body in embarrassment. She prevented herself from covering her cheeks with her hands. Instead, she cleared her throat and took a step back. "A gentleman wouldn't mention such things."

He leaned closer. "Aye, well, I'm not a gentlemen."

Fraser's flashing pupils didn't distract from the heat of his gaze. It was almost as if he were thinking of ways to devour her.

She finally glanced to his firm lips and imagined them kissing her neck, her shoulder, and finally her breasts. He would tease and torture her nipple before his hot, wet mouth finally licked and lapped between her thighs. No doubt, the dragonman would tease her until she begged for him to make her come.

Fraser growled and his expression turned hard. Pulling away, he retreated to the greenhouse door. "I have work to do."

Without another word, Fraser headed back out to the garden. Holly watched his back and arse as he walked away.

As his scent dissipated, Holly's heart rate slowed down a fraction.

Bloody hell. No man had ever affected her to such a degree. She'd been very close to kissing him. Thankfully, Fraser had had more sense and left before that happened.

Holly lightly patted her cheeks. "Get a grip, Holly. Dad's counting on you."

Busying herself with picking peppermint, Holly tried to imagine how her meeting with Fergus would go. After all, she needed to sleep with him in the end.

The memory of Fraser's lips a few inches from hers sent a rush of heat through her body again and Holly closed her eyes. To try and forget about the dragonman she couldn't have, Holly concentrated on former patients and their fear and joy over the years. The memory of smiling parents gazing at their newborns with love helped to calm her heart and her nerves.

"Right, then." With a nod, Holly went back to picking enough peppermint for some tea. She was done with fancying the forbidden. Holly would do her duty if it killed her.

With the peppermint in hand, Holly exited the greenhouse. Careful not to look over her shoulder to check out Fraser's broad back or intense blue eyes, she made a beeline for the glass sliding door and into the house.

As she washed the leaves, Arabella's voice rang out, "Are you almost ready with whatever you're making? Finn should be here soon."

Turning on the kettle, Holly peeked from the kitchen into the living room. "Give me three minutes. It took me a while to find what I needed."

The dragonwoman studied her intently. "Did Fraser give you any grief?"

Careful to keep her expression neutral, Holly shook her head. "No. He's pretty determined to weed the garden."

THE DRAGON'S DILEMMA

"For all his faults, once Fraser sets his mind on something, he'll go to ridiculous lengths to see it through. Next time you talk with him, ask him about Loch Ness."

She blinked. "Loch Ness?"

Arabella smiled. "Let's just say his prank to prove Nessie was real to the local humans didn't go as planned."

Despite her burning curiosity, Holly merely nodded. "I'll keep that in mind. I think I heard the kettle, so let me fix your tea."

Holly dashed into the kitchen and went to work tearing the peppermint leaves. After placing them in a teapot she'd found on the counter and pouring hot water over them, she leaned against the counter and crossed her arms while the tea steeped.

She may not know Arabella at all, but her words about Fraser focusing on what he wanted worried her. She was fairly certain that the near-kiss in the greenhouse had run both ways.

Holly only hoped Fraser hadn't set his sights on her. She couldn't imagine he would betray his twin like that.

Glancing to the clock, Holly willed Lochguard's clan leader to get home. The sooner he started drowning her in protocols and advice, the sooner she could focus entirely on her reason for being on Scottish dragon-shifter land.

Holly was Fergus's sacrifice. No matter how much her heart pounded or her skin tingled in Fraser's presence, she couldn't have him.

Nodding to herself, Holly made a decision. She would keep her distance from Fraser and be as civil, yet distant, as she could manage. She might even ask Fergus to take her to bed sooner than the week allocated for her to get to know the clan. Until recently, all of the sacrifices had only two days to adjust to their new homes. Holly didn't see why she couldn't do the same.

Yes, she would find a way to get Fergus alone and flirt with him.

Of course, she had to meet Fergus MacKenzie first. Looking to the clock again, Holly sighed. Three minutes had passed.

As she poured Arabella's tea, Holly took one last look out the kitchen window. But all she saw was Fraser climbing over the wall.

Good. The man clearly had some sense to put distance between them.

~~~

Fraser climbed over the rear garden wall, jumped down, and started running. He didn't trust himself around Holly. Especially with his dragon clawing at the latest maze he had constructed. For once, Fraser wished he would have listened to Fergus and Finn go over how they made elaborate mazes to keep their beasts occupied for hours.

Fraser was currently paying for always indulging his dragon.

Pushing his legs to run faster, he hoped the exercise would help to ease his dragon's nervous energy. The pacing inside his mind was driving Fraser crazy.

His beast finally broke free and huffed. *You had the chance to kiss her. You should've taken it. We could be fucking our mate right now.*

No. As I've said thirty times before, she's not ours.

His dragon snarled, *Yes, she is.*

Are you willing to risk the clan's future? Finn worked hard to get Lochguard back into the good graces of the DDA. If we kiss Holly, let alone fuck her, they may not trust us for another decade.

His dragon snarled. *Finn will find a way. We're family.*

THE DRAGON'S DILEMMA

Fraser gave a strangled laugh. *Family or not, the clan comes first. Even Arabella knows that.*

I want Holly. She will make us happy and give us a child.

Fraser couldn't stop his mind from picturing Holly smiling as he chased her through the forest, her long hair trailing behind her. As she turned, her slightly round belly was full with his child. *I won't risk the clan.*

You will regret this.

His dragon huffed and disappeared to the back of his mind.

Great. His beast was throwing another tantrum.

With a sigh, Fraser pushed his legs to move faster. He had only a few more minutes before reaching home and he needed to think of an excuse. And not just any excuse, but one that his mother would actually believe.

An idea hit just as he finally approached the MacKenzie household.

The second he stepped foot inside the door, his mum's voice rang out. "Fraser, come here."

Since he'd long ago figured out which battles to fight with his mother, he moved toward the kitchen. "Hey, Mum. Whatever you're cooking smells fantastic."

Lorna turned with a wooden spoon in her hand. Her eyes darted to his cheek and hair before returning to his eyes. "What happened to you? Please tell me you weren't found rolling around in a field with a lass again. Most of the dragon-shifter parents with females your age already give me the stink eye."

He shrugged. "All of their daughters are of age. They can make their own decisions."

He reached for an apple, but his mum smacked him with the spoon. "I need those for my tarts."

With a dramatic sigh, he answered, "I guess I'll just go hungry again."

41

Lorna rolled her eyes and turned back toward the cooker. "Find your own place if you don't like it."

"What and have to cook all of my own food? The horror."

Lorna snorted. "You truly would starve then."

"Speaking of one of your children moving out, where's Fergus?"

"Upstairs, doing what you should be doing right now: showering." She glanced at him. "If you want to eat at my table, you'd better clean up."

Time to test his excuse. "I'll shower, but I'm going to miss supper, Mum."

Lorna turned around again. "Tonight is important, Fraser Moore MacKenzie. Unless you're dying or fending off a horde of dragon hunters, you're coming to supper."

Despite being twenty-eight years old, it still took every ounce of self-control Fraser possessed to not fidget under Lorna's piercing amber-colored gaze.

But for both the good of the clan as well as his brother's happiness, Fraser stayed strong. "There's been a setback at the new warehouse project at the edge of our land. If I don't go and figure out a solution to the foundation problem, the whole project might have to be scrapped." When Lorna eyed him even more closely, he added, "Finn needs the warehouse for his grand plans for the clan. Without it, we can't stockpile crafts and wooden furniture to sell during the high tourist season. You know how he wants to add to our fish and agricultural income."

Lorna waggled her spoon. "You have three hours before supper, which is plenty of time to go to the site, check it out, and come back. Your brain always works best after a night's sleep on an issue." She nodded toward the door. "Go. I expect you back in time for supper."

THE DRAGON'S DILEMMA

The problem with arguing with your mum was that she knew all of your tricks. The bloody female was right—Fraser always worked best by finding out a problem and sleeping on it. Nine times out of ten, he'd wake up with an answer.

Since he didn't have a better excuse, Fraser sighed. "Fine. But if Finn is upset about the delay, you can explain it to him."

"Fraser, stop wasting my time and get your arse out the door. I have too much to do here to argue with you any more."

"I feel the love, Mother. I feel the love."

"Go, you bloody rascal. I don't care how old you are, I will smack your bum with my spoon to get you out of my kitchen."

As Fraser exited the kitchen and made a beeline for the door, his dragon laughed. *That's why I didn't fight you too much. I knew Mum would make you attend.*

Shut it, dragon. I'm not in the mood.

I need to reserve my strength for our female later, anyway. Have fun creating and solving a made-up problem. You know Mum will ask about it.

As his dragon laughed again, Fraser gritted his teeth. So much for trying to be noble and give Fergus a chance with Holly. Thanks to his mother, Fraser was going to be sitting at the same bloody table with her.

Not only that, but in full view of his family.

Supper was going to be the ultimate test. Not being charming would set off red flags to his family. They would expect him to flirt and charm the human female.

He only hoped Fergus didn't pick up on anything more. His twin knew Fraser better than anyone else in the world, even their Mum.

Sighing, he ran toward the edge of Lochguard's lands. Maybe physical exhaustion would be a good enough excuse to leave supper early.

CHAPTER FOUR

Holly sat across from Finn and frowned. "There was nothing in the contract about having to live with my assigned dragonman. My only duty is to sleep with him."

"Aye, that's true. But both the DDA and myself think it's best if you get to know Fergus a little better. Unlike in the past, we want sacrifices to keep in contact with their children."

The word "children" brought back reports she'd read about survival birth rates amongst human women who bore a dragon-shifter's child.

The fact she had a fifty-fifty chance of surviving the birth reminded her of something Arabella had mentioned. "I will live with Fergus from next week on one condition."

Finn raised one blond eyebrow. "Oh, aye? You have conditions already?"

Holly refused to back down at his intense gaze. "Yes. I want to assist in the surgery and have access to any research done related to the effects of dragon-shifter hormones on humans."

Finn sat back and steepled his fingers. "It's possible, but it's not me you're going to have to win over, lass. It's Dr. Gregor Innes, the head doctor here on Lochguard. And let's just say he's not the most gregarious of dragon-shifters."

"I've worked with all types of nurses and doctors. I'm sure I can handle it."

THE DRAGON'S DILEMMA

Arabella shouted from the next room, "Let her try, Finn. She's the only one who's been able to help with my nausea so far."

Concern flashed in Finn's eyes. "Are you all right, Ara? Do you need me to bring you something?"

"Just go back to your meeting. I'm fine," Arabella answered.

Finn looked about ready to stand up, so Holly drew on her strength and said in her sternest voice, "Stop fussing."

Finn met her eye and his pupils flashed to slits and back. "Careful, lass. You're a guest on my land."

Holly leaned her elbows on Finn's desk. "And you're suffocating your mate. If she wants your help, she'll ask for it. Believe me, the most frequent complaint I get about a pregnant woman's other half is that they stifle them and walk on eggshells. I may not have experience with pregnant dragon-shifters, but I'm fairly certain they want the same thing."

"And what's that?"

"To be treated as a normal person." Holly leaned closer and whispered, "Most of the time. Save your fussing for when she really needs it."

Finn whispered back, "And how will I know?"

Before Holly could answer, Arabella shouted again. "Because I'll tell you, you bloody idiot. Okay?"

Finn raised his voice to normal speaking levels. "We'll talk about it later, love." He looked back to Holly. "Before we discuss any position or opportunities with the clan we need to get two things straight right now, lass."

Holly refused to be intimidated and sat back in her chair. "What?"

"I'll allow you to order me about on matters concerning Ara's pregnancy when we're alone. But outside of that, I won't tolerate it. You're a guest on my land and I'm trying to create the best possible environment for you. However, I am the law here on Lochguard. Are we clear?"

Holly nearly blinked at the change in Finn from the smiling, teasing bloke he'd been a few minutes ago to the steely-eyed, intimidating presence. The dominance in his voice nearly made her want to just nod and say nothing.

However, that wasn't Holly's way. "I agree, provided you're not embarrassing me or doing something worth a scolding."

Holly swore she heard a bark of laughter from the other room, but Finn replied before she could think about it. "Provided our definitions of 'something worth a scolding' are the same, then I can accept that. Any clan member would do the same."

Holly nodded. "Good. And what's the other condition?"

Finn's face relaxed and he smiled as he leaned back in his chair. "You need a recommendation from my Aunt Lorna before you can approach Dr. Innes about working in the surgery. And before you ask, she's Fergus and Fraser's mother."

Holly sensed there was something Finn wasn't telling her, but she'd find out soon enough. "I'm sure she'll give me a glowing review by tomorrow evening at the latest."

Amusement danced in Finn's eyes. "Aye, maybe. Let's see if you survive dinner first." Finn stood up and motioned out the door. "Go freshen up, lass. We'll be heading over in less than an hour."

Holly motioned toward the paperwork on the desk. "But we've barely gone through the first stack."

Finn waved a hand. "No worries. We have plenty of time. After all, you have a week before you move in with Fergus and try to fulfill your contract."

Holly was careful to keep her expression neutral. The last thing she needed was Finn guessing her plan to entice Fergus into her bed earlier than that. "You're right." She stood. "Should I dress formal?"

"It's just a family dinner." He lowered his voice. "But all straight dragon males appreciate a lass in a pretty top. Even Arabella figured that out."

Arabella's form appeared in the doorway. "Finlay Stewart, leave her alone." Arabella looked to her. "Wear what you like. Meeting Fergus will be stressful enough. You don't need to add uncomfortable clothing to the mix. Fergus will understand."

Finn walked over and put an arm around Arabella's waist. After he kissed the top of her head, he laid his cheek there and met Holly's eyes. "All clan leader dominance and rules aside, Fergus is a good male. He's patient with lasses, even if he's not overly patient in other areas of his life."

Arabella slapped his side. "It's all Fraser's fault. Speaking of which, Fraser offered to clean up our garden."

"Offered?" Finn asked dryly.

Arabella chuckled. "Okay, I sort of coerced him. But I had a good reason. Let Holly go upstairs and I'll tell you all about it."

Finn grunted and Holly took that as her cue to leave. Skirting around Finn and Arabella, she headed toward the stairs.

As she ascended them, she mentally cursed Arabella for bringing up Fraser again. Simply mentioning his name had brought the moment they'd shared inside the greenhouse, with his hot breath on her cheek and his wonderfully masculine scent surrounding her, to the forefront of her mind.

If the sacrifice contract hadn't been hanging over her head, she wondered if she would've kissed him.

Entering her room and shutting the door, Holly closed her eyes and inhaled deeply. Thinking about "what ifs" was a waste of time. She was there to bear Fergus a child, not Fraser.

And at dinner, Holly would do everything in her power to forget about the forbidden twin.

Decision made, she opened her eyes and moved to her suitcase. Surely she had something revealing to wear. She needed it if she was to kill two birds with one stone—both to tempt Fergus to kiss her or more and to also drive Fraser crazy to the point he might leave early, allowing her to focus. If all went according to plan, she might even be able to convince Fergus to spend some time alone with her.

As she rummaged through her bag, Holly found a wee present hidden under her stack of trousers.

Her dad must've put it there.

Sitting down, she tore off the wrapping paper and tears formed in her eyes. She traced the title of the book, "Medicinal Plants of the Scottish Highlands." How her dad had managed to order the book and hide it without her knowledge, she didn't know. But the token made her eyes wet.

She hugged the book to her chest and closed her eyes. Her dad's gift reminded her of the bigger picture. Fraser, Fergus, or any of the other dragon-shifters didn't matter. Holly needed to survive her time on Lochguard so she could go back to Aberdeen and take care of her father. She was all he had left.

She wouldn't let him down.

Carefully laying the book down on the bed, Holly picked out her sexiest clothes. They were tame compared to some of the women she'd seen on Friday nights in the past, but they would have to do.

It was time to catch a dragonman.

~~~

Fraser ran his fingers through his wavy hair one last time before exiting his bedroom. Between the jogging and his shower, he was tired yet slightly more relaxed. If he was lucky, his exhaustion might give him the reason he needed to be less than charming at supper.

Popping into his younger sister's room, he met her eyes in the mirror and Faye frowned. "You didn't knock."

He shrugged. "Our whole lives, you've always been ready five minutes before everyone else. You mention it every chance you get." He changed his voice to mimic his sister's. "'Fraser, why did you take so long? You must be arranging every strand of hair individually.'"

Faye turned and threw a stuffed tiger at him. When it bounced off his chest, he made himself look affronted. "Dear sister, that was uncalled for."

"I'm not in the mood tonight, Fraser."

The words were out of his mouth before he could stop them. "As of late, you never are."

Faye's face turned neutral. "I used to be Finn's go-to Protector for the clan. Now, I can barely jump in dragon form and still can't fly. Excuse me for not being all charming and full of smiles."

Fraser had mostly tiptoed around the subject of Faye's injury since it had happened two months earlier. But as his dragon paced inside his head, pushing for him to go downstairs and wait

49

for Holly, his patience snapped. "Stop pitying yourself, Faye. You're not the only one with problems."

"Oh, aye? Are you having trouble deciding between two females? Or, let me guess, you can't sneak off with Fergus anymore to cause trouble in the neighboring towns and villages?" She rolled her eyes. "Those aren't real problems, Fraser."

Growling, Fraser took a step toward Faye. "There's more to me than lasses and getting into trouble."

She raised an eyebrow. "That's pretty much what you've been doing for the last decade. What's changed?"

He teetered on the edge of telling Faye about Holly. His sister could keep a secret if she wanted to. After all, she'd been one of the top security officers for Lochguard.

But at the last minute, he decided not to. Fraser wanting Fergus's sacrifice might be a big enough problem for Faye to go to Finn or their mother. "Never mind. It's not that important and we don't want to keep Mum waiting." He put out an arm. "Shall I escort you to dinner?"

Faye's amber-brown eyes scrutinized him a second and she almost looked like her old self, from before the accident that had damaged her wing.

Finally, she stood up and threaded her arm through his. "I would be honored, Fraser Moore."

He bowed his head. "As am I, Faye Cleopatra."

She scrunched her nose. "I still don't understand why you and Fergus are named after Roger Moore and I'm named after an Egyptian pharaoh."

He winked. "It could've been a lot worse if Dad hadn't wanted that middle name. Mum could've gone with Connery or even Sean. You know how she loves the James Bond films."

Faye's voice turned somber. "I wish I could've known Dad."

They rarely talked about it, but their father had died the night before Faye's birth.

Fraser squeezed his sister's shoulders. "I don't much remember him myself, but at least we had Mum. She has as much personality and strength as any two parents combined." Anxious to change topics, Fraser tugged his sister's arm and they started walking. "I hope Fergus's meeting with his sacrifice is going well."

Faye looked up at him. "I hope so, too. He may hide it, but he's a romantic at heart. If he can't find a mate in this Holly woman, then I'm not sure where else he can look. He's tried everyone on Lochguard, to no avail, and he's determined to stay in the Highlands. Without accepting a foster position in one of the other clans, I'm not sure how Fergus could ever meet someone else."

Fraser's dragon snarled at the idea of Fergus having Holly, but Fraser just managed to shove his beast to the back of his mind. *She's off limits, dragon.*

Forcing his tone to remain light, he replied, "He'll make it work. Fergus may not be as charming as myself, but he'll still manage to win the human over. Remember, it's more than just Fergus's happiness at stake—Holly's final report on her time here will help determine if we ever have another sacrifice."

"Maybe. But I don't want our brother to merely settle. He should choose a mate for love."

Fraser looked down at his sister. "Since when are you a romantic? I seem to remember you stating a mate would only get in the way of your career."

"Aye, I did. But I don't have much of a career to look forward to these days, do I?"

Fraser stopped them in their tracks and turned Faye toward him. "Stop with the pity, Faye. You're a MacKenzie. We're stubborn and never give up. Even if I have to find a scientist to design a customized dragon jet-pack, you'll fly again."

Faye smiled and it pleased both man and beast.

She tilted her head. "I'd like to see that. Although, I'm sure the humans wouldn't approve of dragon jet-packs."

"Who cares what the humans think?" Fraser patted her arm. "Right, how about we survive dinner first and then we can discuss the jet-pack option later."

"Because it's such a believable option," Faye answered. Fraser growled and she patted his arm. "Okay, okay. We'll start with dinner and go from there."

Guilt flooded his body at keeping the truth about Holly from his younger sister, but Fraser pushed it away. Unfortunately, he couldn't stop his dragon from bursting free. *I will fight for Holly and you won't be able to stop me.*

Are you really going to betray our family to do it?

She's our true mate. Tell Fergus. He'll understand.

I wish it were that simple, but he didn't take it well the last time we stole a lass from him. Besides, I'm not sure Finn would agree to transfer the contract. It may not even be possible.

You never know until you try.

Listen, dragon. I won't hurt my twin or take away his last chance for happiness, so stop pushing.

His beast snarled. *You've made your opinion clear. I'll make my next move without you.*

As his dragon retreated to the back of his mind, Fraser's stomach turned heavy. If his dragon took control, the bloody beast could do all kinds of damage. Not only scaring Holly, but testing the bonds of his family.

52

THE DRAGON'S DILEMMA

Fraser may not have tried to resist his dragon's wishes in the past, but that was changing from this moment forward.

His dragon's laugh echoed inside his head and Fraser clenched his jaw. *Just wait, dragon. I'm stronger than you think.*

His beast's silence spoke volumes. Some might think it meant his beast agreed, but in Fraser's experience, his dragon usually fell quiet when he didn't think arguing a point was worth his time.

His dragon's response only strengthened his resolve. For the remainder of the walk to the kitchen, Fraser recalled every detail he'd heard over the years on how to construct a complicated maze to preoccupy his dragon. If he could manage that, then he could devise a way to leave supper early. The longer he stayed in the room with Holly, the greater the chance his dragon would take control and do who the hell knew what to her.

Faye's voice interrupted his thoughts. "You're quiet, brother. What's wrong?"

Forcing a lazy smile, he shook his head. "You know me, I'm just devising trouble. I'll have to give Fergus a big send off before the mating ceremony."

As he rambled off pub names and the best hunting grounds to fool his sister, Fraser built his maze piece by piece. There was no bloody way he was allowing his dragon to ruin things for his family.

~~~

Holly tucked a section of her hair behind her ear. She usually wore it up, but her friends had always mentioned how pretty she looked with it down. Combined with her blue low-cut top, she just might be able to convince Fergus to kiss her.

Picking at her trouser leg, she resisted pacing the floor of the small study. Finn should return with the aforementioned Fergus at any moment.

Even though she was having dinner at the MacKenzie household, she was meeting Fergus at Finn's place first. Finn had muttered something about keeping the family's overbearing curiosity out of the way for her first introduction to her assigned dragonman.

It would also give her a chance to admire Fergus without his bloody twin brother distracting her.

The doorknob turned and she took a deep breath. *This is it. Time to meet your future.*

The door opened to reveal Finn's smiling face. "Ms. Holly Anderson, may I present Fergus Roger MacKenzie."

Behind him, she heard a male murmur, "No need for the middle name, Finn."

Finn grinned as he stepped aside. "Blame your mum if you don't like it, not me."

With a sigh, a tall dragonman with wavy auburn hair and blue eyes stepped into the room. From his broad shoulders to the slight indentation in his chin, Fergus looked exactly like Fraser, except the man in front of her lacked a scar near his left eye.

Despite Fergus having the same build and face as his twin brother, the look in Fergus's eyes was kind and missing the twinkle or heat of his brother's. Fergus also didn't have a late-day stubble like Fraser. And most importantly, Holly had no desire to stare at Fergus's lips.

Catching herself before she remembered about the incident in the greenhouse yet again, Holly held out a hand. "Nice to meet you, Fergus."

Fergus took her hand and shook. His touch was warm, but lacked any sort of fizzle. It was almost as if she were shaking the hand of a patient or coworker.

In contrast, just the heat of Fraser's breath on her face had sent warmth rushing between her legs.

Stop it, Holly. Fergus and not Fraser is your future. Think of how happy Dad will be when he gets to see you again back in Aberdeen.

Fergus released her hand and smiled. "I know everything must seem strange to you, but I'll make sure your stay here is pleasant. There's nothing to fear from Lochguard."

A small part of Holly wanted much more than pleasant; she wanted hot, uncontrollable passion.

Instead of voicing her thoughts, she nodded. "I sense that already."

Finn moved back to the door. "I'll give you two a few minutes. But after that, we really should leave." He looked to Holly. "Aunt Lorna hates tardiness."

She smiled. "I'll keep that in mind."

Finn grinned and shut the door, leaving her alone with Fergus.

Fergus smiled wider at her. "I hope Finn and Arabella are treating you well." He lowered his voice. "Don't tell Ara, but her pregnancy has made her extra grumpy. I'm not sure how Finn puts up with it."

The corner of Holly's mouth ticked up. "If you kept throwing up your food, I'm sure you'd be extra grumpy, too."

"True, true. I'm grateful every day that I'm not a female."

She raised an eyebrow. "Some might take that the wrong way."

Fergus put up his hands. "I apologize. I'm used to speaking my mind. I'll try to be careful."

"No, don't. I like straightforwardness."

"Good, then you should get along famously with my family."

As silence fell between them, Holly resisted comparing Fergus to Fraser. She wouldn't think of how much easier it was to talk with the other twin. Or, how the other twin would never be so cautious around her. Fraser might even push her up against the wall and try to win a kiss if she so much as batted an eyelash in his direction.

Stop it. Holly needed to work on Fergus and forget all about Fraser MacKenzie. The sooner she sealed the deal, the sooner Holly could fulfill her sacrifice contract and count down the days until she could return home.

Deciding she needed to speed things up, she walked over to stand in front of Fergus and placed a hand on his chest. "Maybe we should go. I need to make a good impression with your mother."

Fergus placed his hand over hers and squeezed. "Don't worry. Compared to my brother and sister, you're going to be like a breath of fresh air."

"How so?"

He grinned and his eyes crinkled at the corners. Fergus was a handsome man, but not quite as handsome as Fraser.

Before she could mentally scold herself again, Fergus answered, "Let's just say that 'quiet' is never used to describe my family." He squeezed her hand again. "I warn you, though. To win them over, don't back down. Even if my mum says something out of turn or is flat out wrong, call her out on it. That's the fastest way to earn her respect."

Holly's mum had been similar.

But her mother had died years ago. Holly missed her voice and offer to make a cup of tea first thing in the morning every day.

However, she didn't feel comfortable talking with Fergus MacKenzie about her mum.

And more importantly, the MacKenzies didn't need to learn of her past and end up giving her looks of sympathy all night. "Right, shall we go?"

Fergus moved their hands between them until he could thread his fingers through hers. "Come. The sooner you meet my family, the sooner I can sneak you away and we can talk. I won't pry your secrets out just yet, but I'm always here to talk when you're ready."

Holly's respect for Fergus raised a notch. The dragonman was observant, she'd give him that.

Not knowing what else to say, Holly merely nodded. Silence fell and Fergus tugged her hand. "Let's go."

The silence continued. Before Holly could think of what to ask Fergus that wasn't something daft such as, "What's your favorite color?" they joined Finn and Arabella in the front hall.

Finn's eyes darted to their clasped hands and he smiled. "I see you two are off to a fine start."

Fergus squeezed her hand. "Don't scare her off, Finn. She has a week and not even your bawdiest joke will convince me to rush her."

Holly kept her expression neutral. Fergus would be in for a surprise later when she planned to all but jump him.

Well, maybe not jump him. But certainly she was determined to kiss him before the night was over.

Holly raised an eyebrow. "I spent some time volunteering in the East End of London. There's little you can say that will surprise me."

Finn grinned as he pulled Arabella closer. "Aye? Well, I look forward to hearing some of those jokes later. We could always use some new ones around here."

Arabella rolled her eyes. "Finn, you can ask for dirty jokes later. Unless you want to face Aunt Lorna's wrath, we need to leave right now."

Finn motioned with his head. "Then let's be off."

Thankfully, Finn did most of the chatting en route to the MacKenzie house, explaining about one legend or another. Holly half-listened, but her mind was preoccupied with the dragonman holding her hand.

Fergus was nice, but Holly had wished for more than that. After the spark with Fraser, she'd hoped his twin would cause the same reaction.

Unfortunately, he hadn't.

Holly would just have to make the best of it. She didn't think she'd be abused whilst on Lochguard, for one. If she did have a child, survived the birth, and came back to visit, she had a feeling Finn would allow her to do so, even if she didn't stay with Fergus.

The hard part would be surviving dinner with Fraser's eyes on her face. If she had affected Fraser half as much as he'd affected her, then they would be stealing glances all evening.

And if that were the case, Holly had a feeling Finn or Arabella might notice.

CHAPTER FIVE

Once Fraser and Faye reached the kitchen, Fraser released his sister's arm and swiped an apple tart from the nearest plate. Just as he was about to take a bite, his mother didn't so much as turn around as she said, "Put it down or you won't eat anything else tonight."

He looked to Faye mouthed, "How does she do that?"

Lorna turned and raised her brows. "I've been your mother for nearly three decades, Fraser Moore. There isn't much you can do that would surprise me."

Faye smiled. It was good to see since his sister hadn't smiled much of late. "If you're hungry, just ask." Faye looked to their mother. "Mum, may I have a tart?"

Lorna waved a hand. "Go ahead, child. You're the grumpiest of the lot when you're hungry."

Faye stuck out a tongue at her brother as she plucked a tart from the plate. Putting his own down, he muttered, "Brownnoser."

His mother merely shook her head and went back to carving the roast. "Start taking the food out to the table."

Faye dramatically brushed the crumbs from her hands and he growled. "Stop rubbing it in."

His sister shrugged. "I had to clean my hands."

Grabbing the basket of rolls, he walked to the dining room. After the past few weeks, with Faye being grumpy and a recluse, he'd forgotten how annoying she could be at times.

Fraser was just about to return to the kitchen for another side dish when he heard the door open. Finn's voice boomed down the hall. "We're here, Aunt Lorna."

If Finn had arrived, so had Fergus and Holly.

His beast spoke up. *Good. I can watch them and figure out how to make my move.*

It's not going to happen, dragon.

You underestimate me.

Finn walked into the dining room with Arabella at his side. "Hey, cousins." Finn looked at him with a twinkle in his eye. "Thanks for offering to clean up the garden. I've been meaning to do it for some time."

Fraser rolled his eyes. "You would scrub a toilet before you would ever weed, let alone plant something."

Finn grinned. "You're right, but I'm looking forward to watching you do the backbreaking work."

Fraser opened his mouth to reply, but Fergus walked in with Holly.

And they were holding hands.

Before he could stop it, a resounding, "*No bloody way*," rang inside his head.

The scary thing was he didn't know if it was from man, beast, or both.

If Holly and Fergus holding hands wasn't bad enough, the human female had on a dark blue top that dipped down to a V to display the tops of her creamy, pale breasts.

Breasts that should only be his.

Fuck. His dragon laughed and he ignored his beast. Instead, Fraser forced his voice to work. "Hey, brother. Holly."

Fergus frowned. "You two have met?"

Fraser shrugged. "I was at Finn and Ara's place today. We met then."

Fergus narrowed his eyes. "Please tell me you didn't do anything to frighten her or give the wrong impression of me."

Fraser motioned toward Holly. "Ask her yourself. She's standing right there, in case you've forgotten."

With a sigh, Fergus looked down at Holly. "Forgive my brother. He's pretty much a full-time pain in my arse."

When Holly smiled up at Fergus, Fraser clenched the fingers of one hand.

His dragon chimed in. *We can have her. Just talk to Fergus. Shut it, dragon. Holly might be Fergus's only chance for happiness. And what about ours?*

Constructing a rough maze, he shoved his beast inside. The maze wouldn't last long since Fraser was a novice, but it would at least allow them to start eating supper.

Fraser glanced at Finn and Arabella, both of whom were studying him.

Faye entered the room carrying a giant bowl of salad. That was his cue to leave. "I need to help Mum with the roast. You lot can settle down around the table and chat for a bit before supper."

Before anyone could reply, Fraser rushed into the kitchen. When the scent of beef and potatoes hit his nose, it helped to calm his anger a fraction. Now that he'd seen his brother and Holly together, he was prepared. If he drew on every ounce of stubbornness he possessed, he just might be able to survive the meal.

Careful to keep his voice neutral, he asked, "Do you need help carving the meat, Mum? Fergus and the human have arrived. If you want to talk with Fergus and his sacrifice, I can do that for you."

Lorna turned around slowly, complete with a knife and pronged meat fork still clutched in her fingers. After assessing his eyes, she demanded, "What did you do?"

"Nothing. I just wanted to give you a rest."

Lorna remained quiet for a few seconds. Then she motioned with the utensils in her hands. "Come. I'm not about to turn down one of your rare offers of help."

"Oh, come on, Mum. I help with the dishes all the time."

She handed him the knife and pronged fork. "Only because you know I won't cook anything if you don't do them."

Fraser motioned with his head. "We can argue later. Go meet the possible mother of your first grandchild."

Lorna washed her hands and dried them on a towel. "To be honest, given your way with the lasses, I was convinced you'd be the first one to give me a grandchild."

There was no way in hell he was talking about sex and babies with his mother. "I don't have any children. I'm careful. But isn't it your duty as head of the family to vet Holly?"

"Finn vetted her first. I trust the lad."

He was running out of options to convince his mother to leave. As she watched him in silence, a new one hit him. "Then go to satisfy your curiosity. Otherwise, Meg Boyd will be spreading facts about Holly before you even have a proper conversation with the human."

"Meg hasn't met her." Fraser raised an eyebrow and his mother sighed. "You're right. As much as I love that dragonwoman, she was probably a detective inspector in her previous life. I won't have her knowing more than me about Holly. Especially since her unmated son, Alistair, will probably never take a sacrifice and I won't be able to get her back later."

He nearly released a breath in relief. "Exactly. Go and find out as much as you can. Then you can lord it over Meg tomorrow."

Lorna walked up to him and took his chin in her hands. Fraser had long ago practiced keeping his true thoughts hidden from his mother. It only worked about half the time, but maybe he'd be lucky.

Lorna searched his eyes before lightly slapping his cheek. "For all my harping, you're a good lad, Fraser. I love you."

"Mum, please."

Shaking her head, Lorna moved toward the exit. "Sometimes, I wish I'd had all girls."

He was about to tease his mum about female hormones, but she was gone.

Alone at last, Fraser worked on reinforcing his mental maze as he carved the roast. If Finn and his mother were already suspicious that something was wrong, he needed to up his game.

There was no bloody way he'd let them know how he wanted to whisk Holly to a private cottage and fuck her until she carried his child.

Oh, but not before he'd punched Fergus in the face first for daring to touch the human or glance at her breasts.

~~~

Holly's hand was sweaty from prolonged hand-holding, but she thought it might be rude to tug it out of Fergus's grip and wipe her hands on her trousers.

63

The meeting with Fraser had gone well enough. Neither of them had acted familiar beyond names and Holly had tried her best to focus her attention on Fergus.

Just as a young woman with brown hair and eyes entered with a large bowl in her hands, Fraser left and Holly let out a breath. Trying to entice Fergus would be much easier with Fraser out of the room.

After setting the bowl of salad in the middle of the table with flair, the young, brown-haired dragonwoman looked straight at Holly. "You must be Holly. I'm Faye, Fergus's favorite sister."

"You're my only sister," Fergus replied.

Faye stuck out her tongue at Fergus and then smiled at Holly. "I warn you that most nights when we all dine together, food ends up on the walls."

Holly blinked. "Pardon?"

Arabella's voice was amused as she said, "The MacKenzies and Stewarts may look to be in their twenties and thirties, but they have a mental age of about thirteen whenever they're in the same room together."

Finn, Faye, and Fergus said at the same time, "Hey."

Arabella shrugged. "See what I mean?"

Holly grinned. "I'm starting to."

Fergus released her hand and touched her lower back. "Let's sit down before Arabella starts telling more tales to scare you." He increased the pressure against her back. "Besides, it's been a busy day. You must be exhausted."

She was about to say she was a nurse and she was used to standing on her feet for hours on end, but the second she saw the kindness in Fergus's eyes again, she backed down. "Thank you."

Just as she settled in the wooden chair, a middle-aged woman with graying blonde hair came from the kitchen. She was tall, and slightly overweight. The older dragonwoman's brown eyes reminded Holly of both Faye's eyes as well as Finn's.

The older dragonwoman met her gaze and smiled. "There she is at last. I'm Lorna MacKenzie, Faye, Fraser, and Fergus's mother. I hope my kin haven't frightened you yet. They always seem to find trouble when they're out of my sight."

From the laugh lines around Lorna's mouth to the crinkles around her eyes, Holly guessed the older MacKenzie might complain about her brood, but spent a good deal of her time laughing with them. "No, they've been pretty well-behaved so far, Mrs. MacKenzie."

Lorna waved a hand. "Call me Aunt Lorna for now."

Holly understood what was left unsaid—Holly might one day call her mum.

But if she stayed and did that, Holly would be cut off from her father.

No, the best thing was to fulfill her contract and go home. In order to do that, she needed to not think of a future on Lochguard.

Wait, since when did she want to stay on Lochguard? Maybe Holly was more exhausted than she'd thought.

Faye's voice cut into Holly's thoughts. "Are you sure it's wise to leave Fraser alone with the roast? He'll probably eat all of the best bits or save them for himself."

Lorna placed a hand on her hip. "Faye Cleopatra, there is enough roast in there to feed a small army. Have a little patience."

Fergus leaned to Holly's ear and whispered, "Faye is really grumpy when she's hungry."

At that moment, Fraser walked in carrying a large tray. His blue eyes met hers. At the intensity in his gaze, a flash of heat rushed through her body.

When his pupils flashed to slits and back, her heart skipped a beat.

Fraser was the first to break eye contact. He laid the platter on the table. Since the room had fallen silent, the clatter of the porcelain against the wood echoed in the room.

Lorna was the first one to speak. "See, Faye? There's plenty of meat for you to eat, even if Fraser ate some already."

Faye looked away from Holly and toward Fraser. "You didn't spit on it, did you?"

Laying his hand on his chest, Fraser put on a mock expression of horror. "And face Mum's wrath? Are you mental?"

Fergus leaned away from her. She dared to glance at him from the corner of her eye. Fergus was studying Fraser's face.

Her heart rate kicked up. Had their shared glance stirred up suspicion?

Calm down, Holly. Even if anyone had noticed, Holly hadn't done more than talk with Fraser and share a few glances. She hadn't violated her contract.

And she would make sure she never did.

Holly's determination renewed, she touched Fergus's bicep. "Would you pour me some wine?"

Fergus finally looked from his brother's face to hers. "Of course."

He reached for the nearest bottle of red wine and poured her half a glass. The second he handed it to her, Holly took a sip and then another. She needed all of the liquid courage she could muster if she had to spend the next however many minutes not looking at Fraser.

Faye chimed in. "Can we eat now, Mum? The longer the food sits on the table, the higher the risk of a food fight breaking out and I'm pretty damn hungry."

Lorna clicked her tongue. "Language, Faye."

Faye muttered something Holly couldn't hear, but Fergus chuckled at her side. "Just wait until I leave and it's just you and Fraser in the house. Mum will have more time to focus on you two with me gone."

From the corner of Holly's eye, she just made out Fraser shrugging. "I probably won't be home much, either. Without you around, brother, I'll have more lasses for myself."

Fraser's words were a stab to her heart. She must've read too much into their shared glances and near-kiss in the greenhouse.

Fraser MacKenzie clearly wasn't worth her time or worry.

Using her newfound determination, Holly glanced to Fraser. Yet as soon as he met her eyes, Fraser looked away and smiled at his brother. "This may actually be your last potential food fight for life. Holly doesn't strike me as the type."

Arabella's voice chimed in. "You mean she acts older than a teenager."

Holly took a sip of wine and then turned toward Fergus. "If a food fight breaks out, will you shield me?"

The corner of Fergus's mouth ticked up. "That depends if you start it or not."

Holly leaned closer. "I was thinking more of you starting it by hitting your brother with a cooked potato."

Fergus grinned, making his eyes crinkle at the corners. "I like your way of thinking, lass." Fergus leaned down and whispered, "It's best to wait until Fraser isn't expecting it. But no worries, I have a few tricks up my sleeve. I'm the food fight champion."

Fraser growled. "He's lying, Holly."

Lorna clapped her hands. "Now, now children, let's play nice." Lorna's voice turned to steel. "Let's eat."

Holly hid her laugh by taking a drink.

Things were going well with Fergus. Each minute in his company helped relax her. Especially ever since Fraser pretended his meeting with her earlier hadn't happened.

As Fergus lightly bumped his shoulder against hers, he murmured, "I'll shield you, Holly. Always."

She forced a smile. The words were meant to be romantic, yet they didn't stir any flutterings or heat. Maybe with time the heat and awareness would come.

Glancing at Fraser one last time, he met her eyes. Heat flared briefly before his expression turned to a slightly cocky yet carefree one.

The flare of attraction only reminded Holly of what was at stake. Nothing would keep her from returning to her father.

Fergus slid a few slices of roast onto her plate and Holly focused on her food. The sooner she ate, the sooner she could convince Fergus to take her out of the room. She needed to sleep with the dragonman as soon as possible. Maybe even tonight.

Holly couldn't afford to stay on Lochguard any longer than necessary or a certain auburn-haired, blue-eyed dragonman would get her into trouble.

~ ~ ~

Fraser gripped his knees under the table. His dragon was roaring and trying to claw his way out of the maze. Fraser wasn't sure how much longer he could restrain his beast.

Yet if he left supper without eating, Finn, his mother, and maybe even Fergus would try to talk with him and see what was wrong. If there was one thing that was always true in the MacKenzie household, it was that meals were never missed and all of the siblings fought over the food. If someone missed supper, they either had a bloody good reason or something was wrong.

As long as he could make it through dinner, Fraser could spend the rest of his time working on the warehouse project and clearing Finn and Arabella's garden. He wouldn't have to see Holly again until after she'd slept with Fergus and possibly carried his brother's child. By then, his dragon might even give up.

Fraser gripped his fork so tightly his fingers turned white. Who was he kidding? If his dragon's tantrum was anything to go by, seeing Holly pregnant with anyone's child but theirs would set his beast off. He needed to think of a plan to get him away from Lochguard. He might even request to be fostered at Stonefire. He could meet an English dragon-shifter female and forget all about Holly Anderson.

He just needed to make it through dinner first.

Faye plucked the basket of rolls from in front of him and piled three on her plate. Reinforcing his mental maze one last time, he decided to play his part and swiped one of his sister's rolls and took a bite. "Thanks, Faye."

Faye glared. Even when she'd been pitying herself after her injury and had been stuck in a wheelchair for four weeks, his sister had always been protective of her food. "You have five slices of roast and a heap of potatoes. Eat those first. You know rolls are my favorite."

Fraser took another bite and replied with his mouth half-full. "But they're warm."

A pea bounced off his cheek from the other end of the table. Fraser glanced to both Finn and then Fergus. "Not now. We have a guest."

Holly took another sip of wine and he watched the red liquid slide between her lips before she swallowed. The human had slender, pink lips he would love to nibble and then taste.

Before he was caught staring, Holly lowered her glass and spoke up. "Fergus here said he'd protect me. So, don't hold back on my account."

Fraser raised a brow. "Oh, aye? Did he, now?"

Fraser tossed the remainder of his roll in Holly's direction, but Fergus snatched it out of the air. "You're going to have to do better than that."

As Fergus and Fraser grinned at one another, Fraser nearly forgot about Holly coming between them.

Then the bloody human took the roll from Fergus's fingers—did she have to brush her fingers and linger so?—and tossed it back in his direction. "How about we eat first and play later?"

Fraser's dragon snarled and tried harder to escape Fraser's maze. No doubt, the beast had his own ideas of play.

Before he did something daft, Fraser poured some wine and took a swallow.

It was Lorna who broke the silence by tapping her knife against her plate. "I call a time-out. I didn't slave away in the kitchen all day so you could toss my food across the table. If this is how you appreciate all of my hard work, then next time I'll take the easy route and make fish, chips, and mushy peas."

Finn smiled. "That's not much of a threat, Aunt Lorna. You know that's my favorite."

Lorna sighed. "Okay, then how about I order some frozen human foods that taste like cardboard and then reheat those?"

Fraser scrunched up his nose. "That is an actual threat, Mum."

Lorna readjusted her bum in her chair. "Good, then eat and postpone the food fights for later."

Everyone but Arabella and Holly murmured their assent.

Lorna turned her head toward Holly. "So, lass, how fares your father? Is he doing better?"

Holly swallowed her bite of potato and answered, "The doctors think so. But his recovery is going to take a while and they're going to monitor his body for the further growth of any cancer cells. The treatments are experimental, but if they succeed, the process has a far higher survival rate than regular chemotherapy."

Lorna smiled. "I'm glad you were able to help your father. When he's feeling better, maybe he can come visit. I'm sure Finn can arrange it."

Holly blinked. "I didn't think human visitors were allowed."

Finn answered, "The DDA and the Home Secretary office are issuing a few visitor's passes to both our clan and Stonefire in England. I'm sure I can work something out, provided your father's health is strong enough."

Holly's eyes lit up and Fraser sucked in a breath. Hell, when the lass was happy and excited, she became even more beautiful.

Fraser wanted to try and make her happy as often as possible.

Stop it, Fraser. He took another sip of wine and half-listened as Holly and Finn talked about visitation passes. Their conversation gave Fraser a chance to study the human more closely without being overly obvious about it.

He loved how her long, dark hair tumbled past her shoulders to nearly her elbows. The gentle waves of her hair softened her face and if Fraser had a say in how she wore her hair, Holly would never wear it in a bun ever again.

Although the idea of him tugging out the pins and releasing her hair had its own appeal.

Resisting a frown lest he give away his thoughts, Fraser took another swig of wine. It was going to be a long evening. How he would survive watching Holly and Fergus for the next six months or more, Fraser had no idea. Fostering with Stonefire was his only real option.

His beast banged against the top of his mental maze at the thought of leaving Holly behind and the structure gave a little.

If his beast acted this way with Fergus merely touching Holly, Fraser hated to think what would happen once Fergus started sleeping with the lass.

Finn kicked his leg under the table. "Earth to Fraser. Are you listening?"

Damn. "What did I miss? I was too busy concentrating on this fine glass of wine."

Finn merely raised his brows. Fraser's cousin was unconvinced.

Bloody hell, if Fraser didn't get his act together, he would be cornered and interrogated before the night was over.

Holly answered, "Don't worry, it wasn't important."

Fraser should resist looking at the lass yet again since everyone was watching him at the table, but he turned his head. The human's cheeks were flushed from the wine, laughter, or both. Combined with the sparkle in her eyes, all he wanted to do was tug her out back, pull her close, and kiss her.

His dragon roared again.

Holly finally looked away from Fraser and to Fergus. She touched his brother's bloody bicep again. "I need to use the toilet."

THE DRAGON'S DILEMMA

Fergus smiled. "I think you're just trying to escape the madness for a bit."

Holly winked and Fraser dug his nails into his thighs as she said, "It is a bit exhausting having dinner with your family, if I'm honest. Of course, for all I know, it's like this with all dragon-shifter families."

Arabella snorted. "Definitely not. If you ever meet my brother, then you'll see what I mean."

Fergus whispered, "Ignore Arabella. Her brother's a bit of a bastard and she knows it."

Arabella growled. "Watch it, Fergus. I'm not even two months pregnant yet. I can still kick your arse if need be."

Fergus grinned. "I would, but Finn would have my head. We can have a rematch in about five years, when you can send your kid to school." Arabella rolled her eyes and Fergus met Holly's gaze again. "Go up the stairs and turn left. The toilet's the first door on the right."

Holly squeezed Fergus's arm. "Thank you."

As the lass exited the room, Fraser's dragon finally succeeded in breaking through the top of his mental maze. *Go after her. Now is our chance to kiss her. She will choose us.*

No way, dragon. She isn't ours.

His beast snarled. *Then you leave me no choice.*

His dragon pressed to the front of his mind. Fraser pushed back, but his dragon's need to kiss Holly and brand her with their scent was strong enough to hold Fraser off.

Dropping his head into his hands, Fraser closed his eyes. *No, we can't.*

You had your chance. We're going after her. I won't allow Fergus to take her. She is ours.

Wait—if you don't want to make the others overly suspicious or instantly follow us, then let me give them an excuse.

His beast paused and then replied, *I give you two minutes. Try to stuff me back into a maze and next time, I won't pause before I take control.*

Afraid his dragon might scare Holly, Fraser had little choice but to answer, *I won't.*

Two minutes.

His dragon relinquished control and moved toward the back of Fraser's mind, ready to pounce if Fraser showed the first sign of deceit.

With his beast no longer growling and snarling, Fraser finally heard Faye's voice asking. "Fraser, are you okay? What's wrong?"

Taking a deep breath, he lifted his head. "I think I drank too much wine too quickly. I'm just going to splash some water on my face."

Finn wasn't smiling, but his tone was light. "Or, put your head in a toilet."

Aware the clock was ticking, Fraser merely nodded and stood. He looked to his mother. "Sorry, Mum, but I'll be right back."

Not wanting to give his mother a chance to read his face and guess what was happening, Fraser quickly grunted and exited the dining room.

As he ascended the stairs, his dragon's voice boomed, *Find her.*

I will, but allow me to explain what's going on, first. Otherwise, she might run.

She had better say yes.

Trust me, dragon. I can get a lass to kiss me.

Despite the confidence in his tone, Fraser's stomach rolled. Never in a million years had he expected to trick his true mate into kissing him. With any luck, Holly wouldn't hate him afterwards.

It wasn't as if he had a choice. Unless Fraser left the clan, his beast would want Holly as long as she was nearby. And given how Fraser had spoiled his dragon over the years, what his beast wanted, his beast would take.

He couldn't allow his dragon to scare the lass. Fraser could take her hate later, but he never wanted to see fear or tears in her eyes when looking at him.

An idea hit and Fraser said to his dragon, *Let me talk to Fergus and Finn, first. They might be able to help us.*

No. You waited too long. I need to kiss her and claim her. She is ours.

If you would give me five minutes—

His dragon roared. *No. Kiss her and talk later.*

The need to kiss and fuck Holly rushed through Fraser's body and his step faltered. *You said I could talk to her.*

That was before you tried to make excuses and prevent us from kissing her.

Fine, I'll kiss her. But let me prepare her first.

His beast paused a second before replying, *This is your last chance. Kiss her or I will take control.*

Understood.

As his beast went back to pacing, Fraser cursed at his future being stolen from him. Yes, he was attracted to Holly and would love the chance to woo the feisty lass. But not with trickery and his dragon driving his actions.

That sort of deceit would only solidify the rumors about dragon-shifters being beasts. Not to mention Holly would probably flee Lochguard as soon as she'd birthed his child. Even knowing how important family was to her, Holly would probably try to find a way to take her child away from Fraser, the monster.

Taking a deep breath, Fraser pushed aside all of his doubts and fears. He couldn't risk his dragon taking over his mind and running amuck. If that happened, the Department of Dragon Affairs would probably hunt him down and lock him up.

There was no bloody way he would allow that to happen.

He reached the toilet door just as Holly opened it. She blinked. "Fraser? What are you doing up here?"

He could make up excuses about needing to use the loo, but each second he wasted talking was a second more that Finn or Fergus could come check on either one of them.

Reaching for her hand, Fraser tugged her into his room across the hall and shut the door. His dragon hissed. *Pin her against the wall and kiss her.*

Not yet.

Hurry.

Fraser leaned against his door as Holly frowned at him. "What the hell are you doing, Fraser MacKenzie?"

He clenched his jaw at the thought of what he was about to do.

~~~

Holly's heart beat double-time. One second she'd been exiting the toilet and the next she was alone in a room with Fraser.

With no one else with them, Holly could do nothing but stare at the blue-eyed dragonman who kept invading her thoughts. Surely he wouldn't try to flirt with or touch her again. After all, Fraser had dismissed her at the dinner table.

Hadn't he?

THE DRAGON'S DILEMMA

The dragonman's pupils flashed to slits and back. Something was going on with his dragon, but she had no bloody idea what.

Not one to back down from getting answers, she frowned and willed her voice to be strong. "What the hell are you doing, Fraser MacKenzie?"

He growled out, "Do you know what a true mate is, Holly?"

Holly nearly did a double-take at the strange question. "Yes, the DDA told me. A dragon-shifter's true mate is their best chance at happiness. Why?"

Locking the door, he took a step toward her. "What else did they tell you?"

Her heart raced faster. She took a step back and her legs hit the edge of the bed. "That if a dragon-shifter kisses their true mate, it starts a frenzy." She swallowed. "Why are you asking me this? Fergus is waiting for me downstairs."

Fraser curled his upper lip. "Don't mention Fergus."

Taking a deep breath, Holly straightened her shoulders. She wasn't about to let Fraser frighten her. "He's the one I'm here to be with, Fraser. You know that. Now, let me go."

Fraser closed the distance between them until he was only a few inches away and placed a hand on her back. Despite his flashing eyes and alpha attitude, heat flared at his touch.

Fraser smiled. "I'm the one you want, lass. Not my brother."

He pressed her closer until her breasts touched his chest and she sucked in a breath. "Stop it, Fraser. I can't."

Fraser leaned down and nuzzled her cheek. Each pass of his late-day whiskers against her cheek caused heat to flush through her body.

Fraser's breath was hot on her ear as he murmured, "Kiss me, Holly, and you'll be mine."

The huskiness of his voice made her breasts heavy and nipples harden. Damn the man and his effect on her. "I can't, Fraser. If I go to jail, then I won't be able to take care of my father."

Fraser nibbled her earlobe and she had to lean against his chest for support. "We'll find a way to make it work, Holly. I promise you that."

He gently bit her neck. From between her thighs to her breasts to even her lips throbbed in anticipation. Kissing Fraser MacKenzie would be much more than pleasant.

Isn't that what you want?

It was, but she had her father to think of. A compromise flashed inside her mind. One that might solve all of her problems.

Holly leaned a little closer and whispered into his ear, "If you can find a way to transfer the contract, then I'll consider it."

Fraser growled as he nipped her neck again. The slight sting made the pulsing between her legs increase.

Moving back to her ear, he murmured, "I will. But kiss me and let me fuck you now, Holly Anderson. I burn for you."

The rational side of her mind battled with her hormones. Fraser mentioning true mates had to be relevant. But each time he nibbled and licked her neck, it made it harder for her to connect the dots.

She was about to say yes when someone pounded on the door and shouted, "Open the bloody door, Fraser MacKenzie, or I will kick it down."

It was Finn.

Chapter Six

At the knock at the door and the sound of Finn's voice, Fraser's dragon roared and tried to push to the front of his mind. Fraser pushed him away. *No. You stay back.*

His beast snarled and hissed. *Kiss her. That will send Finn away and make her ours. Why are you waiting?*

I want to talk with Finn. That is a better way. Holly would be willing if we transferred the contract.

No. She's about to say yes anyway. Kiss the human.

Fraser stared at Holly's wide-eyed expression. Him kissing her and fondling her with his cousin banging on the door wasn't how he wanted to share their first kiss.

Holly deserved better.

Drawing deep inside of himself, Fraser shoved his beast to the back of his mind and threw up a wall. His dragon beat and pounded against his prison, but it held. At least, for the moment. But his beast would escape in the next few minutes, so Fraser had to make them count.

"Stay here," Fraser ordered Holly before going to the door.

Finn pounded again, but Fraser turned the lock and opened the door.

Gone was Finn's carefree expression and smiles. In their place, Finn's jaw was firm and his eyes were flashing to slits and back. His clan leader growled out, "What the hell are you doing,

Fraser? Why are you alone with Holly not only in your room, but with the fucking door locked?" Fraser opened his mouth to explain, but Finn cut him off. "And don't give me an excuse about giving her a tour or some such bullshit. You two have been stealing glances at each other all night. I want to know why."

With each second that passed, his dragon was closer to breaking free and taking control. Fraser could explain it all to Finn in this moment, or he'd lose his chance.

Finally, Fraser whispered, "She's my true mate, Finn. And my dragon is about to lose his head and take control."

Finn cursed. "Why the hell didn't you tell me this?" He motioned for Holly to come. "We need to get you out of here, lass. And quickly."

Fraser put out his arm to block the door and growled. "You're not taking her from me without a guarantee she's mine and not Fergus's."

Finn's eyes flashed. "I will take her away. Either lower your arm and move out of the way or I will make you."

The dominance in Finn's voice nearly made him follow the order. Then his dragon's need to mate pounded through his body and Fraser could barely put two words together. "No, I won't let you."

"Last warning, Fraser. I'll give you ten seconds to explain your answer before I knock you out cold and snatch Holly away."

His dragon roared and snarled. Fraser had maybe another minute before he'd lose the battle with his beast.

Gripping the edge of the door for support, Fraser bit out, "Transfer the contract to me." Finn opened his mouth but Fraser beat him to it. "Promise me you will and I'll let you knock me out so you can take Holly to safety."

Finn merely stared at him.

Fraser's dragon clawed to get free. Fraser had about thirty seconds. "Please, Finn."

Finn's jaw turned firm. "I'll see what I can do. Now, close your eyes."

Fraser trusted Finn to make things right. After all, they were brothers in all but blood.

Closing his eyes, Fraser focused his remaining energy on restraining his dragon long enough for Finn to knock him unconscious.

After a few beats, a fist connect with his jaw and the world went blissfully black and silent.

~~~

Holly clenched her fingers tighter over her chest as Finn's fist connected with Fraser's jaw.

The smacking sound filled the room before Fraser's body went limp and crashed to the floor.

She was torn between checking to see if Fraser was all right and pushing past Finn to run out of the cottage to somewhere safe.

Finn took the choice out of her hands and moved to stand in front of her. His amber eyes were full of concern. "Are you okay, Holly?"

"I—" She paused, took a deep breath, and made her mouth work again. "I'm fine. But explain to me what just happened."

Finn pressed his lips together before answering, "Fraser is a bloody idiot, that's what happened."

Holly raised an eyebrow. "That isn't exactly helpful."

Finn sighed. "The DDA is required to explain how you could turn out to be a dragon-shifter's true mate, aye?" She nodded. Finn half-turned and motioned toward Fraser. "Fraser recognized you as his but didn't tell anyone, the bloody idiot."

Before Holly could ask a question, Lorna's scowling face appeared in the door. Her eyes darted to Fraser and then to Finn. "Why is my son out cold on the floor? I'm sure there's a good reason, but I'm curious as to what it is."

"Holly is Fraser's true mate and the bastard didn't tell us."

Lorna shook her head. "Idiot." Lorna's eyes turned kind and looked straight into Holly's. "Are you okay, child? He didn't hurt or force himself on you, did he?"

"No. But it would be nice if someone explained to me what's going to happen from here." Holly's heart rate kicked up again. "You aren't going to turn me into the DDA for breaking my contract, are you? Nothing happened. We didn't even kiss. I can still do what I came here to do and try to bear Fergus a child."

Lorna waved a hand. "Don't be ridiculous. The second Fergus touched you, Fraser would beat his brother to a bloody pulp."

Relief flooded her body, but she wasn't out of the woods yet. Just because they wouldn't force her to be with Fergus didn't mean they wouldn't turn her over to the DDA.

Holly forced her shoulders back. The action helped to give her strength to push. "You still didn't answer my question about reporting me."

Finn answered before Lorna could open her mouth. "Right now isn't the time to be making promises. I told Fraser I would see what I could do, and I will. I'm more concerned about Fergus." Finn looked to Lorna. "Is he downstairs?"

Lorna nodded. "Aye. He volunteered to keep watch over Arabella and Faye, in case an intruder had broken in."

THE DRAGON'S DILEMMA

Finn lightly jabbed Fraser's side with his shoe. "I rather wish it had been an intruder. That would've been a whole hell of a lot simpler." Finn turned back to face Holly. "I need an honest answer, Holly. Are you composed enough to give one?"

She bobbed her head and ignored her thundering heart. "Yes. What is it?"

Finn replied, "If I can manage to transfer your sacrifice contract, would you accept Fraser?"

Holly looked down at Fraser's face, relaxed in unconsciousness. "Will I have to deal with his dragon again?"

Finn's voice filled the room again. "Clever lass. And the answer is yes. Since you are his true mate and Fraser is not very good at containing his dragon, Fraser will go into a mate-claim frenzy the second he kisses you. As you probably know, that means Fraser and his dragon will continue to have sex with you until you're pregnant. The charming, flirty dragonman you know will most likely disappear until the frenzy is over since the idiot never learned to control his dragon properly."

While her body wanted nothing more than to strip Fraser and lick every inch of his muscled body, her mind had a conscience and wasn't ready to commit just yet. Holly met Finn's gaze again. "And what about Fergus?"

Finn crossed his arms over his chest. "I'm not going to lie to you. Fergus will be devastated at both his brother's betrayal and his loss of you. Fergus had his heart set on winning you over, Holly."

Holly's heart squeezed with guilt. "I never planned for this to happen, you know."

Lorna walked around Fraser's unconscious body and put an arm around Holly's shoulders. "We know that, child. A dragon's instinct is unpredictable." Lorna took Holly's chin between her fingers. "This isn't your fault. Fraser is the one who allowed this disaster to happen."

Holly could remain silent and allow Fraser to take all of the blame. However, she'd never be able to sleep soundly until she told the truth anyway, so Holly decided to get it out of the way. "He isn't the only one. I ignored the connection between us." She darted a glance to Finn, but he was merely watching her without judgment, so she continued, "We nearly kissed inside Finn and Arabella's greenhouse this afternoon." Holly met Lorna's gaze again. "But I really was trying to do what I was sent here to do. I never intended to hurt Fergus. He's a nice lad and he'll find a lass. Please just make sure he knows I never would've hurt him on purpose."

Lorna squeezed Holly's chin. "I'll tell him myself once he cools down." Lorna released her grip. "Speaking of which, how do you want to handle this, Finlay?"

Finn uncrossed his arms. "I'll call Grant to come over and help carry Fraser to my cottage. Holly will stay here for the time being, in Faye's room. That way, Faye can watch over her."

Lorna asked, "Do you think Faye's ready?"

Finn frowned. "The job should give her a purpose, even if it's small. I think it'll do Faye good."

Holly found her voice. "You want me to stay in the same house as Fergus? I'm not sure if that's the best idea."

Finn shook his head. "I never said that, lass. I'll let him cool off in one of the empty cottages before I have a chat with him in the morning. I have a job for him on the Isle of Skye, which should keep him preoccupied for some time. I was going to assign it to someone else, but with the recent happenings, I'll give the assignment to Fergus."

Lorna clapped her hands. "Right, then. Let's set things in motion. I don't know how much longer Fraser will be unconscious and I certainly don't want him to wake up with Holly in the room." Lorna placed a hand on Holly's back. "Come, child. You can wait in my room with the door locked until everything is sorted."

Lorna gently pushed against her spine, but Holly stood her ground. "When will I see Fraser again?"

Finn answered, "Probably tomorrow." Finn took out his mobile phone and typed something. "I'm going to ask the doctor to come over and put Fraser's dragon in a time out for at least a day. That way, he can have a rational conversation without his beast clawing for control." Holly wanted to ask what that meant, but the second she opened her mouth, Finn cut her off. "Not now, Holly. I know you have questions, but they'll have to wait until morning. If all goes to plan, you can see Fraser during a supervised visit at the surgery tomorrow."

Lorna pressed harder and Holly finally followed the older dragonwoman's lead. As they walked around Fraser, Holly's training urged her to check on him.

However, Lorna's grip moved to one of her wrists. The dragonwoman had fingers of steel.

Lorna gently tugged her arm. "Leave him be for now, hen. If Fraser wakes up before the doctor sees him, all hell will break loose."

With a nod, Holly took one last glance at Fraser before she moved with Lorna out the door and into the hall.

She barely registered Lorna telling her how to lock the door before Holly was standing alone in the middle of a strange room.

Up until fifteen minutes ago, Holly had known what to expect during her stay with the Scottish dragon-shifter clan.

But now, everything had turned uncertain. If that wasn't bad enough, she would have all night to think about what might or might not happen with Fraser. Even if Finn could transfer the contract, there was so much she didn't know about her auburn-haired dragonman, let alone his dragon.

Her biggest concern was the mate-claim frenzy. She knew it consisted of lots of sex and a dragon-shifter's dragon half being in charge for a good chunk of it, but she had no idea if Fraser's dragon-half would ever stop until she was pregnant. The thought of not showering or eating for days was bad enough, but a cold thread of fear shot through her body at the image of her being tied to a bed and used like a brood mare.

No. Deep down her gut told her that Fraser would never allow his dragon to treat her that way.

Of course, that wasn't Holly's only concern. The DDA had never explained what happened once the mate-claim frenzy cooled. Holly needed to return home to Aberdeen for her father's sake since humans weren't allowed to live on dragon-shifter territory unless they were a sacrifice. But she had no idea whether a dragon-shifter would allow his true mate to leave or not once the child was born.

Holly resisted placing a hand over her lower abdomen. A frenzy with a true mate always resulted in pregnancy at least once. It was no longer the case Holly might become pregnant; she would for certain.

And she could die.

She growled. Holly wanted answers, damn it, but no one was around to give them to her.

Holly clenched her fingers and started pacing to ease some of her tension. Once she was allowed to see Fraser, and provided the dragon doctor could honestly put his dragon half into a "time out," she was going to tie the dragonman down if need be and demand some answers.

Because no matter what happened or how much Fraser's touch made her heart race, Holly Anderson was going home as soon as her time was up.

~~~

Arabella MacLeod watched as Fergus paced from one window to the next, and then from one door to the next, checking for any signs of trespassing. If only Finn would hurry the hell up and tell them what was going on upstairs, then her cousin-in-law would sit his arse down and stop making her dizzy with all of his pacing.

Adjusting her position in the hard, wooden chair, she sighed. "Fergus, calm down. If it had been an intruder, Finn would've shouted and asked for your help by now."

Fergus turned with a growl. Gone was the usually kind, calm expression. In its place was a snarl and flashing dragon eyes. "It's taking every iota of restraint I have not to rush up the stairs and check on Holly." Fergus ran a hand through his auburn locks. "This isn't how the night was supposed to go."

Arabella's dragon spoke up. *In more ways than one.*

Just because you think there's something between Holly and Fraser doesn't mean it's true. You shouldn't jump to conclusions.

Dragons have a sense about these things. Between the pregnancy and extra hormones, I'm hyperaware of attraction and sexual energy. Speaking of which, where's Finn? I want him again.

Arabella mentally sighed. *As I've told you, no sex tonight. Today's the first time I've kept anything down in weeks. I'm not going to risk it.*

Finn will make us feel good.

Ignoring her dragon, Arabella answered Fergus, "Don't start playing the 'what if' game just yet, Fergus. For all we know, it could be one of the clan members who left two months ago when Finn gave them the option."

Someone in the clan had betrayed Finn by giving the Dragon Knights the codes to the back gates. The knights had wanted Arabella's head. Once Finn and the DDA had cleaned up the mess, Finn had had enough and told anyone who didn't support him and his mate to leave.

Every day Arabella wondered if the clan deserters would come back to wreak havoc.

Fergus growled. "That isn't helping, Ara."

She hated how people other than Finn would only trust her when it suited them on Lochguard. No matter how much the MacKenzies had welcomed Arabella into the clan, she was still an outsider.

Her dragons spoke up again. *They will learn to trust us with time.*

Time is what we don't have right now.

Needing help, Arabella looked to Faye and raised her eyebrows.

Faye took the hint and walked to her brother's side. "Grant would've told me if he or the other Protectors had picked up on a possible threat. I saw him today and he didn't say anything. I highly doubt it's the clan deserters or an intruder, unless they've recruited former Special Forces to their cause."

Fergus met Faye's eyes. "Forgive me, sister, but you haven't been in the loop on inside security threats for nearly two months. After this, I should pay Grant a visit. He's in charge of the Protectors now and he needs to up his game."

Faye jabbed Fergus's chest. "Don't go blaming Grant for some nonexistent threat, Fergus Roger MacKenzie. He's been making all sorts of upgrades since the last attack."

Arabella should stay out of the siblings' conversation, but her curiosity burned to know more. "Since when are you defending Grant McFarland?"

Faye raised her chin. "He's Lochguard's head Protector. We all should be defending him."

Interesting. Finn had mentioned Grant being a bastard to Faye several years ago and them no longer being friends. If Arabella could tame her nausea and exhaustion long enough to ever move about the clan freely again, she would have to be more observant.

Hell, she might even try to tap some of the clan security feeds to finally figure out where Faye spent her days.

Arabella's dragon spoke up. *If we start feeling better, we're not walking about the clan. We're going to drag Finn into a room, lock the door, and ride him hard.*

She mentally sighed. *I enjoy Finn's cock as much as you do, but there is more to life than constant sex.*

Maybe for you. I hardly ever get to fly anymore because of the baby making us sick. Sex is all I have to look forward to.

Arabella was trying to think of how to respond to her beast when footsteps pounded down the stairs. A second later, Finn stood in the doorway with his lips pressed together and a frown on his face. Some called it his pissed off face, but Finn couldn't frighten her. Her mate would rather take his own life than hurt her.

Arabella folded her hands over her stomach and asked, "So, what happened?"

Finn growled out, "Fraser's an idiot."

Fergus took a step toward Finn. "Is Holly okay?"

Finn waved a hand in dismissal. "Holly is a little shook up, but fine. We have a much bigger problem on our hands."

It was Fergus's turn to growl. "Just tell me what the bloody hell is going on, Finn, so I can go comfort Holly."

Finn's eyes flashed for a second. She wasn't sure if anyone else had noticed it, but it had been a split-second of sympathy. Narrowing her eyes, she demanded, "Finlay Stewart, stop stalling and just tell us already."

Finn looked to Faye. "Stand by your brother." Despite the puzzled expression on Faye's face, she obeyed. The second she reached Fergus's side, Finn spit out, "Holly is Fraser's true mate."

Arabella cursed as Fergus made a go for the stairs. Only because Faye wrapped her arms around his chest from behind and leaned backward did Fergus stay put.

Fergus tried to jab Faye in the stomach, but the dragonwoman dodged it easily. Fergus turned his slitted eyes to Finn. "Are you sure? He used that line once before about a female that I wanted and he was lying."

Finn crossed his arms over his chest. "I had to knock Fraser unconscious to stop him from all but attacking Holly. If he was faking it, then his act bloody well convinced me."

Fergus hissed. "Where is he? I need to talk with him."

Finn shook his head. "No, not until you cool down. You can either take your dragon out for a hunt or bed down in one of the empty cottages. Holly's staying here tonight and your presence will only make her feel guiltier than she already does."

Fergus struggled to get free, but Faye tightened her grip. Fergus bit out, "It's not her fault. It's my bloody twin. I swear, if he's faking this time, I will kill him. Hell, I might kill him anyway."

"No killing your twin. We'll find out soon enough if Fraser is telling the truth," Finn stated.

What was left unsaid was if Holly brought on the frenzy and was pregnant by the end of it, then Fraser was indeed telling the truth.

Even from five feet away, Fergus's anger affected her beast. Her dragon couldn't stop pacing or flicking her tail.

Arabella slowly rose to her feet and went to Finn's side. The second she leaned against his chest, some of the tension eased from her body. She murmured, "What about Holly?"

Finn shook his head. "Let's not discuss this right now."

Arabella's dragon chimed in. *I was correct. The human wants Fraser too.*

Let's hope so. That will make talking with the DDA easier.

Finn will find a way. He always does.

Arabella agreed with her beast.

She patted her mate's chest. "The best thing for everyone is to split up until tomorrow. A good night's rest might clear a few heads."

The corner of Finn's mouth ticked up as he looked down at her. "I highly doubt anyone is going to have a good night's sleep."

"You will. You sleep through anything."

Faye cleared her throat. Arabella and Finn both looked in her direction. When they met her eyes, Faye asked, "Can I release Fergus yet?"

The smile vanished from Finn's face as he met Fergus's gaze. "Swear on your mother's life that if Faye releases you, you'll leave the house directly and check in with me in the morning. I also don't want you talking with Fraser unless I'm present."

Fergus's eyes were flashing, but his tone was even as he said, "I swear. Just let me leave or I will kill my brother."

Finn motioned with his hand and Faye released her brother. Before Finn could say anything else, Fergus exited the front door and slammed it behind him.

Finn hugged Arabella tighter and she leaned more into her mate's side. There was a small possibility Fergus would never forgive Fraser for keeping such a big secret from him. Finn might technically be the twins' cousin, but they had grown up together and were more like brothers. The rift would tear his heart in two.

Yet if Finn was hurting inside, the strength and dominance in his voice masked it well as he said to Faye, "Holly is your responsibility for now. She's going to stay in your room with you and you'll be her guard until I say so. Can you handle that?"

Faye hesitated a second and Arabella held her breath. Faye MacKenzie had avoided any sort of Protector-related duties since her accident. But maybe, just maybe, helping her family would restore some of her confidence.

After a long pause, Faye nodded. "I'll ensure Holly's safety. I assume you're taking Fraser away from the house?"

"Aye," Finn answered. "I'll have Dr. Innes inject him with drugs to force his inner dragon into silence."

Arabella frowned. "Is that really necessary?"

"He'll survive a day or two without his beast." Finn ran a hand through his hair. "I need to sort everything with the DDA first. This was a hell of a way to treat our first sacrifice on Lochguard in more than a decade."

Arabella tilted her head. "You'll make it work. You know I only mated you because of your powers of negotiation."

Finn's smile returned. "Aye, it did take a wee while to woo you, lass."

Finn lowered his head and gave Arabella a gentle kiss, which made her dragon roar. *I want more.*

We'll see. It might help Finn relax.

So you change your mind to make him feel better but not me. I'm going to remember that.

Can we argue this later?

Fine.

Finn's voice interrupted Arabella's conversation. "Ara, are you listening?"

She raised an eyebrow. "When am I not?"

He sighed. "How many more months until the baby's here?"

She punched his side. "About seven. And if I'm suffering, you can suffer along with me."

"We can think of how I can suffer along with you later. For now, make sure Holly's okay until I get back. She's locked inside Aunt Lorna's room."

"Of course."

Finn gave her one last gentle kiss and then released her. "Faye, go with Arabella. I'm going to take Aunt Lorna with me. She'll keep Innes in line."

Arabella smiled. "What, you haven't been able to charm Dr. Gregor Innes yet? He's nice to me." Finn growled and Arabella put up her hands. "Okay, I'll stop. Just hurry. The last thing we need is for Fraser to wake up and go after Holly before she's ready."

Finn's face turned grim. "Aye, I know."

With that, there was a knock on the door and Finn went to answer it. As Gregor's voice drifted down the hall, Arabella looked to Faye. "Come, let's go before the doctor sees me and starts asking a million questions."

"Aye, good idea," Faye answered. "That man is fiercely protective of pregnant females. I understand that his mate died in childbirth, but it's been over a decade. He needs to let it go."

Arabella's heart squeezed, but she pushed aside her sympathy. "Then come on."

Faye nodded and moved toward the stairs. Arabella followed.

Two steps up, Arabella's stomach churned and she willed its contents to stay put. There was much to do and she didn't know how much longer she could go without being sick.

Her dragon chimed in. *I will try to help.*

Arabella blinked. *What can you do?*

This.

Her dragon hummed inside their mind and Arabella's stomach settled. She had no idea if her unborn child could hear Arabella and her dragon's conversation, but she wasn't going to question it. She would take all the help she could get.

Rushing past Fraser's room and his unconscious body, Arabella and Faye reached Lorna's room and knocked. Arabella spoke up. "It's me and Faye, Holly. Let us in."

After a brief pause, the lock turned and Holly opened the door. Arabella let out a sigh of relief at the determination in Holly's eyes. Combined with her clenched jaw, the human was more pissed off than scared. "What do you want?"

"Let us inside," Arabella answered. When Holly remained quiet, she added, "You can give me every tip and remedy you know to help with my all-day morning sickness. Before long, I may not have your resources at my disposal."

Arabella knew it was a risk to bring up Holly's possible future, but the human's expression softened and she moved to the side. "Come in, then. If there's one thing that can distract me, it's work."

Arabella smiled. "I'm the same way."

As she entered Lorna's room and sat down on the bed, Arabella thought of as many questions as possible. The longer she distracted Holly, the more at ease the human might become.

Chapter Seven

Fraser groaned as the pounding inside his head grew in intensity with each passing breath.

Although why his head hurt he had no bloody idea. Finn had clocked him in the jaw and not the back of his head.

He half expected his dragon to roar and take control, but his mind was silent.

Maybe too silent.

His mother's voice greeted his ears. "Fraser, lad, open your eyes. We have much to discuss."

Anytime him mum used the words 'much to discuss,' it never boded well for him.

Fraser forced his eyes open and blinked against the dim light until he could make out Lorna's assessing amber eyes. Before he could open his mouth, his mother beat him to it. "First, you're an idiot. Why would you keep something so important from all of us?" He tried to answer, but Lorna cut him off. "Second, do you know the damage you've done? Not just to your brother, but to Finn as well. This questions his leadership. If Finn can't control his own family, how is he supposed to control the clan?"

Fraser growled. "None of that matters right now. Where's Holly? If Finn turned her over to the DDA, so help me, I will challenge him to a fight in public."

Lorna merely watched him. Fraser tried to sit up, but his wrists were restrained.

No matter, he'd gotten out of something similar before. Fraser tried to nudge his dragon awake, but his beast was dead asleep. *Dragon, wake up, you lazy bastard. Holly needs us.*

His dragon remained silent.

Dread pooled in Fraser's stomach. "What have you done, Mother?" He tugged against his restraints. "Let me go. I need to see Holly."

"Aye, and I'd like to go on a date with a handsome film star twenty years my junior. It doesn't mean it's going to happen."

Fraser narrowed his eyes. Even without his dragon's help, he would find a way out. Holly could be on her way to the DDA to receive her punishment for all he knew.

Fraser may not be a soldier, but he'd fight for the lass. She was in trouble because of him. He might not be able to make it right with Fergus, but Fraser would make it right with Holly. Just as soon as he could get free.

If he could get his mum out of the room, Fraser could think of how to escape. "Tell Finn I want to speak with him. Now."

Lorna clicked her tongue. "Demanding, aren't we?"

Fraser had never minded his mother's behavior before, but as he lay there thinking of what could be happening to Holly, he was close to raising his voice and telling his mother to fuck off.

He half expected his dragon to give him advice, but Fraser's beast remained silent.

Fraser didn't like it.

Taking a deep breath, Fraser managed to keep his tone neutral. "Just find Finn. I need to talk with him."

Lorna stood up. "Aye, as you should've done from the beginning."

He sensed there was something else his mother wasn't telling him, but as she opened the door, he held his tongue. The sooner she found Finn, the sooner Fraser could be released and go after Holly.

Not two seconds after the door shut, there was a knock. Since Finn wouldn't bother to knock, Fraser growled out, "What do you want?"

Through the door, he heard Holly's voice. "I was just going to check on you. But if that's the greeting I get, then maybe you need another nap."

Holly. She's here. "Come in, lass. Please."

Even to his own ears it sounded like begging.

Holly opened the door and peeked her head in. He didn't care that her expression was neutral or what she must think of him in that moment. Holly was in Lochguard and not in the hands of the DDA.

Then she smiled at him and some of his unease dissipated. Holly stepped inside the room and shut the door. "Is it wrong that I find you being in restraints funny?"

He frowned. "What the hell are you talking about, woman?"

She crossed her arms over her chest. "Well, think about it. The lady charmer being tied to a bed makes me think of someone's parents keeping you away from their daughter."

"Aye, except it's my own family keeping me away from you."

Holly took two steps toward him. "If I release you, can you restrain yourself and concentrate? Or, will you go into the frenzy?"

Even with everything going on, Fraser was aware that he lay in the same room as his true mate. He didn't like the smudges under her eyes, but her gaze was merely curious. As her long, dark hair swayed against her round face, his heart warmed. "So you don't hate me, then?"

Holly rolled her eyes. "You willingly allowed Finn to knock you unconscious to keep me safe. If that wasn't noble, then I don't know what is."

"That still doesn't answer my question."

"Since when are dragon-shifter males this sensitive?"

Fraser should grunt and let it be. However, as her honey-colored eyes searched his, he decided he would always be honest with Holly. He wasn't about to fuck up a second time. "This male is only sensitive when it concerns you."

She blinked. "You've known me for two days. Why do you care so much?"

Fraser tugged one of his arms. "Let me go and I'll bloody well tell you. I'm not about to have this conversation with you whilst I'm tied to the bed."

"Answer the question first, Fraser."

"Of course my true mate would be stubborn," he muttered. When Holly merely raised an eyebrow, he sighed. "Fine. I've never been drawn to a lass as much as I am to you, okay? Now, let me up."

"Is it only because of your dragon's instinct?"

"Just what has my family been telling you?"

Holly shrugged. "That your inner dragon senses the person who is their best chance at happiness and it brings on the frenzy. Supposedly, it's good news for me as it's less likely for a true mate to die in childbirth."

Fraser chose his next words carefully. "So if Finn transfers the contract, you'll allow the frenzy to happen?"

Holly averted her eyes and traced the skin above the cuff restraints. The soft, gentle motions of her finger made him want to shiver. Only through sheer stubbornness did he remain still.

A section of her hair fell in front of her face and Fraser itched to brush it back behind her ear. Holly Anderson should never hide her beauty from him.

His eyes glanced down at her breasts. He wanted to strip her and simply memorize every curve of her body.

Before his mind could continue with his fantasy, Holly's voice interrupted his thoughts. "That depends." She met his eyes again. "If Finn can transfer the contract, then I want you to try to repair relations with your brother. If you promise me that and put in a good effort, then I'll agree to the frenzy."

Fraser ignored the skip of his heart at her answer. "Did my family put you up to this or is it of your own accord?"

Holly stopped brushing his skin and he nearly begged for her to touch him again.

Bloody hell. Fraser had never yearned for a lass's touch so much in his life. Especially without his dragon going on about it.

He'd put it down to the lingering effects of his dragon's need to mate. There was nothing certain between him and Holly. And Fraser wasn't about to wish for what he couldn't have. Hell, after two weeks, they might not be able to stand each other. True mates didn't always end in true love.

Bloody hell, he was starting to sound like a sappy movie.

Despite his dragon's silence, Fraser swore he heard his beast's growl inside his head. Good. Maybe his dragon was waking up. For better or worse, Fraser missed the randy sod.

Holly finally answered, "It's my own decision. If you think I'm easily swayed by someone taller and much stronger than I, then let me set the record straight: I don't put up with anyone's crap, least of all a grumpy, alpha male. I may be human, but I've dealt with my fair share of alpha arseholes in the delivery room. I won every single time when they challenged me."

Fraser had always wooed and bedded females who flirted or fell for his pretty words. Holly was a completely new challenge for him.

And bastard that he was, he rather liked the idea of winning her over. "That may be, but you have yet to handle a dragon in the throes of a frenzy."

The female raised her chin. "I won't put up with crap from a dragon either."

There was definitely a stirring in the back of his mind. Maybe the lass's backbone was enticing his dragon.

After all, his beast had always urged Fraser to go after more difficult females. To his dragon, Holly was the equivalent of a fat stag waiting to be hunted and devoured. Although, both man and beast had different ideas of how to devour Holly Anderson.

Fraser reached out to touch her, but the leather around his wrists dug into his skin. "Release me, Holly, and I'll make an effort toward my brother."

"If you don't follow through, there will be hell to pay."

The corner of his mouth kicked up. "From a wee lass as yourself?"

"Aye, this 'wee lass' has a few tricks up her sleeve."

Fraser's dragon cracked his eyes open and yawned. *Hurry up, dragon. The silence is killing me.*

His beast shook his head and stretched. His dragon wasn't quite ready to wake up yet.

Holly's voice brought him back to the hospital room. "Is your dragon breaking free again?"

"He'll be groggy for a while yet. Release me, lass. There's much to do before the frenzy starts."

Holly hesitated, but finally undid the cuff on his left hand. The second it was free, he reached up to cup her cheek.

Holly stilled and Fraser held his breath. Maybe the lass's words didn't match the truth in her heart.

Then she leaned into his touch and reached across his body to undo the other cuff. Her long hair tickled against his chest. With his free hand, he tucked a section behind her ear and murmured, "Much better."

Holly freed his other wrist and met his eyes. With her heat and scent surrounding him, all he wanted to do was kiss her.

But not yet. At least, not on the lips. He wouldn't allow his dragon to ruin his second chance with the lass.

Fraser traced her brow, the bridge of her nose, and finally her lips. Holly parted them and he rubbed back and forth across her plump bottom lip. "Thank you, Holly." Before she could answer, he raised his head and kissed her cheek. "I'm glad you met me first."

~~~

Holly's heart thundered inside her chest. She'd entered Fraser's hospital room as nervous as she'd been on her first solo nursing shift. But her heart was currently beating fast for an entirely different reason.

Finn and Arabella had warned her against any prolonged skin-to-skin contact, lest she stir Fraser's dragon and begin the frenzy.

Yet as Fraser's breath danced against her cheek, her resolve fractured slightly. She'd been told not to kiss him on the lips.

She would keep that promise, but she yearned to taste Fraser's skin.

Holly turned her head. Fraser's dark blue eyes were less than six inches from her own. For the first time, she noticed flecks of lighter blue around the iris.

Fraser's pupils flashed to slits and back. His dragon must be waking up, which meant she didn't have much time.

Leaning around his face, she whispered into his ear, "Don't tell the others, but I'm glad I met you first, too."

Fraser growled and she took his earlobe between her teeth. As she teased his flesh with her tongue, his hand wrapped around her waist before sliding down to her arse. "I knew your tightly controlled appearance was hiding the true lass beneath." He slapped her bum lightly. "I look forward to seeing her free and open to my hands, my mouth, and my cock."

She released his ear. "You still have to earn all of that, Fraser Moore MacKenzie."

"What are you talking about?"

Smiling at the disappointment in his voice, she moved her head until she could see his eyes. "It takes more than a few pretty phrases and caresses before I trust you with my body."

He frowned. "Did they not explain the frenzy properly? Because my dragon isn't going to care about games until after you're pregnant."

"We'll see about that, Fraser. After all, your dragon has yet to really get to know me."

Fraser's grip tightened on her bum. "My dragon will have to get in line. You're going to know me first."

Sensing the conversation was heading toward talk of a more permanent future on Lochguard, Holly pulled away and stood. Confusion flashed in Fraser's eyes, but it was gone before Holly could blink.

Tossing her hair over her shoulder, Holly changed topics. "Well, seeing as Finn and Dr. Innes talked about keeping your dragon sedated for days if need be, that might be easier than you think."

"Days? Why?"

She searched his eyes. "Is it really that awful to be without your dragon for a few days?"

Fraser adjusted his position on the bed until he was sitting upright and cleared a space at the edge. Taking the hint, Holly sat down and he answered, "My dragon started speaking to me when I was six. For twenty-two years I've had a constant companion with me. Sometimes he's a pain and most other times he drives me crazy. But he is part of me. I know it's hard for a human to understand, but imagine taking something essential to who you are and ripping it from your life. That's what it's like to have your dragon go silent and remain that way for any prolonged period of time."

Holly tilted her head. "But surely there's more to you than just your dragon."

"Aye, there is. But the silence is uncomfortable. It's probably similar to taking away your ability to nurse, every hobby you enjoy, plus not seeing your dad even though you know he's still alive back in Aberdeen. You could probably live without all of those if need be, but you wouldn't be the same person you are now."

Holly looked away from Fraser. She should tell him about her plans to return home. Much like his dragon was essential to Fraser's being, her dad was to hers. After all, it'd been just the two of them for longer than Holly could remember.

Fraser touched her lower back. "I don't like secrets, Holly. Tell me what's on your mind, lass."

THE DRAGON'S DILEMMA

Deciding it wasn't the time to talk of her future when she barely knew the dragon-shifter beside her, Holly forced a smile and looked back to Fraser's face. "I just miss my father is all. You seem close to your mum, so you understand."

Fraser's voice turned dry. "Aye, we're close but maybe a tad too close."

Holly grinned. "I like her."

"Of course you would, honey. She's always going to take your side against me."

Holly poked his chest. "My name's not Honey."

Fraser reached out and brushed her cheek. "I know that, but I can't help but use it. You have such bonny eyes."

Heat flooded Holly's cheeks. "They're just brown."

Fraser took her chin between his fingers and turned her head one way and then the other. "No, you're wrong, lass. They're dark amber with little flecks of brown and green. If you don't like Honey, then I can call you Kitty."

She rolled her eyes. "Let me guess, I have cat eyes?"

Fraser grinned. The humor dancing in his eyes in addition to his pearly whites made him extremely handsome.

Unable to resist, she traced the scar near his left eye. "Where'd this come from?"

Fraser trapped her hand against his cheek. "Sit next to me and I'll tell you."

"I am sitting next to you."

He tugged and she tumbled onto his chest. Heat radiated off his bare skin. Combined with his masculine scent and light brushing of hair against her cheek, Holly felt safe and wanted to lay against his chest for hours.

Fraser's chuckle rumbled inside his chest before he said, "Now this is what I call sitting next to me."

She looked up. "This is technically laying on you."

He winked and her heart skipped a beat. "Call it whatever you like while I enjoy your soft body against mine."

"I can't help being soft. I'm not a dragon-shifter with a metabolism of a thirteen-year-old boy."

Fraser ran his hand down her back, her hip, and over her bum. "I like it that you're soft. But can I tell you the truth?"

She raised her brows. "Let me guess, something about me needing to be naked before you can make a final judgment?"

The dragonman's grin widened. "Exactly."

Shaking her head, Holly answered, "You're fairly predictable, dragonman."

Fraser's hand slapped her backside. "As soon as I'm out of this bed and not under constant threat of a frenzy, I'll show you just how unpredictable I can be."

She patted his chest. "You can try, but you won't succeed."

Determination flashed in Fraser's eyes. "If there's one thing you should know about me, it's that when I'm told I can't do something, I usually find a way to see it through."

"Oh, really? Then maybe I should tell you not to talk with your brother and then you will."

Fraser's lips pressed together. "I'll handle Fergus."

Holly knew Fergus was missing and hadn't reported in to Finn yet, but she decided not to mention it to Fraser. She didn't need to stir his anger and possibly his dragon just yet.

Rather than speak again, Holly seized the quiet moment to become used to Fraser's touch and scent.

She rested her head back against Fraser's chest and took a second to memorize the firmness of his muscles and the unique scent that was Fraser MacKenzie. It wouldn't be long before she was doing much more than pressing against him.

The Dragon's Dilemma

Holly should be afraid, but the thought of Fraser's deep blue eyes staring into hers as she came sent a flood of heat through her body.

Stop it, Holly. She was about to ask a question to distract herself when Fraser's hand roamed her back and caressed her in slow circles. Each pass helped to relax her muscles and ease her tension.

It was almost as if the bloody dragonman had magic hands.

Not that she'd ever admit that to Fraser. She could just imagine how cocky his grin would become then.

Clearing her throat, she looked up and touched Fraser's scar again. "Tell me about this."

Fraser shrugged, but never ceased stroking her back. "I was trying to scare away a few males following my sister. I tripped over a rock and earned what I like to call my scar of love and devotion."

Holly snorted. "In other words, your scar of clumsiness."

"Hey, now, dragon-shifters need to keep up an image of strength."

She looked up. "Why lie about it? A person can be strong, even if they have faults."

Fraser smiled. "You're too clever, you know that?"

"It's good for you to recognize that now."

With a growl, he slapped her arse. "Once I'm back at full-strength, dragon and all, you'll see just how clever I can be."

Holly should object to Fraser constantly slapping her bum, but she rather enjoyed the closeness. "Oh, really? I look forward to the challenge."

Fraser brushed his finger against her cheek. The humor in his eyes faded and was replaced with something much hotter. "Let's just say I look forward to a challenge as well."

He leaned down as if to kiss her. For a split second, Holly nearly gave in to the temptation. Considering a heated gaze would send a thrill through her body and wetness between her legs, she wondered what actually kissing Fraser would be like.

Then she remembered her meeting with Finn and Arabella earlier in the morning. They'd told her not to kiss him on the lips.

If it would only affect her and Fraser, she would kiss him right this second. But it wasn't that way. There was Fergus, Finn, and hell, the whole clan to think about. After all, she didn't know if Finn had successfully wrangled an agreement out of the DDA yet or not.

Laying her head back on his torso, she patted the firm planes of his chest. "The others should be here any minute. I really should get out of your bed."

Fraser wrapped his arm around her back and hugged her tighter against him. "Stay, Holly."

Glancing back up, she asked dryly, "So you can use me as a shield and Finn won't punch you again?"

"Hey, now, what happened to me being noble before? I liked that better."

She smiled. "Being noble comes and goes. You'll have to work hard to keep it up."

He gave an exaggerated sigh. "And here I thought you would be on my side. Does being the possible father of your child mean nothing?"

Before she could answer, there was a knock and the door opened before Holly could do more than turn her head.

Finn stood in the doorway. He studied them for a second before entering and shutting the door behind him. Finn looked to Fraser. "I see you haven't wasted any time in luring Holly into your bed."

108

The Dragon's Dilemma

Holly turned a little toward Finn and replied before Fraser, "I'm here of my own free will. I'm not easily 'lured' as you put it."

Apology flashed in Finn's eyes. "Sorry, lass. Let's just say that I've had a hell of a day and it's not even half over yet."

CHAPTER EIGHT

At the sight of Finn entering his room, Fraser's dragon rumbled in the back of his mind. While his beast still sounded sleepy, it wouldn't be much longer before his dragon woke up and tried to wrestle away control.

Fraser hugged Holly tighter against his body and then jumped in. "Did you talk to the DDA, Finn?"

Finn's gaze turned neutral. "Aye, I have."

Fraser frowned. "And? From your tone, I'm not convinced it's good news."

Whether Holly realized it or not, she leaned more against Fraser. *Good.* The lass wanted him to be her assigned dragonman.

Whatever it took, Fraser would find a way to ensure it happened.

Finn crossed his arms over his chest. "They transferred the contract." Fraser's heart skipped a beat at the same time as his dragon gave a sleepy roar. However, Finn added quickly, "But it came with a cost."

Holly asked, "What?"

Finn's brows furrowed. "I have to allow a bloody human scientist to live on my lands for six months to do research."

Fraser should feel sorry, but as he caressed Holly's side, all he could think about was that Holly would be his soon enough. "It could be worse."

Finn growled. "The older dragon-shifters are going to have strokes when I tell them a human is coming to study us. You will owe me big time. Once the frenzy is over, we'll discuss terms."

Fraser's dragon stretched one leg and then another. The action reminded him of all that was about to happen. "Fine, but we can do that later. Right now, we need to discuss the short-term future. My dragon's waking up."

Finn answered, "We could drug him again."

Holly spoke up. "No, I don't want that."

Finn searched Holly's eyes and Fraser took a more possessive hold on his female. Knowing Finn was happily mated didn't matter. Until Fraser and his beast claimed Holly, every male was a threat.

Finn finally answered, "Your adjustment period will vanish if we don't, Holly. Are you ready to face Fraser and his dragon? I'm not sure you're truly prepared for what's about to happen."

Holly sat up and raised her chin. "I discussed it with Fraser. I'm ready."

Finn nodded. "Aye, I can see the stubborn determination in your eyes. However, I want a word alone with Fraser first." Finn motioned toward the door. "Faye is waiting in the hall to take you to the cottage you and Fraser will have to yourselves. Faye can answer any lingering questions you might have on the way."

Fraser's dragon snarled. He said in a sleepy voice, *Holly is ours. Don't let her out of our sight. Another male might try to take her.*

It will be for just a short while. Faye will keep her safe.

His beast grunted. *She'd better or I will challenge her.*

Finn's voice prevented Fraser's from answering. "Damn, Fraser's eyes are flashing. Holly, go quickly. Fraser will follow before too much longer."

Holly turned her face toward Fraser. Her honey-colored eyes were concerned. "Will you be okay?"

His dragon roared. *We won't be okay until she's naked and we're inside her.*

Not yet.

Hurry. We must brand her to keep her safe from Fergus and the others.

Fergus won't betray Finn or the clan. And the others won't cross Faye.

His dragon was about to say something else, but Fraser gritted his teeth and ignored his beast to force a nod. "I'll be fine. It'll be easier with you out of the room, honey. Wait for me. I'll come to claim you soon."

Heat flared in Holly's eyes and Fraser's dragon snarled. *She is ready. Take her.*

Only because his dragon was still groggy from the medication could Fraser keep his beast at bay. "Go, Holly."

With a nod, his human moved from the bed and went to the door. After one last look, she exited the room and shut the door behind her.

Fraser clutched the bedsheets with his fingers as his dragon continued to roar and snarl. It wouldn't be long before his beast would be strong enough to take control, so Fraser growled out, "What do you want?"

Finn closed the distance between them and stared down at Fraser. His clan leader's amber eyes were hard. "Fergus is missing. You know him better than anyone else in the world. Where would he go?"

Guilt squeezed Fraser's heart. He really had wanted to speak with his twin before going into the frenzy. But it looked like it wasn't going to happen until afterward. "Fergus has several places he likes to go to escape the family and to think. Mum and Faye know of a few."

"And the ones they don't know about?"

Fraser's dragon flicked his tail, but Fraser managed to keep his beast contained for the moment. "He likes to perch on one of the hills or mountains around Loch Shin. Since the humans in and around Lairg village believe a dragon-sighting is good luck, he can observe them and not be reported to the DDA."

Finn frowned. "Since when has Fergus been observing humans?"

"His whole life." Fraser's dragon roared and then roared some more. Fraser clutched the sheets even tighter in his hand and managed to say, "We can talk about his obsession with human-dragon mythology later. I don't know how much longer I can control my beast."

"Aye, I can see that. Stand up. Grant and I will escort you to Holly."

Fraser rolled to his side and placed his feet on the floor. The second he stood, Finn grabbed his bicep and moved his face closer until it was a few inches from Fraser's. "The second the frenzy is over, you call me. We have much to discuss."

"You're starting to sound a lot like my mum."

Finn growled. "Now is not the time for flippant comments." He tugged Fraser's bicep and they started walking. "Come. The sooner you're with Holly, the sooner I can focus on the half-dozen other problems newly landed on my plate."

"I would say I'm sorry, but would you apologize for Arabella?"

His cousin grunted. "I don't care about an apology. I just want you to bloody well confide in me from now on."

Holly sat on the bed for a few seconds before standing again. Pacing to the window and back to the bed, she tried to focus on anything else but that Fraser was coming to claim her.

Her stomach both fluttered and flipped. The anticipation was killing her.

Since Holly was alone in the cottage, all she could think about was Fraser ripping off her clothes and covering her soft body with his hard one. Fraser the man would be playful and somewhat patient. Fraser the dragon half, however, she had no idea what to expect.

She would be a fool to deny it scared her a little.

Her nerves had been made worse by Faye muttering something about not wanting to be there when Fraser arrived. The fact a strong dragon-shifter was afraid of her own brother didn't speak well of what would happen.

Buck up, Holly. Maybe Faye didn't want to see her brother half naked and kissing Holly. Given the option, most siblings didn't like to see their brothers or sisters fondling someone else.

Holly moved back to the window. It was mid-morning and the light drizzle sprinkled against the glass. Born and raised in Scotland, Holly hadn't even bothered to ask for an umbrella on the short walk to the cottage. As a result, her hair was damp and frizzy.

Maybe under normal circumstances, she'd care more about her appearance. But as her stomach flipped again and her heart pounded, Holly wanted to be ready the second Fraser arrived. She didn't have time for a shower or to find some new clothes.

A part of her was sorry for causing Lochguard so much trouble, but another part of her wouldn't apologize. After laying on Fraser's chest and being surrounded by his heat, she wanted Fraser and only Fraser. It was selfish and she knew it. But for at least a short period in her life, Holly wanted to experience passion. Once she left Lochguard, she might never experience it again; human men often held prejudices against women who had sacrificed themselves to the dragons.

Not to mention Holly would want to visit her child at times. It would take a very understanding human man to accept she'd not only sacrificed herself, but also to accept the fact she would have a half-dragon-shifter child.

No, the only passion she would ever have would be her brief time with Fraser.

Rubbing her arms, three shapes appeared in the distance and Holly stopped thinking about what would happen to her after she left. It was time to face the path she'd chosen.

She leaned closer toward the window. But because of the drizzle, all she could make out was two men holding a third man between them. One of them could be Fraser.

She hugged her upper body and held her breath. Two seconds later, the man in the middle looked up at the window. Even from a distance, the intensity of Fraser's gaze made her heart skip a beat.

Holly shivered at imagining that gaze on her body when she was naked. She'd had her fair share of boyfriends, but none had looked at her with half the hunger of Fraser MacKenzie.

She only hoped it wasn't entirely because of his dragon.

Blinking, Holly pushed that thought aside. It wasn't as if she could keep Fraser, not even if she survived the birth. She would have to give up everything she knew—her career, her father, her friends—if she stayed. Could she really manage that and still remain who she was?

Maybe there was some way everything could work out in the end. But as the figures disappeared through the door below, all she could think about was the immediate future and seeing Fraser again.

Holly turned away from the window. Each second that passed made her heart beat faster. As the sound of steps on the stairs and then in the hall grew nearer, she clenched and unclenched her fingers. The wait was going to kill her.

Someone knocked and Finn's voice drifted through the door. "Are you ready, Holly? I'm not sure I can pull Fraser back once he sees you."

This was it. For a split second, Holly's confidence faltered. Could she really handle a dragonman in the throes of a frenzy? Not only that, but would Fraser's human-half disappear completely for the next week or more?

Finn's voice boomed again. "Holly? Are you all right, lass?"

Taking a deep breath, Holly nodded to herself. There was no point in delaying the inevitable. It was time to fulfill her contract. "I'm ready. Let him in."

The doorknob turned and then Fraser was standing opposite her, restrained between Finn and a man she'd seen only once before, when Faye had escorted her out of the surgery. Grant-something-or-other.

Fraser growled as his pupils flashed to slits and back. "Mine. Let me have her. She's my mate."

Holly nodded at Finn and the two men released Fraser, pushed him into the room, and shut the door.

For a split second, neither she nor Fraser moved. But then the spell broke and Fraser stood right in front of her. Looping his arm around her waist, he drew Holly flush against his body. "Are you ready, honey?"

THE DRAGON'S DILEMMA

Her heart pounded harder. Holly placed a hand on Fraser's chest and lifted her face. "Yes, now hurry up and kiss me."

With a growl, Fraser's mouth descended on hers.

~~~

Fraser's dragon roared as their lips touched. *Let me take her until she carries our young.*

Holding out a few seconds longer, Fraser focused on exploring Holly's sweet mouth. His human hesitated at first, but then leaned against him and met him stroke for stroke. With a growl, he moved his hands to her backside and rocked her against his hard cock.

Holly gasped and broke the kiss. Fraser leaned forward and took her lips again.

His dragon snarled. *I need to fuck her. Stop stalling. Give her to me.*

You're going to share.

No. You will stop before she carries our child. Only I can last long enough to brand her with our scent. Only then will the other males stay away.

I need to ensure she's ready. You don't want to hurt her, do you?

His beast snarled. *Never.*

Then give me five minutes.

No more. At the end of five minutes, I won't ask. I will take.

Aware he didn't have much time, Fraser broke their kiss. Holly's breath was hot and fast against his lips as he murmured, "I only have a few minutes with you, Holly, before my dragon takes over. I know I have yet to earn your trust, but will you allow me to undress you? I want to make sure you're ready so my dragon won't hurt you."

Holly's fingers danced against the back of his neck. "If either one of you starts hurting me, I will find a way to stop you."

117

"Holly—"

She placed a finger over his lips. "I can scold you about your lack of confidence in me later."

She ran her finger up and down his lip. Each stroke shot straight to his cock. Fraser nipped her finger and whispered, "Then it's time to get you naked."

Fraser scooped Holly up and tossed her onto the bed. As she blinked in confusion, Fraser ripped her shirt down the middle before extending a talon and slicing open her bra. With a flick of his hands, her breasts were visible. At the sight of her plump, creamy skin, he licked his lips.

He traced her dark pink nipple as he said, "So hard and pretty." He then cupped her full breast. "And slightly larger than my hand. I need to taste them."

Fraser leaned down and flicked his tongue over her other nipple. Holly drew in a breath and he sucked her tight bud between his teeth. As he bit gently, Holly moaned and unconsciously opened her legs in invitation.

His dragon snarled. *She is offering herself to us. Rip off her clothes and devour her pussy. I want to taste her now.*

Humans like patience.

You have just under four minutes.

Silently cursing his dragon, he promised himself to tease Holly into frustration later. In the moment, he needed to make sure she was nice and wet because once his dragon started, he wouldn't stop fucking Holly for who the hell knew how long.

Releasing her nipple with a pop, he moved to kiss the skin between her breasts. He couldn't resist blowing on her skin.

Holly threaded her fingers through his hair and met his eyes. Her pupils were dilated and her cheeks already flushed. "Fraser."

Rubbing the skin of her abdomen in a slow back-and-forth motion, he whispered, "I wish I could spend an hour memorizing every curve and tender spot of your upper body." He kissed between her breasts again. "But my dragon is impatient for more."

Holly's breathing was faster than before and her voice husky as she asked, "Just your dragon?"

He growled as he took a possessive hold of her breasts. "I've been imagining you naked and at my mercy since I first met you, Holly Anderson. Say the word and I'll show you a fraction of what I want to do to your beautiful body."

His human wiggled her hips. "Then you'd better hurry up and show me before your dragon breaks loose."

His beast growled. *I like her. I bet she is already wet. Let me have her.*

No. It's not your turn.

Fraser ran a hand down her ribs and over her round, soft belly.

A belly that might soon hold his child.

Longing surged through his body at the thought of a child with Holly. But he pushed it aside for the moment. He didn't have much time.

He extended a talon again and sliced through her trousers and her underwear. With a quick tug, the fabric ripped and Fraser tossed it onto the floor. The next second, her shoes and socks were gone, too.

Holly closed her legs and then moved her hand to cover the patch of dark hair between her legs, but he grabbed her hands and pinned them to her side. Looking up, he licked his lips. "I need to taste you. Open your legs and show me your beautiful pussy." Holly's cheeks flushed pink, but she opened her legs. When she looked away, he squeezed her hands. "I want you to watch me."

His human frowned and looked back at him. "I never agreed you could order me around."

His dragon spoke up again. *Two minutes.*

Moving her hands so he could keep a grip on them with one hand, he rubbed slow circles on her inner thigh. Holly moaned and he removed his hand.

She growled. "Don't you dare tease me like that."

"Then watch me."

"We're going to talk about this later, Fraser MacKenzie."

He lightly traced the lips of her pussy with a finger and Holly drew in a breath. Taking the sound as encouragement, he ran his finger back and forth through her slit. "Trust me. Watching me will make it hotter."

As soon as he said it, Holly's frown deepened. But as his eyes flashed, she merely nodded. "For now. But this isn't over, Fraser Moore. I very much believe in payback."

He tried not to laugh at the sternness of her voice. "I can live with that."

Not wanting to waste another second, Fraser moved back and leaned between her thighs.

Holly was swollen and glistening already. Just for him.

It would always be for him.

Fraser took a long, slow lick and savored the sweet taste of his female. "You're fucking perfect." Holly averted her gaze and he growled before taking another quick taste. "I will never get enough of you."

Holly refused to look back at him, so Fraser blew up and down her folds. A moan escaped Holly's lips and Fraser murmured, "Watch me devour you."

She obeyed at the same time as his beast spoke up. *Your time's nearly up.*

THE DRAGON'S DILEMMA

Wanting a few more minutes with his true mate, Fraser seeded every bit of dominance he possessed in his reply. *I want and will take a few more minutes. Hush.*

Shocked, his beast merely blinked. Taking advantage of the distraction, Fraser leaned back down and lapped a few more times before swirling up and around Holly's clit but never touching it.

"Fraser."

The unspoken order in her voice made both man and beast happy. She wanted to be claimed.

Caressing her hips, he finally flicked his tongue over her sensitive bud. He swirled faster and Holly moaned his name. She was close.

He might just be able to make his human come before his dragon took over.

Fraser was just about to nibble her sensitive bud when his dragon snarled. *Time's up.*

No. I want more time with her.

You took too long. It's my turn.

In the next second, Fraser was trapped in the back of his mind. He shoved against the invisible wall, but his bloody dragon was strong. The frenzy was about to start.

Fraser tried one last-ditched effort. *Holly is ours. At least share her.*

No. The only way to keep the other males away is to fuck her and impregnate her. She is at my mercy now.

As much as his dragon wanted to brand and claim Holly, Fraser wanted to do it first. His human deserved a little tenderness.

Fraser searched for a way to break free, but his dragon wasted no time in speaking aloud. "You're mine, Holly. I need to claim you now."

121

~~~

One second Holly had been enjoying Fraser's tongue and the next her hands were pinned over her head with Fraser's hard body lying on top of her. Looking at his eyes, the pupils were slitted and didn't flash.

She was currently dealing with Fraser's dragon.

Her heart rate kicked up. As much as she understood Fraser and his dragon were one and the same, the dragon's gaze lacked Fraser's humor. In its place was hunger and desire.

Holly shivered. The action felt like a betrayal to Fraser; she wanted her first time to be with his human half.

The dragon spoke in Fraser's voice, which made the situation even more surreal. "Are you ready? I'm going to brand you now. You're my female." He leaned downed and nipped her neck. "Fraser wants to make sure you're ready." The dragon eyes looked back at her. "Are you?"

As Fraser-slash-dragon continued to nip and lick her neck, Holly nearly gave in. But remembering Fraser's grin and teasing, she pushed down her desire and answered, "Not with you. Give me Fraser the first time. You can have me as many times as you wish after that."

He frowned. "We are one and the same."

"No, I want the other half."

Anger flashed in his eyes. "You are mine. I need to fuck you."

He leaned down and took her nipple into his mouth. Holly cried out in pleasure and realized talking with him wasn't going to work.

While Holly would fulfill her contract, she was going to do it on her own terms.

THE DRAGON'S DILEMMA

Moving her head to the side, she opened her mouth and bit down on the dragonman's arm with all of her might.

With a roar, Fraser's dragon half released his grip on her arm and her breast. Using the split-second advantage, Holly reached down between them and swung a punch toward Fraser's cock and bollocks.

She made contact with a smack.

Not even the dragon half was strong enough to withstand the pain of being punched in the dick and he grabbed himself and rolled over. Holly jumped out of the bed, picked up the lamp on the nightstand, and held it up over her shoulder. She debated hitting him on the head without a warning, but then Fraser turned over. His pupils were round and his voice was strangled as he said, "I should thank you, honey. But seriously, what the fuck?"

While she relaxed her grip on the lamp slightly, Holly didn't put it down. "Your dragon wasn't behaving, so I taught him a lesson."

"Aye, I'd say you did." Fraser groaned again before adding, "Put the bloody lamp down. You've scared him and he's not coming out again until you say it's okay."

She raised an eyebrow. "How do I know your dragon's telling the truth? From what little experience I have with him, he doesn't take suggestions or bother to discuss something first."

"You have no reason to trust me, but my dragon's sulking in the back of my mind. He's never been bested by a human female before."

"Good."

Fraser took a deep breath before sitting upright. "Come, lass. At least let me hold you. The contact will calm you, me, and my dragon."

Holly's heart thundered inside her chest as she scrutinized Fraser's face. His pupils were still round and the lightheartedness

123

had returned to his gaze. "I have a compromise. I can sit with you, but the lamp's coming with me."

The corner of Fraser's mouth ticked up. "As long as you don't try to shove it up my arse, then aye, bring the bloody lamp if it makes you feel safer."

Holly smiled. "Thanks for the idea. Tell your dragon to mind his manners or I might just have to try it."

Shaking his head, Fraser murmured, "You have gumption, I'll give you that."

"I'm just glad my idea worked. Angering a dragon is risky, but he needs to learn some manners."

"I may have spoiled him a bit."

"So not all dragon halves act that way?"

Fraser motioned toward the bed. "Come sit with me and I'll answer your questions." She raised her brows and he added, "It's not like I'm going to ravish you, lass. Not even a dragon-shifter can sustain a punch to the dick without needing a little time to recover."

Darting a quick glance down, Fraser removed his hands. He was indeed no longer standing at attention.

Still, she kept the lamp gripped in one hand as she sat on the edge of the bed. In the next second, Fraser moved her to his lap. The skin-to-skin contact helped to ease her concern and she relaxed a fraction. When Fraser rubbed his hand up and down her arm, it helped a little bit more.

He whispered, "What would you like to know, Holly?"

~~~

Fraser reveled in the soft, heavy weight of the female sitting in his lap.

124

The Dragon's Dilemma

Never before had he sat naked with a female and been content with merely holding her. Yet as he rubbed up and down her arm, Holly's feminine scent helped him to not only forget about the pulsing pain in his cock, but it also helped to slow his dragon's pacing. Fraser said to his beast, *What happened to wanting a challenge?*

His beast huffed. *I didn't expect for her to punch us there.*

At least you'll think twice about trying to force her again.

With a harrumph, his dragon fell silent.

He kissed the side of Holly's neck and her body relaxed a wee bit more. "What would you like to know, Holly? Ask me anything."

She turned her head to meet his eyes. "Why couldn't you control your dragon just now?"

Fraser shrugged one shoulder. "I've never had a reason to try and contain him before. Some might say I've spoiled him. To be honest, we've never really disagreed about anything until we met you."

Holly raised her chin. For all that she was trying to look brave, her wild, frizzy hair and nakedness made him want to laugh. Thankfully, before he did, Holly answered, "Well, if he tries something like that again, I'll be ready. I might even find a taser and use it instead of my fist next time."

Fraser winced. "Whatever you do, don't mention that option to other humans who come here. The last thing we need is a group of dragon-shifter males with fried cocks." Holly smiled and the sight made his stomach flip. He brushed her cheek with one hand. "It's good to see you smiling again, honey."

"That's still not my name."

"Aye, I know. But no one else has used that name for you, have they?" Holly shook her head. "Good. Then it's yet another way for me to claim you."

"I should be offended at that."

He grinned. "But you're not, are you?"

She sighed. "Answering that may feed your ego, and you definitely don't need that."

Nuzzling her cheek, he murmured, "I could do with some ego feeding." He nipped her earlobe. "It might help me forget about the pain."

He released her ear and kissed his way across her cheek until he was less than an inch from her lips. Meeting her eyes, he whispered, "Although I could settle for a kiss instead. One taste of your lips will make everything better."

Holly fought a smile and lost the battle. "You were quite the ladies' man before you met me, weren't you?"

He frowned. "Why would you bring up other women? None of them compare to you."

His human finally tossed the lamp to the floor. It landed with a thud on the carpet and she placed her currently free hand on his chest. "I wonder if that's you, your dragon, or your penis talking."

Fraser growled. "I was trying to make up for my dragon's behavior, yes, but I'm speaking the truth." He took her face in his hands. "No one has ever resisted my charms before, let alone taken on my dragon in a fit and won. That's pretty bloody fantastic, Holly Anderson." He strummed his finger against her cheek. "Just as you are, too." He laid his forehead against hers. "Now, you stubborn woman, I'm going to kiss you and convince you of my words." He moved a fraction closer. "Provided you won't punch me in the dick again."

Holly grinned and mischief danced in her eyes. "Then I guess you'd better make me forget how to think, let alone act, and your dick will be safe." She lowered her voice. "At least, for now. I make no guarantees about later."

The urge to tease Holly some more was strong, but his cock was already hardening and he didn't want Holly, let alone his dragon, to change their minds.

So, Fraser lightly kissed her and answered, "Then I just need to ensure I leave you begging for more. That way, all of me will be safe from your devious mind."

Holly opened her mouth, but Fraser swallowed her reply with a kiss.

CHAPTER NINE

Holly wasn't sure if she was happy or irritated that Fraser shut her up with a kiss. Very few people had ever tried to take charge of her.

Yet as his taste and heat filled her mouth, she leaned into him. As he slowly strummed his thumbs against her cheeks, he took his time in exploring every inch.

The tenderness made her forget about his dragon-half. In time, Holly was sure she would enjoy rough, hot dragon sex. But she wasn't there yet.

Turning toward him, she wrapped her legs around his waist. Fraser moaned as his hands slid down her neck and her back before resting on her bum. He rocked her hips forward and her clit brushed his hard abdomen. When he did it again, she had a hard time focusing on the kiss.

Fraser finally released her lips and whispered, "Will you let me explore your beautiful body properly this time?"

She should just say yes and enjoy Fraser's attentions. But Holly didn't want false platitudes. "You've barely seen my body. How do you know it's beautiful?"

Fraser growled as he lightly slapped her arse. "Do you have to challenge everything I say?" She opened her mouth, but he cut her off. "Lay down on your back and I'll show you with actions just how much I admire and desire your body, honey."

"You better not disappoint me, *ruadh*."

Fraser's gaze turned determined. "Believe me, you won't be disappointed."

The huskiness of his voice sent a shiver down her spine. While she enjoyed his humor and teasing, she was coming to enjoy his dominant, possessive side as well.

"We'll see," she murmured.

After lightly patting Fraser's chest, Holly crawled to the empty side of the bed and lay down. Tapping her fingers in impatience, Fraser eventually turned to face her and stared.

The second he met her gaze, he said, "I should warn you, lass. If there's one thing my dragon enjoys, it's a challenge." He traced a finger along her jaw and then down her neck. "I used to like it easy, but I'm starting to see the appeal of a challenge when it comes to you."

Lifting his finger, Fraser's gaze moved to her breasts. One second ticked by and then ten. The longer he looked, the harder her nipples became.

If it were any other aspect of her life, she'd bark an order and tell him to move along. But just this once, she wanted him to linger.

Holly moved a fraction to better settle her bum and her breasts jiggled. With a growl, Fraser cupped one and squeezed.

His firm grip combined with the callouses on his palms made her breasts grow heavy again. As much as she'd enjoyed his tongue, she wondered what it would feel like to have Fraser's rough fingers dance between her legs.

Fraser finally released her breasts and she just prevented herself from crying out. She wouldn't let him know how much she yearned to have his hands on her body again.

If she did, Holly would never hear the end of it.

Fraser chuckled and she narrowed her eyes. "If you're laughing at my body, then so help me, I will find that lamp and shove it up your arse."

Rubbing his hands in slow circles on her belly, it took everything Holly had to concentrate on his answer. "I was laughing because you bit your lip to keep from begging." He moved his blue-eyed gaze to hers. "Am I right?"

Holly raised an eyebrow. "Wouldn't you like to know?"

Fraser's pupils flashed. Holly held her breath, but they didn't change again.

The next instant, Fraser's face was a few inches from hers. "Don't ever fear me, Holly Anderson. Even if I lose my bloody mind in the process, I will never allow my dragon to come that close to taking you when you're not ready."

She saw nothing but the truth in his eyes. On top of that, his words held such conviction, she believed him. "Well, I'm ready now. Are you really going to keep me waiting? I won't beg, Fraser MacKenzie, so if you're waiting for that, it isn't going to happen."

The corner of his mouth ticked up. "Keep telling yourself that."

Holly opened her mouth but then Fraser tugged one of her nipples and added, "Enough talking." He flicked her other one. "I want to commit every curve and valley of your body to memory."

It was on the tip of Holly's tongue to say something else, but she held back. She and Fraser could probably argue until next summer, if she gave in.

No, as much as Holly enjoyed the banter, she wanted something else.

She wanted hot, passionate sex with the dragonman above her.

Reaching out her hand, Holly lightly brushed Fraser's cock. He grabbed her wrist and hissed, "No touching until I'm sure you'll be gentle."

Holly smiled. "Then get on with it or I may just think of my own form of torture."

Determination flashed in Fraser's eyes before he leaned down and lightly traced her nipple with his tongue. Releasing her hard bud, he blew slowly on her wet flesh. In a much softer tone than before, she murmured, "Fraser."

"Aye, that's the tone I wish to hear, honey."

Sucking her nipple deep into his mouth, Holly arched her back as wetness rushed between her legs.

Fraser took his time, licking and suckling her nipple before releasing it with a pop. "My beautiful human."

Holly opened her mouth to contradict him when he took her other nipple. This time he bit gently before twirling his tongue over and around the taut peak.

She moved a hand to his hair and dug her nails into his scalp. Fraser rewarded her with a deep pull.

Pressing his head closer to signal she wanted more, her dragonman growled. The vibrations made her pussy throb in anticipation.

As if reading her thoughts, Fraser roamed his hand down her belly and between her thighs. Holly opened her legs without hesitation, expecting Fraser to touch her.

But while he continued to nibble her nipple and breast, his fingers danced from her left inner thigh to her right and back again. Not even when she widened her legs did he touch her slit.

She growled. "Fraser, stop teasing me."

He lifted his head. His blue eyes were filled with heat and desire, yet his pupils remained round. "Anticipation will only make you come harder."

The huskiness in his voice sent a thrill through her body. "Then prove it."

"I'm not done yet."

She opened her mouth to reply, but the instant Fraser ran a finger through her slit, she sucked in a breath. The roughness of his skin against her sensitive nerves made her close her eyes and lean her head back.

Fraser moved his hand back to her inner thigh. As he rubbed back and forth, so close yet so far from her pussy, Holly growled out, "No more teasing."

"Look at me, Holly. I want to see your beautiful honey-colored eyes as I touch you." He moved to her other thigh and repeated the same motions. "And as I make you come."

~~~

Fraser continued to caress Holly's skin as he waited for an answer.

His bloody dragon growled. *It's taking too long. At this rate, she will never carry our child.*

Patience, dragon. If she enjoys the first time, she'll enjoy the rest.

His beast huffed. *I don't believe you. But I'm not about to come out again and have her smack a lamp against our cock and balls.*

Good answer, dragon.

Holly opened her eyes and his beast fell silent. His human's half-lidded gaze shot straight to his dick.

When she was open and honest with her expressions, it made her all the more beautiful.

His dragon snarled. *All the reason to brand her with our scent. If any other male sees her, they'll want her.*

Holly's voice prevented Fraser from replying. "I'm ready, Fraser. Make me come."

His mouth went dry at the sultriness of her voice. But he quickly recovered and moved his position so his head was between her thighs. "I think you've waited long enough, my human."

Fraser licked Holly's slit and her sweet juices made him groan. "You're so fucking sweet, Holly." He lapped again. "I will never get enough of you."

Holly opened her mouth, but Fraser plunged his tongue into her pussy and swirled. The arching of her hips told him she was enjoying it.

Removing his tongue, he traced around her clit but never touched it. Then his bloody female wiggled her hips. "Stop moving."

"Then get on with it."

"You asked for it."

Fraser sucked her clit between his teeth and lightly nibbled. Holly's cry only encouraged him to bite a little harder before soothing the sting with his tongue.

Releasing her nub, he went back to lapping her pussy as his finger rubbed the bundle of sensitive nerves in slow circles.

He moved back to her clit and lightly flicked it with his tongue as he dipped two fingers into her slit. Finding the slightly raised area of her g-spot, he stroked up and down a few times before Holly screamed as her orgasm hit.

Determined to feel her gripping his cock, he removed his fingers and covered her body with his. In one swift thrust, he was inside of her and Holly cried out again in pleasure. If that weren't enough, her eyes were not only heavy-lidded, but also full of desire and expectation.

Taking her mouth in a kiss, he moved his hips in slow circles, loving how Holly squeezed and released his cock.

Holly gripped his bum and dug in her nails. The slight sting made him break the kiss. "You asked for it."

Fraser increased his pace and moved a hand to just above her clit. Pinning her in place, he thrust harder. Each movement caused the bed to shake. His human moaned and wiggled beneath him, gasping her pleasure.

Pulling out slowly, he paused and growled out, "You're mine, Holly. Only mine."

She opened her mouth, but he pistoned hard forward. Holly's nails dug deeper into his bum. "Again."

He retreated and held still. Fraser was determined to bring out Holly's boldness in the bedroom as well. He didn't care for her silence. "Tell me what you want, Holly, and I'll give it to you. Otherwise, I'll pull out and take care of myself."

His dragon roared, but Fraser was just able to hold him off.

Holly hesitated a second but then moved her hands to his upper back. "Then I want you to fuck me hard, Fraser MacKenzie, and don't hold back."

Then she scratched down his back. With a roar, Fraser took hold of her hips and let go of his restraint. It was time to please both his female and his beast.

Fraser slammed in and out of Holly's tight, wet pussy. He loved how she gripped his dick as he moved.

His dragon chimed in. *Take her harder. She wants it.*

Channeling his dragon, the sound of flesh slapping against flesh, mixed with Holly's moans, filled the room. Sweat trailed down Fraser's back and the pressure built at the base of his spine.

He was about to come.

But he fought it. His human should always come first.

He used his thumb to rub Holly's clit in quick circles. Holly scratched his back hard enough Fraser smelt blood.

That was his lass.

Fraser increased the pressure against Holly's nerves and she clutched his shoulders as she screamed. The sound of her voice, combined with the image of Holly carrying his scent and possibly his child pushed him over the edge. With a roar, Fraser stilled and spilled his seed inside of his female.

With each spurt of his semen, Holly screamed louder and dug her nails deeper into his skin. As she continued to grip and release his cock, her prolonged orgasm confirmed what his dragon had told him—Holly was his true mate.

Fraser roared as he branded her with his scent. No other male would touch her after this.

His dragon hummed at both the claim and their mate's pleasure.

When Holly finally wrenched the last drop from his dick, Fraser collapsed on top of her. His dragon paced at the back of his mind and Fraser knew it was only a matter of time before his dragon would demand a turn.

Once would never be enough for his dragon. Yet as Fraser brushed a damp tendril of hair from Holly's face, he admitted it would never be enough for him, either.

Holly Anderson was his and always would be.

His female's face was flushed and satisfaction filled her gaze. The sight sent a surge of pride rushing through his body.

His dragon growled. *She wants more. It's my turn.*

Fraser wanted nothing more than to take a breather to cuddle and coax laughter out of Holly so that she would know he wanted her for much more than sex. He wanted her for a lifelong mate.

Then his beast sent a flood of desire and need through his body. Fraser gritted his teeth, but his dragon would take over far too soon.

Still, Fraser wanted a few more minutes. He just needed to fight his beast.

In response to his wish, his dragon roared. His beast sent a torrent of lust to impregnate Holly and brand her through his body.

His cock was already hardening again when curiosity filled Holly's eyes. "Fraser?"

As his dragon joined him in the front of his mind, Fraser bit out, "I can't resist much longer, honey. I need to make you mine in a more permanent way. Either let my dragon have you or you need to run out of the door and lock me inside." His beast roared inside his head again and Fraser wanted to clap his hands over his ears. "He's not patient. I hate to rush you, lass, but I need an answer."

~~~

Fraser clenched his jaw and closed his eyes before rolling away from her. It was plain her dragonman was in pain.

The thought of him remaining that way for who knew how long squeezed her heart.

Unlike before, when his dragon had tried to take her, the thought of Fraser's beast being unleashed and fucking her didn't frighten her. The light, gentle caresses of Fraser the man had eased her fears and anxieties.

Besides, her entire reason for being here was to try to get pregnant. Even though Finn and Fraser were both patient with her, she couldn't expect for it to last forever. The DDA might take back what money she had left from the sale of the dragon's blood and then her father's treatments would stop.

No, it was time to do what she'd come to Lochguard to do.

Decision made, Holly laid a hand on Fraser's shoulder. He hunched further into himself. His voice was strangled as he said, "If you're thinking of leaving, then don't touch me. It makes my dragon want you all the more."

Taking a deep breath, Holly scooted over until her breasts touched his back. "I'm not leaving, Fraser."

In the blink of an eye, Fraser turned over and pinned her to the bed. His pupils were slitted. "Last time I'm going to ask. Are you ready for all of me?"

Holly nodded. "Yes."

With a growl, Fraser kissed her and plunged his cock into her pussy. As he wrapped her leg around his waist, he moved faster than before, each movement reaching deep inside her. She cried out into his mouth.

Fraser pulled away and his pupils were round again. "I don't want to hurt you, Holly."

Smiling, she answered, "Don't stop, Fraser. Kiss me and take me hard. I won't break."

With a growl, he took her lips again as he increased his pace. The bed shook, but Holly could barely concentrate on anything but the tall, muscled dragonman on top and inside her.

Fraser roared and his semen caused a wave of blinding pleasure to rush through her body. Each spasm felt as if it was going to shatter her.

She'd barely come down when Fraser pulled out, flipped her over, and raised her hips. He smacked her bum and then his cock was inside her to the hilt again.

As he guided her hips, she clutched the sheets. She was going to be sore when this was over, but Holly didn't care. She was so sensitive that each long, deep stroke helped to create a fog of euphoria.

Then Fraser smacked her arse and the light sting made her pussy pulse. In the next second, he held her in place as he came again.

As Holly spiraled into her next orgasm, she wondered if it was possible to die from too much sex.

But then Fraser was moving again and she lost all train of thought.

CHAPTER TEN

Fergus MacKenzie kept his wings pressed to his back as he moved his fore and hind legs to swim toward the surface of Loch Shin. His lungs burned when his head finally cleared the water.

He drew in a few deep lungfuls of air and shook the water from his ears. The water might be bloody freezing, but the cold helped to clear his mind.

Still, it had taken Fergus all night and a wee bit of the morning to control his temper. He would no longer kill his younger brother when he saw him.

And yet, his anger toward Fraser remained. His twin was his best friend in the world. It still didn't make any sense as to why his brother hadn't talked with him. More than losing Holly and his last chance at finding a mate in the Highlands, Fraser's silence had wrenched him in two.

Taking a deep breath, Fergus closed his eyes to enjoy the quiet of early morning. However, his dragon used the opportunity to speak up. *Why have you not accepted it? Would you really want another male's true mate for your own?*

That's not the point. Fraser should've talked with me.

Would you have done the same in his situation?

Fergus didn't hesitate. *Of course. I don't keep secrets.*

Liar.

Let me clarify—I don't keep secrets that could hurt my family.

His beast grunted. *Well, Fraser is not as careful as you. His impulses always land him in trouble. You always prevent us from having fun.*

Don't start, dragon. Someone in the MacKenzie family needs to accept their responsibilities.

I'm done arguing. You can sulk by yourself. I'm taking a nap.

As his beast faded into the back of his mind, Fergus dove back down into the depths of the loch. He knew Finn and his mother would start to worry if he didn't return to the clan soon. But he could spare another twenty minutes of solitude before dealing with his zoo of a family.

Twirling in the water, Fergus kicked up and broke free of the surface again. This time he came up about twenty feet from the shore. Blinking the water out of his eyes, he spotted a figure in the distance.

It wasn't unusual for people around the loch or from the village to watch him. According to a tale handed down through the centuries, a dragon had once saved their people from death and disease. To this day, they thought a dragon was good luck.

But after focusing a wee bit longer, he realized the shape was a female and she had her arms crossed over her chest. Her posture signaled she was angry.

Curious, he moved closer until he could see the frown on her face.

She was bonny enough with long, red hair blowing behind her and fair skin with freckles across her nose. Her swollen belly also told him she was quite pregnant and shouldn't be standing in the wee hours of the morning next to a freezing loch. Did she not have any sense?

He couldn't see her eyes, but as the female narrowed them further, he decided to find out why she was glaring at him. He might even convince her to go back inside, out of the cold.

Kicking his rear legs, he arrived in water shallow enough to stand within a minute. He resisted shaking the water from his body. Instead, he peered down at the lass.

Uncrossing her arms, she waggled a finger. "You're not only scaring the fish away, the sheep and cows are having freaking heart attacks. Why do you keep coming back here?"

Her accent told him she was American. Tilting his head, Fraser battled the urge to talk with the female. But to do that would require shifting, and if she was angry with him already, then appearing naked in front of her probably wasn't a good idea. Especially if the father of her child spotted him.

Fergus could take care of himself, but getting into a fight with a human was the last thing his clan needed at the moment.

He let out a low roar and the female answered, "Well, if you can't answer me in English, then you should just go." She took a step toward him and he finally noticed her dark chocolate brown eyes. "And if you know what's good for you, you'll stay away. Otherwise, I'll find ways to keep you away."

Unable to stop it, a chuckle rumbled deep in his chest. The locals living around the lake would never allow the human to report him to the DDA.

But she'd find that out soon enough.

His dragon's voice was sleepy as he murmured, *Stop irritating the pregnant female. Let's just go home. You've pouted long enough.*

For a few minutes, Fergus had forgotten all about Fraser, Holly, and the mess back home. But his dragon's words brought it all back. *In just a moment.*

Fergus leaned down until his head was even with the human's. If he expected fear in her eyes, he was sadly mistaken; she merely shook her head and sighed. "The dragon stare isn't going to work with me. I grew up near Clan BroadBay in the US.

I know your tricks of intimidation." She poked his snout. "Just go or I'll use my secret weapon."

The female reached into the pocket of her coat, but didn't pull anything out. He was tempted to see what a wee female could use against a dragon and win. Her pocket was too small to carry any type of illegal weaponry.

His beast growled. *Leave her alone. I don't like her standing in the cold.*

Since when do you care about random humans?

Since she's pregnant and trying not to shiver.

Fergus studied her body, draped in an overlarge coat, and a few seconds later, her whole body shook.

A sense of guilt flooded his body. *Let's go.*

With a bob of his head, Fergus padded over a safe distance from the female and turned to face her. She merely waited and watched.

The wind blew and her wild, curly red hair danced behind her. Fergus knew the female belonged to another, but he couldn't help but notice how beautiful she was with her pink cheeks and wee nose.

Before he started to think about yet another female he couldn't have, Fergus jumped into the air and beat his wings upward. When he reached a few hundred feet in the air, he glanced below. The female was still standing there, watching him.

Maybe he'd see her again, the next time he came to swim in the loch.

His dragon grumbled. *The longer you linger, the more time she spends in the cold.*

Forcing his eyes away from the red-headed female, Fergus turned toward Lochguard and started on the path home.

The Dragon's Dilemma

It was time to do what Fergus did best—focus on his responsibilities to the clan. Just because Fraser was an idiot didn't mean Fergus could abandon his people. His job was to analyze information and prevent future threats. After the attack on Lochguard a couple of months ago, his skills were more important than ever.

Yet glancing over his shoulder at the retreating red-haired woman, Fergus decided he might have to come back to check on her. Not to irritate her on purpose, but to make sure she hadn't frozen to death in the bloody cold.

She also seemed to help him forget about his problems back home. Maybe next time he'd bring a change of clothes so he could shift nearby and talk with her. He knew all there was to know from the locals about their dragon stories. He'd love to hear a few American tales.

Beating his wings faster, Fergus decided once he could find the time, he would definitely visit the female again.

He was so preoccupied with thinking of questions to ask the lass that he didn't notice his dragon's content rumble at the back of his mind.

Chapter Eleven

Fraser woke up on the twelfth day of the mate-claim frenzy and was surprised to find his dragon snoring at the back of his mind.

The last week and a half had been a constant battle between man and beast. His dragon had wanted Holly all to himself. Only through his sheer stubbornness had Fraser managed to have the lass to himself some of the time.

Fraser was definitely going to work on better controlling his beast.

Glancing at Holly's sleeping face, a sense of peace came over him. A few weeks ago, the mere thought of waking up next to the same female for the rest of his life had made his stomach churn. Yet as he traced Holly's chin with his forefinger, he couldn't imagine not waking up next to her.

The trick would be wooing her to stay.

His beast finally yawned. His voice was full of sleep as he said, *You should be asleep. She already carries our child.*

Fraser stilled. *What?*

She's pregnant. I can smell our scent entangled with hers, so let her rest.

Why didn't you tell me earlier?

I was sleepy.

The Dragon's Dilemma

Fraser cupped Holly's cheek as happiness warmed his heart. He'd never really imagined himself as a father before, but an image of him teaching his wee son how to control his dragon and learn to fly flashed inside of his head. The boy would have Fraser's auburn hair but Holly's amber eyes. He would be too clever for his own good, but Fraser would handle it.

Especially if Holly was at his side.

He may not know much about the lass just yet, but he would find out everything soon enough. After all, he had at least nine months to convince Holly to stay with him.

His dragon stretched inside his mind. *Just order her to stay.*

Yes, because that will work so well.

It might.

Fraser's entire body was exhausted, which included his mind. He'd deal with his dragon later.

For the moment, he wrapped his arms around Holly and breathed in her scent mixed with his.

He'd let his human sleep for a while yet. After all, once she woke up, Fraser would need to contact Finn and address the shitstorm of problems outside the walls of their cottage.

Nuzzling his nose against Holly's cheek, he pushed aside his worries and enjoyed the last peaceful hours he would have with his true mate for a while.

~~~

Holly had lost track of the days during the frenzy, but eventually she woke up in Fraser's arms.

Her Scot was snoring lightly. With his eyes closed and body relaxed, he looked no different from any human man.

145

She traced the dragon-shifter tattoo on his muscled bicep and smiled. Well, he was almost like a human man.

Fraser stirred under her fingertips. Every muscle of her body was sore, but she geared herself up for more sex. Maybe the frenzy would be over soon and she could actually enjoy a conversation with Fraser again.

Yet when Fraser opened his eyes, his pupils were round. Instead of heat, they were full of joy.

Compared to the last however many days, it was a strange sight. "Has something changed?"

The corner of Fraser's mouth ticked up. "Are you always this suspicious first thing in the morning?"

"With you, yes."

"You wound me, honey."

Holly propped her head up with her hand and planted her elbow on the bed. Fraser's glance darted to her breasts and then back to her face. Yet he didn't try to flip her onto her back and kiss her. "Tell me what's going on, Fraser MacKenzie. I'm exhausted and in no mood for games."

"But games are the best part of life."

She sighed. "You try having a cock pounded into you day after day for who the hell knows how long and you see how you feel."

Fraser's eyes turned concerned. "Are you okay? Do I need to call the doctor?"

The sudden change in behavior eased her irritation. "I'm a bit peckish, but otherwise, I'm fine."

Fraser sat up. "Then how about we shower and go get something to eat?"

Holly frowned. "Since when will your dragon allow us to do more than retrieve food left outside the front door?"

146

The Dragon's Dilemma

Her dragonman traced her cheek and tickled the soft spot under her chin. "He's calmed down because we're going to have a baby, Holly."

It took a second for his words to penetrate her fog of exhaustion.

Placing a hand over her lower abdomen, she blinked. "I guess I fulfilled my contract."

Fraser growled and took her face between his hands. His pupils were flashing to slits and back. "You are much more than a vessel for a child, Holly Anderson. You're my true mate. We'll raise the child together." He leaned down until his breath tickled her cheek. "And maybe if I'm lucky, you'll agree to stay with me."

Before the frenzy and the pregnancy, Holly had kept the truth from Fraser. But no longer. She couldn't allow for his hopes to build up. "I can't stay, Fraser. My father needs me. Not only that, my whole life is back in Aberdeen. I'm not sure I can just give it all up."

Fraser placed a possessive hand on her hip. "Don't say that." She opened her mouth, but he cut her off. "At least give me a chance to try and make everything work out. There has to be a way for you to stay with me and to also take care of your father."

"And what about my work? Or my friends? If you think I'm going to keep house and cook food all day, then you don't know anything about me. I would go mad in a week."

Fraser squeezed her hip. "Arabella and the other pregnant females could use your help here. You wouldn't have to give up your nursing."

Running her fingers across the whiskers of Fraser's cheek, she tried to think of another excuse.

But after spending at least a week with her dragonman, she wanted a chance to know him better. If for nothing else, for the sake of their unborn child.

147

Holly knew what it was like to lose a parent. She didn't want that for her own baby.

Searching Fraser's eyes, she finally answered, "If we can find a way for my father to live on Lochguard and for me to help with midwifery here, then I might consider it."

Happiness flashed in Fraser's eyes. "I will find a way, Holly. Once I set my mind on something, I don't give up until it's either seen through or I run into a five-foot-thick steel wall."

Her heart skipped a beat. The thought of not only living with Fraser, but also with her child and the possibilities of helping with dragon-shifter research gave her the most dangerous feeling of all—hope.

No, Holly. She'd never been a woman to hope and wish for something to happen. She'd take it one step at a time. Only when she was physically helping her father move into a cottage at Lochguard would she accept it.

She moved her hand from his cheek to his neck and played with the edges of his hair. "Okay. I'll think about it."

He growled. "No thinking, Holly. We're doing it."

Smiling at his stubbornness, she couldn't help but say, "But we've been doing it for days. Can't we take a break?"

Fraser barked in laughter. "You may be tired, but your sense of humor is intact."

"I sure hope so. If sex with a dragon doesn't bang it out of me, I'm not sure what would."

Fraser gave Holly a gentle kiss and added, "A mini-version of me just might. Ask my mum what terrors my brother and I were as children."

At the mention of Fergus, some of the joy in Fraser's eyes faded. Holly knew they'd have to address the situation soon, but she wanted to keep the tone light between them for just a while longer. She lightly patted his cheek. "That's okay. You can use all of your dragon charms on our child."

"I think it needs to be a joint effort. You have no idea what you're getting into."

Holly sighed. "You might have mentioned this to me earlier."

He winked. "And scare you away? I think not." Holly's stomach rumbled and Fraser frowned. "We need to find you something to eat. Once we do, we can combine your brains and my charm and figure out how to tackle any wee rascals thrown our way."

She raised an eyebrow. "I think before we think of a child in nine months' time, you should learn how to deal with your dragon first. Otherwise, I may need to implement my taser idea."

"After all we've been through, you'd still fry my cock?"

"In a heartbeat."

Fraser placed a fist over his heart. "You wound me, Holly. You really do wound me."

Snorting, Holly sat up. "If you're hurt now, then you aren't going to stand a chance later."

In the blink of an eye, Fraser's gaze turned intense and he drew her into his lap. Even though she had spent most of the last week or more in contact with Fraser's skin, being pressed up against his warm, hard body again felt as if she belonged there.

Then Fraser placed his hand over her lower abdomen and the reality of her future came rushing back.

In other words, her future wasn't guaranteed.

Fraser growled. "I don't like the fear in your eyes, Holly. Tell me what's wrong."

Pasting a smile on her face, she shook her head. "Don't worry about it. I'm just being stupid."

He leaned his head closer. "One day, you will tell me everything."

She wanted to add, 'If I survive the birth,' but decided it would ruin Fraser's current happiness.

Instead, she cuddled against his chest and listened to his heartbeat. "Can we deal with grown-up problems later? I'm starving."

"Then let's shower and go out."

Even though Fraser had spoken their plans, he tightened his grip around her and pulled her closer.

For a second, Holly snuggled against his chest. She didn't want the moment to end, either.

But then they both managed to untangle themselves from one another and head toward the bathroom. It was time to face the real world again.

~~~

As Fraser watched Holly eat her third bacon and toast sandwich, he realized just how worn out she must be. It amazed him that any human survived the mate-claim frenzy.

His beast huffed. *She is strong enough. I never would've killed her because of too much sex or not enough food.*

You say that now, but I'm not so sure about it.

Holly is strong. All will be well.

Fraser wanted to agree with his dragon, but he hadn't even convinced Holly to stay with him yet.

His dragon snarled. *She will stay.*

Oh, aye? I'd like to see you make her.

After her cuddling earlier, it's easy to tell she's becoming attached.

THE DRAGON'S DILEMMA

Fraser sighed inside his mind. *Cuddling doesn't mean she's agreed to be our mate. Sometimes I wish we could just be a full-time dragon. Life is so much simpler for you.*

Maybe. It could be simple for you, too, but you insist on following rules.

Don't even think about breaking any of the DDA's rules. If we're going to convince them to allow Holly's father to live on Lochguard, we need to stay in their good graces.

His dragon flicked his tail. *Fine. But we always have more fun when we break the rules. You're starting to sound like Fergus.*

At the mention of his twin's name, overwhelming guilt flooded his body. He had yet to speak with his brother. The pair of them had only been apart for two weeks once before, when Fergus had gone to America for special job training with the dragon clan in Virginia.

Holly's voice interrupted his thoughts. "You're quiet, Fraser. What are you thinking about?"

He could lie, but as he looked into Holly's amber gaze, the urge to tell her the truth was too strong to ignore. "Fergus."

His human laid down her fork. "I'm sure he's cooled off by now. He didn't strike me as being particularly hotheaded."

"Hotheaded? No. Stubborn as an ox? Yes."

"Don't you mean as stubborn as a dragon-shifter?"

He smiled. "I bet you think you're funny, honey."

Holly picked up her fork again. "I am, actually. I'm saving my best material for later."

Fraser opened his mouth to reply when Finn walked into the small restaurant with a scowl. Fraser stood and moved in front of Holly. Finn stopped a few feet away. "Bloody hell. I'm not about to hurt the lass, Fraser."

"What do you want?" Fraser asked.

Finn raised an eyebrow. "You were supposed to call me."

He growled. "My female was hungry. That was more important."

As Finn and Fraser stared at one another, Fraser held his breath. He wasn't used to challenging his cousin so publicly. But when it came to Holly, Fraser would do whatever it took to care for her.

Finn finally relaxed his posture. "It's important, but you still could've called me. A lot has happened in the twelve days you've been in throes of the frenzy."

Holly pushed against his waist. "Sit down, Fraser." Instead of sitting down, he moved to Holly's side. His female merely shook her head as she added, "Then how about you sit down, Finn, and tell us what happened while we were in seclusion."

Finn raised an eyebrow in warning. "Remember what we talked about before the frenzy, Holly." Finn dropped his voice to a low whisper. "I haven't done anything worth a scolding, so be careful of your tone."

Fraser was about to say something, but Holly beat him to it. Her voice was sweet as she asked, "Won't you sit down and tell us what happened, oh great clan leader?"

Finn muttered something about strong females before taking an empty chair.

Fraser maintained his post at Holly's side as he raised his brows. "Well? What's so important you needed to interrupt our breakfast, cousin?"

Finn pointed to the chair next to Holly. "Sit your arse down first. You really are an idiot if you think I'm going to touch Holly. Remember, I have my own pregnant female waiting for me at home."

THE DRAGON'S DILEMMA

Fraser's dragon chimed in. *He's right. Arabella would kick his arse if he hurt another person's mate.*

His dragon's words helped to clear the cloud of possessiveness inside Fraser's mind a fraction.

Still, sitting down, Fraser put a hand on Holly's leg and growled for good measure.

His female sighed at the action, but didn't scold him. Instead, she picked up her fork again. "While you two have your alpha stare down, I'm going to eat some more."

As she took a bite, Finn finally smiled. "There's no stare down, lass. Fraser knows he can't win against me."

Fraser narrowed his eyes. "Things have changed, cousin."

Finn studied him a second. "Aye, they have. More than you know." Crossing his arms over his chest, Finn looked between Fraser and Holly as he continued, "The DDA have finalized the contract transfer. In three months' time, a human scientist will come to live with the clan."

Holly pointed a fork at Finn. "We already knew that was going to happen. There must be something more important going on."

Fraser's dragon spoke up again. *She is clever and quick. We must keep her.*

Ignoring his beast, Finn answered, "Fergus left yesterday for an assignment on Skye."

Fraser's heart skipped a beat. "When will he be back?"

Finn shrugged. "A month, maybe more. He waited as long as he could, Fraser. He wants to talk with you."

Fraser squeezed Holly's leg under the table. "Probably more like he wants to punch me."

Holly swallowed and cut in, "Stop being so overdramatic. I'm surprised you lot haven't killed one another by now."

Finn grinned. "It's been a close call in the past. And only because the twins teamed up on me."

Fraser grunted. "Believe it if you like."

Finn opened his mouth just as his mobile phone beeped. He took it out and read his text message.

With a curse, Finn looked to Holly. "We need to talk, but not here."

Fraser's dragon growled. *If they try to take her away, I will hunt them down and hurt them. Holly is ours.*

Wait a second before you start planning revenge. Holly's right next to us.

Holly dropped her fork with a clang. "I'm ready."

Fraser didn't like the circles under Holly's eyes. His female needed more sleep and time to recover from the frenzy.

Yet he knew she wouldn't just go to sleep if he ordered it. Fraser would go with a compromise. Standing up, he waited until Holly was also on her feet before he scooped her up into his arms.

Holly squeaked. "What are you doing, Fraser MacKenzie? I'm perfectly capable of walking."

He frowned. "You're tired."

His human wiggled in his arms. "Stop being ridiculous."

Finn touched Fraser's shoulder. "It'll have to do, Holly. Believe me, you don't want to wait for this information and Fraser will argue for twenty minutes if you let him."

Holly sighed. "Fine." She poked Fraser in the chest. "But just don't get used to doing what you want without asking. We are going to set some boundaries later."

"Boundaries I can handle. It signals you want to stay," Fraser answered.

She fell silent and Fraser's stomach dropped. Maybe he'd misread her answers and body language before.

Thankfully, Finn's voice prevented him from thinking of how to respond. "You two can sort things out later. Come on."

Finn exited the restaurant.

Tightening his grip on Holly's body, Fraser followed.

~~~

As Fraser carried her out of the restaurant and toward Finn's cottage, Holly's heart beat double-time.

Sometimes it was hard to read Finn, but her gut told her something was wrong. Not only that, she had a feeling it had something to do with her.

Tightening her grip on Fraser's shirt, Holly leaned her head against his chest. If the DDA had changed their minds, she would have to think of something. There was no bloody way she was going to prison. She wanted to stay on Lochguard and also take care of her father. There had to be a way to make sure it happened, even if the DDA gave her grief.

As if sensing her distress, Fraser kissed her forehead. The brief contact helped to ease some of her tension. Whatever the problem, she knew deep down that Fraser would face it with her.

A small part of her wanted to keep him. Only time would tell if that could happen or not.

A few minutes later, they arrived at Finn's cottage. Arabella opened the door before they even reached it and ushered them inside.

The instant the door closed, Holly spoke up. "Tell me what's going on, Finn. The DDA haven't changed their minds, have they?"

Arabella was the one to speak up. "It has nothing to do with the DDA."

Fraser growled. "Stop stalling and just tell us what the fuck is going on."

Arabella raised her brows. "I'll let that slide this time, Fraser. But only for Holly's sake." She looked to Holly. "We received a message yesterday morning that your father had stayed overnight in the hospital. Since his first update signaled signs of improvement, we didn't think it necessary to interrupt the frenzy."

Holly clutched Fraser's shirt with her fingers. "If he was better, you wouldn't have rushed us over here." She looked to Finn. "What did the text you received in the restaurant say?"

Finn's brown eyes turned sympathetic and Holly's stomach dropped. "He's still alive, but he's taken a sharp turn for the worse. They aren't sure he's going to make it."

Fraser squeezed her closer. Holly looked from Arabella to Finn and back again. She couldn't afford to cry or become emotional. Much like during her time as a midwife, Holly pushed away her fears and focused on finding out information. Only then could she try to solve the problem. "What happened exactly? When I left him, he was looking so healthy. The doctors were surprised at how well he'd been handling the treatment."

Finn answered her. "We're still waiting on the details. But Dr. Innes should have them soon."

Fraser gently lowered her until her feet were on the floor and he said, "Then why are we still standing here? We should be at the surgery."

Finn answered his cousin. "Because we need to talk about Holly visiting her father. The DDA has granted a week's leave, with my permission."

Holly blinked. "So I can leave and see him?"

"Aye," Finn answered. "But with a few conditions."

Fraser growled. "Her father might be dying. Now's not the time to place conditions."

Finn raised his brows. "Isn't it? Someone snapped a photo of Holly at Lochguard's gates and her face was flashed all over the media whilst you two were in the frenzy. Outed sacrifices aren't treated well outside of a dragon clan's lands, Fraser. You know that."

Holly straightened her shoulders. She wasn't about to let anything get in the way of seeing her father. "If I can handle you and your dragon, then I can handle a few harsh words."

Fraser turned toward her. "If anyone so much as dares call you an idiot, let alone worse, I will flash my dragon eyes and extend a talon or two. That should scare them shitless."

She raised an eyebrow. "The dragon hunters may be mostly in England, but they exist in all the major cities of the UK. Doing that in Aberdeen might be dangerous and the last thing I need is to visit you tied up in yet another hospital bed."

"It doesn't matter. I will do anything to protect you and our child, even if it costs me my life."

Searching his eyes, she saw sincerity. Before she could stop herself, she blurted out, "You've changed a lot since I first met you."

He leaned close and laid his forehead against hers. "Oh, that version of me still exists. But you are my future, Holly, and I will bloody well fight to keep it."

The truth in his words warmed her heart, but she couldn't think about the possibilities with Fraser. She needed to help her father first. "Fine. But if you start growling at people, I'm sending you home."

Fraser cupped her cheek and she leaned into his touch. "There's no way in hell I'm allowing you out of my sight in public."

Finn cleared his throat. Holly and Fraser both looked toward him as he chimed in, "As lovely as it is to see you two getting along so well, there are a few things you're forgetting. If you think I'm letting you two travel to Aberdeen alone, then you're crazy. Faye and Iris will go with you."

Holly frowned. "Who's Iris?"

Arabella answered, "She's Lochguard's best tracker. If someone is luring you to Aberdeen, then she'll spot it a mile away."

Holly put her hands up. "Wait a second. Why would anyone want to lure me anywhere? I'm just a midwife from Aberdeen. There's nothing special about me."

Fraser interjected, "That's not true and you know it, Holly."

Finn answered before she could. "I know you're trying to be romantic, Fraser, but I'm going to speed things up since time is of the essence." Finn met her eyes. "Between the dragon hunters, knights, and other dragon-shifters, who have a grudge against me, there could be hundreds if not thousands who want to use you to tarnish the clan's reputation." Holly opened her mouth, but Finn cut her off. "You've just survived a twelve-day mating frenzy and you're newly pregnant with a dragon-shifter's child—congrats, by the way. That means you're exhausted and need the help. As much as I love Fraser, he's not a soldier. He'll need the help, too. Faye and Iris will go with you, or no one goes at all."

The dominance in Finn's voice signaled the topic wasn't up for negotiation.

Knowing when to pick her battles, Holly merely nodded. "Okay, but when can we go? I need to see my father, and soon."

"While he's still alive," was left unsaid.

No. Holly refused to believe her father would die in the next few hours. Hell, the doctors had predicted his death six months ago. But Ross Anderson was a fighter.

She only hoped her dad would keep on fighting.

Someone knocked on the front door. Arabella went to answer it and Finn motioned them toward the living room. "That should be Faye, Iris, or both of them. As soon as everyone's debriefed, you can leave. There's already transportation waiting for you at the rear gates."

Fraser rubbed slow circles on her back as they moved. Looking up at him, she murmured, "Thank you for being on my side. I can't imagine it's easy to go against your cousin."

He smiled. "Don't worry, honey. I can be loyal to Finn while still defending you. He has a mate, so he understands."

"This whole mate thing is starting to sound a bit caveman-like."

He kissed her nose. "We can debate that later, on the way to see your father." His expression turned fierce. "We'll be with your father soon. And knowing your stubbornness, I'm sure you'll find a way to keep him alive."

"I hope so, Fraser. I really do."

Finn called their names and they picked up their pace. The sooner they were debriefed, the sooner they could leave.

Holly only hoped they weren't too late.

CHAPTER TWELVE

Three and a half hours later, Fraser drummed his fingers against the car door as the scenery rushed past at a speed much slower than if they had flown.

It also didn't help that Faye was driving slightly under the speed limit. "Faye—"

"Don't, Fraser. Or I swear I will tape your mouth shut at the next opportunity," his sister answered.

"I'd like to see you try, little sister."

Faye growled. "If not for Holly, I would turn off the motorway right now and teach you a lesson."

"I'm sure Holly is the only reason," Fraser replied.

Iris's voice boomed out, "Enough."

Iris may not be clan leader, but Fraser believed she could be if she put her mind to it. How Grant had taken over the Protectors instead of Iris, Fraser had no idea.

Not wanting to irritate the strong dragonwoman, Fraser went back to looking out of the window. His dragon spoke up. *Admit it, flying is always better.*

Only if you want to be spotted from miles away.

That's why you fly at night.

Fraser glanced over at Holly, who was closing her eyes and opening them in a cycle, trying to fight off sleep. "It's okay to rest, honey. There's nothing we can do until we arrive at the hospital."

Holly lightly slapped her cheeks. "No. I should be reviewing my father's medical records again. My gut tells me something is off, but I can't place it. If only I were a doctor, I could spot it."

Fraser shook his head. "Not necessarily. Dr. Innes couldn't find anything unusual."

"He's a dragon-shifter doctor. He may have human medical training, too, but he doesn't practice it."

His dragon growled. *Find a way to comfort her. Distress isn't good for her or our baby.*

As if I didn't know that.

No need to get huffy. I'm just trying to help.

Ignoring his beast, Fraser punched the driver's seat in front of him. "How much longer till we arrive?"

Faye's voice was low as she spit out, "I don't give idle threats, Fraser. I'm pulling over at the next exit and taping your mouth shut. Punch the seat again, brother, and I will tie you to the roof as well."

Holly's voice was kind as she chimed in. "Faye, at least tell me how much longer we have."

Faye briefly looked in the rearview mirror before focusing back on the road. "What you see in my brother, I'll never understand. But we should be there in another twenty minutes."

As Fraser hugged Holly, he murmured, "Then drive faster, sister."

Before Faye could answer, Iris's calm, cool voice filled the car. "We have bigger things to worry about."

Both man and beast stood at attention. "What's going on, Iris?"

The black-haired and brown-eyed dragonwoman turned around in her seat. "Someone is following us."

Faye demanded, "Why didn't you speak up sooner?"

Iris shrugged. "I wanted to make sure. Besides, it's not like there was a place for us to turn off without drawing attention. We're approaching Aberdeen and it'll be much easier to lose them there."

Faye tightened her grip on the wheel. "Just make sure to let the Protectors back on Lochguard know their number plate. We need to identify the threat."

Fraser's dragon snarled. *It's time to shift and protect Holly. I won't allow anyone to hurt her.*

We're on the same side, dragon. But give Faye and Iris a chance. They have experiences we don't have.

His beast huffed. *Fine. But if I think Holly's life is in danger, I'll take control and whisk her to safety.*

Holly's voice interrupted his conversation. "What's the plan, then? Because I'm not about to be scared away from visiting my father. For all we know, whoever is following us might target my father, too."

Faye nodded. "Exactly. You are a Protector at heart, Holly Anderson."

Fraser grunted. "Don't encourage her. Holly is human and more fragile."

Holly poked his side. "When this is over and everyone is safe, we're going to address your overprotectiveness. There's no way I can survive nine months of it."

Iris spoke as if there were no other conversations going on inside the car. "It's the dark green SUV three cars back, Faye. When I give the word, I want you to take the next available exit."

Faye replied, "I'll do it, but I don't know Aberdeen very well by car."

Holly jumped in. "I've lived here most of my life. I'll tell you where to go. The A90 is coming up. Turning onto the motorway might be a good way to tell if they are truly following us or not."

Iris answered, "We'll try that, first. But if they follow us, then we switch from being cautious to protect and attack mode."

As Faye and Iris continued to talk about tactics, Fraser wished he had something to add. But he didn't. He was an architect and a builder, not a soldier.

His beast spoke up again. *We can still protect Holly. She is our true mate. My instincts will keep her safe.*

Let's hope it doesn't come to that.

His dragon snarled. *If they try, they will be sorry.*

Fraser didn't want to face Finn's wrath because of his dragon going rogue. Fraser needed something to preoccupy his beast.

Deciding he would take his sister's jabs later, he spoke up. "Give me a task, Faye. I need to do something or my dragon will go crazy."

Faye briefly met his eyes in the mirror. "Then take out your mobile phone and be ready to call Lochguard to let them know what's going on. Finn and Grant can also reach out to contacts and find a way to check on Holly's father."

Fraser took out his phone. As much as he hated any threat to Holly, at least his sister Faye was acting like her old self again.

Which was good, considering they might need her brain and fighting skills if things turned south.

~~~

Holly's stomach flipped as Faye took the exit onto the A90 motorway. Between battling her lingering exhaustion and her fears about her father, Holly was on the verge of breaking down.

While she'd thought often about how she could die in childbirth, she never once imagined someone going after her and her father to get back at the dragon-shifters.

To think everyone on Lochguard lived with this constant threat over their heads made her heart squeeze. Finn, Fraser, and the rest of Lochguard hadn't been anything but kind to her. They didn't deserve the hatred aimed at them and their kind.

Iris's voice cut through her thoughts. "The bastards are still there. Where to next, Holly?"

After Holly gave her suggestions, Faye and Iris went back to talking about options and possible threats.

Fraser leaned down and whispered, "I trust Faye with not just my life, but yours and our child's as well. We couldn't ask for a better dragon-shifter to protect us."

She met Fraser's eyes. "I don't doubt Faye, but what about my father? The thought of someone going after him too and doing who knows what to him makes me sick to the stomach."

He rubbed up and down her arm. "Even if Finn and Grant don't have any contacts in Aberdeen, Clan Stonefire should. I could say not to worry and nothing will happen. But you're clever and know it could. Instead, I'll just say that you're part of Lochguard now. And Lochguard does everything in its power to protect its own. If there's a way to save your father, Finn will work to find it."

The steel in his voice helped to calm her stomach a fraction. She also knew Fraser's words about being part of Lochguard were significant, but she would have to digest that statement later, when she wasn't fretting about her father's life.

Holly snuggled into Fraser's side and took a deep inhalation. His scent helped to slow her heart rate a little. "If this is what it takes to be accepted at Lochguard, you might want to reevaluate your criteria."

Fraser's voice was lighter as he replied, "You can mention that to Finn the next time you see him."

Faye took a sharp left turn and Holly was thrown against Fraser. Her dragonman wrapped his arms around her and whispered, "Even if it takes my life, I'll fight to keep you and your father safe, Holly."

In any other moment, Holly might have made a skeptical quip. But as her heart pounded and head throbbed with worry, she merely melted in Fraser's side. She was exhausted and needed all the support available.

Faye's voice cut through the silence. "The bastards are quite good. I can't lose them. I think we're going to have to pull over and take a stand, Iris."

Iris unclicked her seatbelt. "I agree. Fraser, when we stop, you take Holly and run. They may have sent photos of our car to others, so driving is out of the question. I don't care where you go, but take her as far away from us as possible. Do you understand?"

Before Fraser could answer, Holly asked, "What about my father?"

Iris motioned toward Fraser. "Your male can contact Lochguard and set things in motion. Once Faye and I figure out who we're up against, we can formulate a better plan of attack. If we're lucky, they're only after us."

Faye made a high-speed turn into a side alley. Only the combination of Fraser's arms around Holly and her seatbelt prevented her from being tossed to the other side of the car.

For the first time, she was glad to be newly pregnant. A high-speed car chase would be hell when combined with morning sickness.

The car stopped with a jolt. As Faye undid her seatbelt, she ordered, "Take Holly and run, brother."

Fraser nodded. "Take care, sister."

"I will," Faye answered and then she was out the door and jogging down the alley. Iris wasn't far behind.

Fraser threw open the door and guided Holly out of the car. "I'm only going to ask this once, Holly. Do you want me to carry you or can you run?"

Holly hated running, but that didn't give her a reason to burden Fraser. "I can handle it for now. Come, let's go. Since it's the middle of a work day I'm sure we can find an empty home to duck inside. The sooner you call Lochguard, the better."

They started running and Fraser added, "And lucky for you, I've had my fair share of getting in and out of houses undetected."

"We can talk about your criminal history later."

Holly tugged Fraser's hand. He muttered, "Criminal history, my arse," but then fell silent.

As they exited the other side of the alley and turned right, Holly tried her best to keep her breath. Apparently a twelve-day sex marathon hadn't helped her to get in shape at all.

Of course, not that any of that mattered. All they needed to do was to find an empty home, preferably a detached one. There would be less chance of neighbors hearing them move about if they didn't share a wall.

Fraser pointed toward the left. "I see some houses in that direction."

Holly didn't see anything but a blur of shapes. "Are you using your super-dragon senses?"

"Yes. Trust me, honey. I don't hear any running behind us and we can find safety to the left."

Nodding without hesitation, Holly pushed herself to run faster. "Then let's go."

~ ~ ~

Fraser appraised the house at the end of the block. It was detached, with no cars parked in front, and a fence that could be climbed around the back garden. And, most importantly, the lights were also out.

Holding his breath, he listened for any signs of life, but there was no TV, no music, and no talking.

He was fairly certain the place was empty.

Squeezing Holly's hand in his, he whispered, "Follow my lead."

For once, his human didn't try to argue with him and together they made it to the rear of the house to just outside the fence. Fraser was tall enough to look over it, but when his last check of the windows and for noises came up negative, he released Holly's hands and laced his own together. "Come on. We need to climb the fence."

She sighed, but put her foot into his hands and he lifted her. The second Holly landed with a soft thud on the other side, Fraser took the top of the fence in his hands, jumped, and swung over to the other side.

Avoiding the scattered toys in the yard, he guided Holly to the rear door. Some humans tended to keep a spare key of some sort, so Fraser rummaged through the nearby flower pots and bushes. Eventually he found one and opened the door.

The second he and Holly were inside, he took out his mobile phone. "Keep a watch on the front windows. I'll watch the back as I call Finn and let him know what's going on." Holly hesitated, and he cupped her cheek. "What happened to my strong lass? I need her right now."

Holly took a deep breath and then stood tall. "I'm still here. Do you have a code word or something I should use in case I see something?"

Despite the enormity of the situation, the corner of his mouth ticked up. "How about 'intruder' or 'danger'?"

Holly rolled her eyes and the sight helped to ease some of his own nervousness. "Smartarse."

He grinned. "Hey, you asked."

Shaking her head, Holly moved toward the front of the house and Fraser pressed his speed dial for Finn's mobile number.

After two rings, his cousin answered. "What's going on, Fraser? You're thirty minutes early for our next check-in. Are you okay?"

"I don't have time for pleasantries, Finn. Someone was following us on the motorway. Faye turned off into some section of Aberdeen so that Faye and Iris could face the intruders whilst Holly and I found a place to hide."

Finn's voice turned serious-but-distant, as if he were holding the phone away from his mouth as he barked, "Arabella, I need your help." Finn's voice returned to normal volume. "Tell me where you are and I'll send reinforcements as soon as possible."

"I'm not entirely sure where I am. But before I ask Holly, can you have someone check on her father? She's worried about him."

"Rightly so," Finn answered. "I'll reach out to Stonefire and see what their humans can do to help us. Between the female reporter and the former DDA employee, I'm sure we can do something."

"Good. Once you know anything, call or text me."

Holly's loud whisper drifted through the house, "Someone's coming, Fraser."

Fraser was already moving. "Finn, I need to go. We may have been followed."

"Don't hang up, Fraser. Even if you have to toss the phone to the side, keep the connection open so Ara can trace your call."

"Fine, but just don't speak. I need to keep it silent."

"Just be careful."

With that, Fraser slid his phone on top of a bookcase in the living room before joining Holly, who was peeking through a gap in the curtains. Fraser kept his voice low when he asked, "Can I have a glance, honey?"

Holly moved and he peeked outside. There was a man with his dog on a lead and the dog was taking a crap on the grass. "I'm not sure he's a threat, lass."

"Not just him. I swear I saw a dragon high in the sky."

He frowned. "There aren't any rogue dragons in this part of Scotland."

"Do you want to chance it? Maybe we should move."

Fraser shook his head. "No. If it was a dragon, then they'll be able to see us move anyway. Our best bet is to stay here for the time being."

Holly touched his arm. "So that means we're basically sitting ducks?"

He touched Holly's chin. "Maybe not, lass." Fraser motioned toward the window. "Keep watch again. I have Finn on the line." She opened her mouth, but he cut her off. "And yes, he's trying to check on your father."

"Thank you."

Seeing Holly vulnerable, with fear in her eyes, did something to his heart. All he wanted to do was whisk his mate to safety and protect her.

Holly's eyes darted to his mobile and back.

He got the message. Fraser picked up his phone and he whispered, "Did you hear all of that?"

"Aye. I have more Protectors on the way, but it'll take some time. If there is an unidentified dragon in the sky, then lay low until the Protectors get there."

"We'll see." Finn started to talk, but Fraser cut him off. "Does Ara have the trace?"

As soon as Finn said, "Aye," Fraser cut the connection. He had no doubt Finn was about to tell Fraser not to shift and distract the dragon. But if the dragon attacked the house, Fraser would be the only one who could keep Holly safe. He hadn't been bluffing earlier when he said he'd die to protect her.

Fraser was about to ask Holly if she'd seen anything else when something thumped on the roof a split-second before a dragon's hind legs crashed through the ceiling. Fraser yelled, "Run, Holly, and call Finn," before imagining his face elongating into a snout, wings growing from his back, and his nails extending into talons. Two seconds later, Fraser broke through the ceiling and stood in his black dragon form. From the corner of his eye, he spotted Holly running into the distance.

THE DRAGON'S DILEMMA

Satisfied his mate was safe for the moment, Fraser focused on the older blue dragon standing opposite him. The dragon looked familiar, yet Fraser couldn't place him.

But then the blue dragon lunged for his throat and Fraser embraced his dragon's instinct. He swerved his head to the side and slashed his right front talons. Whether out of luck or by surprising the older dragon, his talons made contact and ripped through the flesh.

However, the wound wasn't fatal and the dragon jumped forward to pin Fraser to the ground.

With the remains of the house about him, he couldn't move properly. Waving his tail around, he knocked down the walls as he used every iota of strength he possessed to keep the dragon's jaws from his throat.

When the last wall fell, Fraser kicked his hind legs against the blue dragon's belly. The blue dragon flew over him. Taking the split-second advantage, Fraser jumped into the air and beat his wings. He may not be the best fighter, but he was one of the best at tricks and maneuvers in the sky. If he could last long enough, he might be able to draw the older dragon-shifter away from Holly as well as tire him out.

With a roar, Fraser glanced over his shoulder just as the blue dragon jumped into the air and moved toward him. Turning, Fraser hovered in place. The instant the blue dragon was twenty feet away, Fraser dove down sharply toward the ground. The other dragon turned to follow. One second passed, and then five. A lesser dragon would have crashed into the ground, but thanks to years of challenging his twin, Fraser pulled up and shot straight toward the blue enemy.

The older beast's reaction time was too slow and Fraser collided his shoulder into the dragon's belly. A slight twinge caused pain to shoot through his wing, but Fraser ignored it. All that mattered was giving Holly enough time to flee to safety.

His opponent snarled in pain before dropping down. Not wanting to take chances, Fraser swooped down and slashed one of the dragon's wings. The blue dragon roared and tried to flap the injured wing, but the tear in the membrane prevented him from moving upward. Fraser hovered in place as his attacker smacked to the ground with a crack.

The beast didn't move again.

Fraser's dragon snarled. *We must find Holly.*

Sirens blared in the distance. It was now a race against the clock to find his mate before the authorities tried to shoot him out of the sky.

CHAPTER THIRTEEN

Holly's side ached from running and yet she still pushed herself to go down one alley and then the next.

She hated leaving Fraser behind. But Holly staying would only distract her dragonman. Her best chance to help him was to find a way to contact Finn. Or anyone from Lochguard, for that matter.

The DDA might be willing to help her, but she wouldn't try that until she was out of options. They might not acknowledge that Fraser's shifting inside of a city was a matter of self-defense. The thought of him going to jail made her stomach churn.

Get a grip, Holly. You're used to high-tension and risky situations. You can do this.

True, her life had never been on the line before. But she'd kept a cool head to save a countless number of mothers and newborn babies. Holly could do the same for Fraser and herself.

A small, wooded park came into view and she made a beeline straight for it. She'd have a better chance at watching the skies from a park versus fleeing into another house.

Making it to the edge of the copse of trees, she pushed her way deeper into the park until she stood at the edge of a clearing. Careful to stay in line with the tree trunks, Holly scanned the sky. All she saw were clouds.

Then a dragon snarled in the distance and her heart skipped a beat. Clutching a hand over her chest, she willed the noise to be from the blue dragon who'd crashed into the house and not Fraser. If he died protecting her, their child would grow up without a father. Not only that, a future without Fraser brought tears to her eyes. Any man who would willingly risk his life to save someone else's was someone you kept around.

A dragon roared in pain in the distance. Could it be Fraser?

Taking a step out to better see the sky, a red dragon hovered above her.

Shit. Holly ducked back into the trees. The dragon could be from Lochguard, but she had no idea and she wasn't about to chance it.

Keeping her breathing even, she remained immobile. *Please let them move on. Please.*

After about sixty seconds, Holly debated if the dragon had fled or not when a red forelimb broke through the trees and grabbed her around the middle. Holly screamed as she was lifted into the air.

The sudden climb in altitude made her a little lightheaded, but she fought against the feeling. If she fainted, it was game over. Not just for her, but possibly for Fraser as well.

With a deep breath, she tried to focus on their surroundings and get her bearings. That's when she noticed a large, black dragon hovering in the sky.

When the beast's eyes fell on her, he roared. Her gut told her it was Fraser.

Sirens blared below and someone started blasting over a loudspeaker. Yet with the wind whipping around her, Holly couldn't make out what they were saying.

THE DRAGON'S DILEMMA

Just as her dragonman charged toward her, the red dragon released her.

Holly fell toward the ground and screamed hard enough to hurt her throat. She was going to die.

~~~

The human police were using a loudspeaker to order Fraser to land. He was debating his next step when his eyes landed on Holly, who was clutched in Gordon's foreleg.

The bastard. Gordon had been one of the dragons who had left Lochguard rather than stay under Finn's leadership.

His beast spoke up. *We'll teach him a lesson, just like the other dragon.*

Careful. We need to extract Holly first. Help me think of a plan.

Move toward him. I may have an idea.

His beast fell silent. Since his dragon had helped him escape a dangerous situation or two in the past, Fraser trusted his beast implicitly.

Just as Fraser started toward Gordon, the bastard released his grip on Holly.

Acting on reflexes learned during his boyhood training, Fraser dove down toward Holly. He needed to find a way to slow her descent without hurting her. Grabbing her too roughly would snap her neck.

He pressed his wings against his back to increase his speed. His human was being clever and keeping her limbs sprawled, which helped to slow her descent. That was when something Faye had mentioned about her time with the British Army flashed into his mind. He would use one of the paratrooper tactics for when a parachute didn't open.

Reaching Holly's speed, he used his wings to match her pace. Then very gently, he wrapped a foreleg around her middle. Once they were falling together, he hugged her close and opened his wings. Within a few beats, Fraser was moving upwards again.

The red dragon roared and moved toward Fraser. Apparently, Gordon didn't want Holly alive.

Anger burned through his body, but before he could think of how to take care of Gordon all whilst not harming Holly, a blue dragon approached. The beat of her wings was unsteady and a little irregular. He expected the dragon to falter at any second, but she kept moving with purpose. The determination in her eyes alone told him she wasn't going to give up.

It was Faye.

And she was flying.

His dragon spoke up. *Think about that later. We need to get Holly to safety.*

Fraser glanced toward the human in his grasp. The sight of her motionless body made his stomach drop. Then he heard her heartbeat and pushed his fear aside. He would ensure Holly was okay, even if it was the last thing he did.

Faye touched her front talons to her ear, which was the signal for him to retreat. His sister missed a beat of her wings and fell a few feet, but then she pumped them again. Without another glance, she flew straight toward Gordon.

A purple dragon shot past him; it was Iris.

As he watched Iris and Faye tackle the red dragon, Fraser turned and quickly ascended into the sky to a height that wouldn't freeze his delicate human yet should also act as a buffer between him and the human authorities. The last thing he needed was for the human police to shoot him down.

THE DRAGON'S DILEMMA

As much as he wanted to take Holly directly to Dr. Innes or Layla, the junior Lochguard doctor, Holly could be in serious condition. Aberdeen had the closest hospital, but he couldn't risk going there since the authorities might be waiting for him. No doubt, there was a high alert in progress to keep watch out for a black dragon. Fraser would take her to the next closest human NHS hospital in Elgin.

He tucked Holly closer against his body to protect her from the wind.

Fighting his creeping exhaustion, Fraser focused on moving his wings in a fast, steady pace. The next twenty minutes were going to be the longest of his life.

His dragon growled. *Holly must live. Fly faster.*

Are you holding back?

No.

Then this is it. I'm doing the best I can considering I was in a dragon fight and am still recovering from the frenzy.

Holly's heart still beats. That is all that matters.

Fraser agreed. When Holly stirred against his chest, he glanced down.

She was awake, but then she turned her head toward his chest and closed her eyes. Fraser wanted to squeeze her in reassurance, but didn't want to risk hurting his female.

Holly's actions pushed him to fly faster. For all he knew, she could be hurting. Maybe even dying.

No. He refused to believe it. They had barely started their life together. There was no way he would let Holly go without a fight, even if it was against death itself.

The ground passed below them in a blur. He distracted himself the rest of the way to Elgin by keeping an eye out for threats. If Gordon had paired up with some of the other exiled dragon-shifters, they could be lying in wait anywhere from Aberdeen to Lochguard. After all, they knew northern Scotland as well as any of the Lochguard clan members.

Elgin finally came into view and he nearly let out a sigh of relief. Holly would soon have the help she needed.

Scanning the buildings, he found the hospital and moved toward it. While there were specks of humans milling about on the ground, he didn't see any police or DDA enforcers.

Of course, they could come at any time.

Careful to land in an empty section of the car park, Fraser touched down as gently as he could. Humans were already rushing out of the building to gawk. The urge to snarl and scare them away from his female was strong.

His beast spoke up. *She needs them. For once, I'm going to say let her go.*

Fraser knew his beast was right. Holding Holly close for one last second, he lowered his head and touched her cheek with his snout.

Holly stirred and hope surged through his body.

All Fraser wanted to do was shift and hold his human close. But his need to protect was stronger. With every ounce of strength he still possessed, he removed his forearm from Holly's body. Her knees buckled and she fell against his foreleg. He crooned in concern, but Holly stood up and motioned with her hands. "Go, Fraser. You can't stay here."

He grunted and shook his head. Holly's jaw set and she barked, "Go, Fraser. I don't want you here."

Her words were as if she'd stabbed him in the heart. Fraser knew he'd failed her, but she couldn't honestly want to send him away.

Holly pointed toward the sky. She said, "Go," before turning her back on him.

Fraser's heart squeezed. Yet as more humans came toward them, he knew he should go. Holly refusing him put his life in danger if he stayed. It could give the impression he'd snatched her against her will.

Jumping into the sky, Fraser beat his wings and rose up. He gave one last glance down, only to see Holly being supported by two human males. He bared his teeth at the sight. They shouldn't touch her.

Then police sirens blared in the distance. Fraser didn't have much time. Who knew what they'd try to do with him if they caught him.

His dragon spoke up. *She needs the medical attention more than she needs us. We can talk with her later.*

When did you become so wise?

It's not wise so much as instinct. I will always say what's best for our mate.

His beast using "mate" only reminded Fraser of what Holly had said. *We weren't able to protect her and we might've lost her trust because of it. She must be angry.*

No matter. She will calm down and we'll woo her back. She is worth it.

For the first time since Holly had ordered him away, Fraser felt confident. *Yes. She may be stubborn, but we are more so. I will win her back once she's well again. She's contractually bound to return to Lochguard.*

Then let's go home and think of a plan. She is safe inside the human hospital. Not even the traitors will attack the NHS. Because if they do, they are attacking the British government and they have powerful allies the world over.

Only when Holly's small figure disappeared inside the building did Fraser start flying home.

His lass may be cross with him at the moment, but he would fix it. Holly's future was with Fraser. He just needed to make sure she accepted that.

~~~

The nurse did her final check of vital signs and smiled at Holly. "Everything looks good for now. I'll be back in an hour."

Too tired to do anything but nod, Holly did so and the nurse finally left Holly alone inside her hospital room.

As she lay in the barren room, every muscle and bone hurt in Holly's body.

But nothing hurt worse than her heart.

The look in Fraser's eyes, when she'd ordered him to go, would haunt her for the rest of her life. Crestfallen was the only word she could think to describe it.

Yet if Fraser had stayed, the DDA would've come to get him. They might have even taken him away and locked him up. She couldn't bear the thought of her strong, brave dragonman chained inside a cell. Because of his overprotectiveness, Holly's only option had been to say she didn't want him and force him away.

And yet, she missed his strong presence.

Looking at the door, a part of her longed for Fraser to walk through it and envelop her in his arms.

She may have only known Fraser a short time, but she'd learned to lean on him. Hell, if not for his strength back at the house in Aberdeen, she might've broken down and become a blubbering mess. Yet a few words from Fraser, and she'd found her core of steel once more.

Holly blinked back tears. Hopefully she hadn't hurt him too badly.

At least she would have plenty of time to talk with him later once she returned to Lochguard and apologized.

That is, if they would accept her back at Lochguard. She'd started bleeding and there was a chance that she'd lost the baby.

Placing her hand over her abdomen, Holly fought back her tears. It was bloody ridiculous since she was only days pregnant. Yet the thought of losing her baby still made her heart ache.

And not just because of possibly losing the baby itself. There was also the possibility Lochguard would turn her away. After all, her contract allowed a dragon clan to send a sacrifice away if she miscarried.

She should be ecstatic to have a loophole to leave so she could take care of her father as well as return back to her job and friends. Yet she wasn't as happy as she would've been even two weeks ago.

The only good news was that even though her father's condition was still serious, a note had arrived earlier saying he was safe and under protective custody. No one would be able to kidnap him and use him against Holly or Lochguard. As it was, she still didn't know if her father had been an additional target earlier, when she'd been chased.

Picking up the letter next to her bed, Holly opened it and traced the single "F" at the bottom. While it could be from Finn, Fergus, Faye, or Fraser, she wanted to believe it was Fraser who had sent it. That way, it would show that he didn't hate her.

There was a knock on the door and Holly laid the letter down. Wiping her damp eyes with her forearm, she took a deep breath and said, "Enter."

The door opened to reveal a short, curvy woman with brown hair and green eyes. While Holly had never met the woman personally, she recognized her face from the news reports. "You're Melanie Hall-MacLeod."

Smiling, the woman entered and shut the door behind her. Her short, clipped American accent filled the room. "That I am. And call me Mel."

Holly frowned. "Why don't you first tell me why you're here?"

Mel pulled over a chair and sat down. "Arabella MacLeod is my sister-in-law. She asked me to come, and since she rarely asks anyone for favors, I agreed."

"That still doesn't really tell me why you're here."

Mel grinned. "I can see why Arabella likes you." Holly opened her mouth, but Melanie cut her off. "She sent me because she's worried about Fraser, but she can't come herself without being targeted. Finn is also concerned about the phone lines being monitored by the DDA or even the ones who went after you back in Aberdeen. Since I'm human, I can come and go as I please. Well, mostly. Half a dozen, um, people are watching me at the moment. It was the only way my mate allowed me to come." Mel leaned forward and whispered, "I'm sure you understand a little about dragon males and their overprotective behavior by this point."

Despite Melanie trying to lighten the mood, Holly couldn't move past the bit about Fraser. Her heart beat double-time as she asked, "What happened? Did Fraser not make it back to Lochguard?"

Melanie studied her a second before answering, "Oh, he did. But after the way you dismissed him, I'm not sure why you care."

Holly turned a little more toward Melanie. "I hate to be rude as we've only just met, but you shouldn't make assumptions without all the facts."

Gesturing with her hand, Mel leaned back in her chair. "Then enlighten me. Because even dragonmen have feelings and you've stung his."

Holly clenched her fingers at Mel's words. "I didn't have a choice. He was already breaking the law by shifting inside Aberdeen. I couldn't risk the DDA or police arresting him for arriving at a hospital with an injured human. Dragon-shifters are always presumed guilty until proven innocent. I didn't want him to go to jail." Melanie shook her head, which only made Holly clench her fingers tighter. "If you don't believe me, then you should just leave."

Mel raised an eyebrow. "I never said I didn't believe you."

"Then why were you shaking your head?"

Mel grinned again. "Because your way of thinking is more akin to a dragon-shifter's than you may realize. Especially when it comes to mates and love."

Holly ignored Mel's remark about love. "Fraser risked his life to protect mine. I would do anything to protect him, too."

As soon as the words came out of her mouth, Holly blinked. She hadn't thought much about it before, but it was true. Despite Fraser not being a soldier or a Protector, he'd battled a dragon for her. If it came to it, she'd try to do the same for him.

Mel's voice interrupted her thoughts. "Good, you've passed my test. So if we can put aside the defending and questioning, I can fill you in on what's happening."

Learning about the future was far more important than shouting at Melanie for her stupid test. "Right then, I'm listening. What do you know?"

"The dragons who attacked you were former Lochguard clan members. Unfortunately, the first one died crashing into the ground and the other, a dragonman named Gordon, got away. There's more to it, but it's up to Finn to fill you in on the rest."

Holly could keep the full truth from Melanie, but that wasn't the best way for the woman to trust her. Without a smidgen of trust, Mel wouldn't tell her any more details. And cut off from Fraser and Lochguard, Holly was desperate for details. "I'm not sure if they'll welcome me back." Holly took a deep breath and spat out, "I might've lost the baby. And dragon-shifters usually turn away humans who miscarry."

Mel's eyes softened. "I'm sorry if it is true, but stop being stupid."

Holly blinked. "What?"

"The rumors about dragon-shifters are usually half full of shit. If you had read my book, you'd have known that."

"My life has been too busy to do much else but work and take care of my father. Besides, your book is recent. It's going to take a long time for that information to become general knowledge."

Mel shrugged. "Still, asking the dragon-shifters directly is always the best way. Since that's impossible right now, you'll have to just take my word for it that Finn and his clan won't toss you aside for something beyond your control."

She searched Melanie's eyes. "Do you speak for Lochguard now?"

"Of course not. But if you have such little faith in them, then maybe you should just go home and forget about them. Dragons need strong mates who believe in them. If you're not up to the task, then just tell me now."

The Dragon's Dilemma

Holly studied Melanie for a second. Fire and protectiveness flashed in the woman's eyes. Holly had heard a little about how Melanie was the first to really champion the dragon-shifters in modern times. Yet the woman had always seemed kind and collected on TV.

For the first time, Holly was seeing the Melanie Hall-MacLeod who had not only won an entire dragon clan's loyalty, but who had singlehandedly managed to change many of the rules concerning dragon-shifters.

Holly sat up a little more. "I'm more than ready. But I want to make sure my father is well again, first."

Mel nodded. "Family is important. As I sacrificed myself to save my brother, I understand your devotion more than most."

Holly relaxed and put out a hand. "We've gone about this a bit backwards, but nice to meet you, Melanie."

Melanie smiled, took her hand, and shook. "I just needed to make sure of your intentions and determination. I've witnessed firsthand a sacrifice who didn't want anything to do with the dragon-shifters, and it destroyed her in the end."

Holly released her hand. "I want to live on Lochguard, but there is one problem. Maybe you can help me."

Mel raised an eyebrow "What's that?"

"I'm the only family my father has left. He's battling cancer and I want to take care of him. But in order to do that, he needs to live close by. Is there a way to legally allow my father to live on Lochguard?"

Mel tapped her chin. "Well, if Fraser accepts you as his mate, then I'll see what I can do. I can't make any guarantees, but if I can't make it happen, along with Evie's help, then no one can."

There was a small flutter of hope in her stomach. "Then help me get out of the hospital and to my father's side. The sooner he's healthy enough to be discharged from the hospital and is fit for travel, the sooner I can focus on winning Fraser back."

Mischief danced in Mel's eyes. "My mate will kill me later, but I have a few ideas of how to get you out of here as soon as possible." Mel assessed her for a second before adding, "But not until we know if you've truly lost the baby. If moving you too soon does that, Fraser will try to kill me. The last thing we need is discord between Stonefire and Lochguard."

Holly sighed. She'd briefly forgotten about her child. "The doctors said they'll know by tomorrow evening at the latest. We'll move then."

Mel leaned forward and laid a hand on Holly's arm. "Whatever happens, you have me on your side, Holly Anderson. Being a human amongst a clan of dragon-shifters isn't easy. Even if you do miscarry, Fraser will welcome you back. And if he's stupid enough to turn you away, then you're welcome to live on Stonefire. We'll protect you against anyone who wishes to hurt you."

Even if Holly had turned Fraser away, she couldn't imagine him dismissing her. If he tried, then Holly would just have to smack him on the head and get his dragon on her side.

However, to keep her thoughts from showing, Holly smiled at Mel and replied, "Thank you."

Mel squeezed Holly's arm and leaned down to pick up her handbag. Lifting it, Mel plucked a deck of cards from it. "If you're tired, I'll let you rest. But if I were you, and had just been dropped from the freaking sky, I'd be too hyped up to sleep. Cards can prove a mindless distraction. I learned that lesson myself when I stayed by my brother's side. He had cancer too, you know, but pulled through." Mel wiggled the cards in her hand. "So, what do you say? Are you ready for me to beat your ass in Go Fish?"

Despite everything going on, Mel's good mood was infectious. "I think I can manage that. I need all of the distractions I can get."

"Right, then." As Mel shuffled and dealt out the cards, Holly glanced over at the note on the table next to her bed. As much as she appreciated Mel's presence, Holly wished it was Fraser trying to cheer her up.

The next day would give her a better idea of her future. For the moment, Holly focused on winning a game of Go Fish.

CHAPTER FOURTEEN

Fraser yanked out another weed from the ground and tossed it to the side. Not even the menial work of clearing Finn and Arabella's garden could distract him from thinking about a certain honey-eyed human female.

It'd been just over two weeks since he'd last seen Holly. Every time he tried to remember her smiles or laughter, the image of her ordering him away flashed inside his mind.

Fraser growled and tossed aside another weed. He hated waiting. Each day away from her only strengthened his resolve to win her back.

Yet they'd barely heard anything from the human doctors or the DDA about Holly's future, let alone if she would be returning to Lochguard or not.

With a grunt, he yanked out the largest weed he could find and threw it against the back wall. As he watched the dirt fly every which way, he felt a little better. What he really needed was to drop a few boulders from the sky since destroying things always helped ease his tension, but Fraser was currently restricted to the clan's lands. Finn was still working out details of Fraser illegally shifting inside a city.

Fraser glanced to Finn's cottage and considered asking his cousin yet again if the DDA had ruled his shift a necessity of self-defense. However, before he could do more than stand up, his dragon spoke up. *Finn wouldn't keep that secret from us. To be honest, I don't understand why we're still here. I'm sure with Faye's help, we could sneak into the hospital and see Holly.*

Aye, and face Finn's wrath. He's still trying to smooth things over with the DDA. Until that happens, we're a wanted dragon-shifter.

Then we fly at night. No one will see a black dragon against the night sky.

Fraser was tempted. *For once, let's be responsible. I don't want to give the DDA any fodder to use against us.*

His dragon huffed. *I miss the old Fraser. He was adventurous and had more fun.*

We'll still have fun. But not until after everything is settled with Holly.

Just as his beast was about to reply, Finn's voice drifted from the open kitchen window. "The DDA finally sent Holly's medical status report."

Fraser stilled. He didn't want to give Finn any reason to halt his conversation.

Arabella's voice answered, "Just tell me what it says, Finn. Patience is not a virtue I possess whilst pregnant."

Fraser heard Finn kiss Arabella's skin. His tone was soft as he answered, "She miscarried. They're now asking me what to do next."

Fraser closed his eyes and ran a hand through his hair. It couldn't be true. He'd been so careful about retrieving Holly from the sky. But he must have screwed up and hurt his female somehow.

She might not want to be his female anymore. After all, Holly was alone and hurting because of him.

Maybe she'd had every right to dismiss him back at the hospital.

No. He refused to believe that. Even if Holly was upset about what had happened two weeks ago, he would find a way to make it right. And not just because she was his true mate. Fraser missed Holly's wit and brains as much as having her heat snuggled up against him.

Truth be told, he was already half in love with her. Considering Fraser had never really felt that way about any female before, it was a big deal. There was no way he'd let Holly go without a fight.

Arabella's voice garnered Fraser's attention. "You should let Holly decide what to do. I'm pretty sure Fraser would still want her, child or not."

Fraser's dragon roared. *Of course we still want her. She is so much more than a way to increase the clan's population. She is our future happiness.*

Fraser was still thinking of how to reply to that when Finn's voice floated through the air again. "I'll talk with Fraser in a few days. That will give the lass some more time to spend with her father. And even though she miscarried two weeks ago, seeing Fraser might only heighten her grief or remind her of what she lost."

Fraser's heart skipped a beat. The mere thought of his presence saddening his female made his stomach churn.

Arabella answered her mate, "It's a good thing Holly's location is a secret. If Fraser knew she was in Inverness, he would've gone to talk with her by now."

His dragons spoke up again. *We need to find a way to go to Inverness. And before you say we should wait until the DDA gives approval, I'll take control if I have to. Holly needs us.*

Knowing what we know now, there's no bloody way I'm going to wait around.

THE DRAGON'S DILEMMA

Fraser moved to stand, but his dragon added, *Let's make sure Finn and Ara don't have any other information we need.*

I thought you didn't want to wait.

A few minutes might make all the difference.

As much as Fraser wanted to rush off, all he could hear was Fergus's words over the years about finding out as much as you can before charging into battle. Fraser had never seen the necessity before, but clenching his fingers, he strained his ears.

Finn answered Arabella, "Aye. We'll reveal Holly's location in the main NHS hospital later. Although I must admit Fraser's docile behavior is a bit worrying."

"I'm sure it'll pass as soon as he mends things with Fergus. It's usually when the two of them are together that Fraser acts out."

Finn sighed. "Fergus is yet another problem I'm trying to handle. Sometimes, I wonder how I ever managed all of my clan duties without you at my side."

Arabella's voice turned teasing. "Only through pure charm, but that was bound to run out before too much longer."

Arabella squeaked and then Finn murmured, "I seem to remember my charm working on you."

As Finn and Arabella went quiet, Fraser clenched and stretched out his fingers. *Can we go now?*

Yes, although check the location. It's been a while since we've driven to Inverness.

Right, then. As Fraser moved toward the back wall, his heart pounded. He would go to Inverness to find Holly and convince her to come back to Lochguard. He hadn't done much wooing the first time around, but Fraser could charm a lass as much as his cousin Finn any day. It was time to put his charm to use on the only female he wanted by his side.

His dragon spoke up again. *Good. We need to make our true mate happy. Let's win her back.*

And we will, even if it's the last thing we do.

Fraser slinked over the back wall. The second his feet touched the ground, he ran toward the cottage he and Holly had used during the frenzy.

Wanting to be reminded of his female, Fraser had never moved out.

With man and beast in agreement, Fraser ran all the way to his cottage. Inverness was nearly a two hour drive from Lochguard. The sooner he left, the sooner he could see his female and make her smile again.

~ ~ ~

Arabella MacLeod listened as Fraser scaled the back wall and ran into the distance. When she was certain Fraser could no longer hear her, she looked to Finn. "Do you think it worked?"

Finn nodded. "Of course. If you'd been hiding out somewhere and in pain, I would've gone after you as soon as I knew where to look."

"Then why did you wait two weeks? You received this report the day after Fraser dropped her at the hospital."

Finn's face turned neutral, but there was sorrow in his eyes. "Between her father's health and losing the bairn, the last thing she needed was for an overprotective dragon-shifter to hover around her and drive her crazy."

The urge to hug her male surged through her body, so Arabella walked up and laid her head on Finn's chest. "Holly is a strong woman. While I don't wish a miscarriage on any female, it will give her the option to accept Fraser on her own terms. Most sacrifices don't have that chance if they turn out to be a true mate."

Finn hugged her closer. "Aye, I know. Nothing has turned out the way I'd imagined. After all of this, I'd be surprised if the DDA will ever work with us again."

Arabella leaned back until she could see Finn's amber eyes. "Just stop it. If it were anyone else in the clan, you would accept what had happened and then come up with a new strategy. I know he's your family, but Fraser doesn't want your pity. Believe me, I of all people know how awful that is. Fraser probably just wants you to treat him normally again."

Finn frowned. "What he needs more than that is his twin. If Fergus were back, then the rest of us would settle a wee bit more."

Arabella tilted her head. "Then call Fergus back. I'm sure talking with the humans there can wait."

He lightly tapped her bum. "Let Fraser sort things out with Holly first."

"Are you sure that's the best idea?"

"Aye, I do. Winning Holly back is something Fraser needs to do on his own."

Raising a hand to Finn's cheek, she ran her palm against his late-day whiskers. "If nothing else, all of this drama and commotion has forced Fraser to grow up."

"I'm both sad and happy about that." Finn kissed her forehead. "Come, I think we could both use a few scones with clotted cream and jam. Aunt Lorna probably has a new batch in the oven right now."

"There is no bloody way you can smell it from here."

He winked. "No, but I know she always makes them about this time every week."

Arabella tried to frown, but broke into a smile. "Then we'd better hurry before Faye finds them or there won't be any left."

As they turned and walked out the front door, Arabella took comfort in her dragonman's heat and scent. He might have distracted Arabella with food, but Finn was worried about Fraser. Her mate cared deeply for his family.

Her dragon spoke up. *You both worry too much. Fraser will win the female back or he won't. There's nothing we can do but wait.*

Waiting isn't always easy, dragon.

No, but sometimes it gives the greatest reward.

Agreeing with her beast, Arabella looked up at Finn. He had most definitely been worth waiting for.

CHAPTER FIFTEEN

Holly watched the gentle rise and fall of her father's chest. The steady rhythm, combined with the approving look in the doctor's eyes, gave her hope that everything would be okay.

She should remain quiet and wait for the doctor to finish. After all, Holly knew well that too many questions could delay an examination; she'd experienced it herself as a nurse. Yet as the doctor jotted another note on her clipboard, Holly couldn't help but blurt out, "Is he doing any better?"

The female doctor smiled at her. "He is, actually. We should be able to discharge him tomorrow, provided you can take him home and keep a close eye on him."

She gestured with her thumb toward the door. "Will they come with me?"

The doctor lowered her clipboard. "I believe so. The DDA is afraid of you and your father becoming targets again. But from what I've heard, the DDA enforcers usually keep watch from outside your house to give you a little privacy."

"But not much."

The doctor smiled. "You've pretty much lived inside of this hospital for the past two weeks. Being home should be a nice change."

The only problem was that Holly was torn about where to call home—Aberdeen or Lochguard.

Since Holly had also been watched closely because of the miscarriage during her stay at the hospital—the DDA was concerned about suicide and/or depression—she quickly pushed aside thoughts of Lochguard or any of its inhabitants. She didn't want to give the doctor anything to change her mind about discharging both Holly and her father.

Holly nodded. "Thank you, Dr. Brodie. I'm sure it will be."

Dr. Brodie eyed her a second and then nodded toward the door. "How about you go get yourself something to eat? You've been using your special privilege to stay with your father and don't go out often enough. If you don't keep up your strength, then you won't be able to help him." Holly opened her mouth, but Dr. Brodie cut her off. "Either go eat something or I might reevaluate your father's discharge for tomorrow."

Since Holly had spent most of the last two weeks in the hospital, she was too tired to argue. As it was, she couldn't remember the last time she'd eaten. Maybe breakfast time?

Dr. Brodie raised an eyebrow and Holly sighed as she stood. "Fine, I will. But I'll only be gone for ten or twenty minutes."

"Take at least thirty. I'll have a nurse stay with your father, just in case."

Touching her father's arm, Holly whispered, "I'll be back soon, Dad."

Then she drew on what little strength she had and trudged to the door. The short walk made her lightheaded, which told Holly her blood sugar was too low.

Exiting the room, Holly glanced at one of the two DDA guards posted at the door. His name was Andrew. He frowned. "Where are you going?"

"Just to the cafeteria. I'll be back in half an hour." The same guard opened his mouth, but Holly put up a hand to stop him. "No, I don't need one of you to come with me. But if you want some coffee, I can bring some to you."

Andrew flashed a smile. "That would be heaven, Ms. Anderson. The night shift is always bloody difficult."

She looked to the other guard, but he shook his head. While Andrew was nice enough, the other guard rarely spoke two words together.

Not that Holly minded. Being social wasn't high on her priority list at the moment.

Before either of them could change their minds about accompanying her, Holly went down the hallway and turned left to the elevator. Just after she pressed the down button, a familiar heat came up behind her.

Holly's heart skipped a beat. There was no way Fraser MacKenzie would risk stepping foot inside a human hospital.

Then his familiar lilting voice filled her ear, "Hello, Holly."

She turned to face him and she drew in a breath. Her handsome dragonman had circles under his eyes and red stubble on his cheeks. An average person might not recognize him, but Holly would know the shape of Fraser's face anywhere.

He was finally here.

Before she could stop herself, she blurted out, "You look like hell."

The corner of his mouth ticked up. "Some males might try to use pretty words about your appearances. Hell, I would've done it a few months ago. But you look worse than me by at least a mile."

Sadness flickered in his eyes and in that second, in her gut, she knew Fraser was aware of what had happened to the baby.

Not ready to have that conversation, Holly turned around. "You're an idiot for being here, you know. All I have to do is shout and the DDA guards will come running."

Fraser moved a fraction closer and Holly resisted leaning back against his hard chest. He whispered, "I call your bluff. If you truly want me gone, then shout. Otherwise, stop with the idle threats and talk to me."

The elevator doors opened and Holly hesitated. The last thing she wanted was to talk with Fraser about losing their baby and discover Lochguard didn't want her any more.

Yet she'd missed his comforting presence over the last few weeks. Just hearing his voice helped to ease her tiredness; she could just imagine what would happen if he held her close.

Given her lack of food and sleep, she might even breakdown.

And yet, she didn't care if that happened or not. Because she would have her dragonman to lean on.

Making a decision, Holly stepped into the elevator. She turned around and raised an eyebrow. "Are you coming?"

Fraser grinned and the stubble on his cheeks only made him more attractive.

Her dragonman moved to stand next to her, yet he kept a small distance between them. Holly wanted to reach out and touch his cheek, but she clenched her fingers instead. If Lochguard had wanted her to come back, she would've heard of it by now. There was no reason to torture herself with dreams and wishes of what she couldn't have.

It was best to find out the truth and get it over with as quickly as possible.

As the elevator descended, Holly met Fraser's blue eyes. "Well? Why are you here, Fraser MacKenzie?"

THE DRAGON'S DILEMMA

~~~

Fraser's gaze darted to the stray hair resting on Holly's cheek. The sight reminded him of their first time alone, back in the greenhouse at Finn and Arabella's house. Much like then, he wanted to tuck the dark tendrils behind her ear.

Yet he knew it might be too soon. The lass's reaction to his grin told him she was still attracted to him. But Fraser wanted more than attraction; he wanted her heart.

His dragon huffed. *Then get on with it already. I don't like these games.*

Hey, you're the one who wanted a challenge. Holly is definitely turning out to be our biggest challenge to date.

Just woo her. She looks tired and sad and I don't like it.

Fraser watched as Holly leaned against the side of the elevator. Her cheeks were definitely too pale and the redness of her eyes spoke of little sleep.

Or, he hoped it was only because of lack of sleep. The image of his strong lass crying didn't sit well with him.

His dragon growled. *Pull her close and comfort her. She wants it, but fights it.*

I won't force it. Let me talk to her first. She's been through hell, after all.

Don't wait too long or we could lose her.

Give me some credit, dragon.

His beast fell silent and retreated to the back of his mind. Fraser met Holly's eyes again. They were unreadable. He decided to screw being gentle. "I'm here for you, Holly Anderson. Why haven't you bloody tried to call me or even send me a message?"

She blinked. "Why would I?"

Fraser moved in front of Holly until their bodies were mere inches apart. "I know I fucked up and couldn't protect you. But if you think I'm just going to let you get away, then you're crazy."

"Why? Because I'm your true mate and your dragon's needs tell you to go after me?"

He leaned his face down until it was a hairsbreadth away from hers. "If you haven't noticed, the frenzy is over and I still came for you." He gently took her biceps in his fingers. "I want you to come back to Lochguard." He squeezed her arms. "I want you to come back to me."

Holly's eyes turned wet. "I can't, Fraser. I think you already know, but I lost the baby. Finn will probably turn me away in favor of finding another sacrifice who can see her contract through to the end."

Fraser growled. "Fuck that. Even if I have to challenge Finn in public to keep him from turning you away, I will. Give us a chance, Holly. That's all I'm asking for." He brushed the hair from her cheek. "Even if we're never gifted with a child again, I still want you by my side."

She searched his eyes for a second before replying, "I—" Holly swallowed and then continued, "I don't know." He opened his mouth, but she placed her forefinger over his lips. "I want to make sure my father is doing okay first."

He growled and she removed her finger. "And then you'll come back to me?"

She looked away and it took everything he had not to force her gaze back. He wanted to know what she was thinking.

Holly finally answered, "Maybe. We've had little chance to really get to know each other, Fraser. I can't decide my life without being more certain."

"Then I will erase all of your doubts, honey. Just wait and see. I'll win you back if it's the last thing I do."

The elevator doors opened and Fraser moved to Holly's side. Thanks to his long-sleeved jumper and careful use of language, no one had guessed he was a dragon-shifter yet. He needed to keep it that way.

Wrapping an arm around her waist, Fraser murmured, "Have supper with me. We can consider it our first real date."

When his female smiled, some of his tension eased as they started walking. "Having a first date with you now, after everything, seems a bit ridiculous."

"You're the one who wanted us to get to know each other better. If it were up to me, I'd take both you and your father home to Lochguard and make it my life's purpose to see you smile every day."

Holly looked away from his gaze. "I'd like to see you try."

Fraser whispered into her ear, "You should know to never challenge a dragon-shifter. I'll have to see it through now."

His female shivered and Fraser's dragon rumbled in approval. *She doesn't hate us. Just like I told you. She will come home with us.*

Confidence doesn't make it truth.

It usually does for me.

Holly looped her arm around Fraser's waist and he forgot all about his beast. The simple gesture made his heart rate tick up.

Looking up, Holly gave a small smile. "Have you ever had hospital food before?"

"No. Why? Is it full of secret vitamins or something?"

Holly merely shook her head and Fraser started to worry. Surely the lass wouldn't try to poison him.

~~~

For the first time in a week, Holly had nearly forgotten about the dragon dropping her out of the sky, her father's health, and the loss of her child.

Despite everything hanging over her head, Holly was feeling mischievous. For whatever reason, Fraser MacKenzie's mere presence helped her to forget about her problems.

A small part of her wondered if she'd been an idiot to assume the worst of Fraser and his clan. Yet Holly had learned a long time ago to be careful. Her mother's death had taught her that lesson the hard way.

No. She wouldn't allow anything to ruin her supper with Fraser. She sure as hell could use a small break from real life.

Holly nodded toward a table at the far end of the room. "Sit there and wait for me. It should be somewhat private."

He grunted. "I'm not sure it's wise to allow you to choose my food."

She raised an eyebrow. "I find it hard to believe you're a picky eater."

Fraser glanced toward the section of the cafe selling food. "As long as it is food."

She smiled. "Some might say it's not, but it shouldn't kill you."

Fraser looked back to her eyes. "The 'shouldn't' part of your sentence worries me."

Shoving Fraser's side, she motioned toward the table with her head. "Just go, already. I'll be there in a second."

After giving her an assessing glance, Fraser headed toward the far side of the room.

As she took a tray and surveyed the choices, Holly felt a little evil and selected the blandest items on offer for Fraser and her favorites for herself. She paid for them and soon slid into the chair across from Fraser. Her dragonman scrunched his nose. "That doesn't smell right."

Holly bit her lip to keep from grinning. "That's how it always smells."

Poking it with a finger, Fraser asked, "What is it?"

"Stop being a baby and just try it."

Fraser furrowed his brows, but he picked up a fork and scooped up a bit of mashed potatoes.

As Fraser made a face, Holly finally let out a laugh. Her dragonman growled out, "That isn't real food, Holly. What the hell are you trying to feed me?"

When she could stop giggling, she motioned toward Fraser's plate. "It's potatoes."

He dropped his fork with a clang. "That is not bloody potatoes. It's as if someone mixed cardboard with a wee bit of butter and served it on a plate." Fraser looked to her plate of fish and chips. "How about we share yours?"

Swiping a chip, she popped it into her mouth. Not even the hospital cafe could ruin the greasy, salty heaven of a hot chip. "They're mine." She ate another and moaned for effect. "And they're good."

Fraser growled, "Cheeky wench," before swiping a few of her chips. After sniffing one, he took a nibble and then ate the whole thing. "That's more like it. Mum never let us have chips. Something about making our dragons fat and lazy."

Holly replied, "My mum was the same." She took a bite and then continued, "But once a month she'd cave to my dad's wishes and we'd have fish and chips on the last Friday of the month."

"What happened to your mum?"

She sobered a fraction. Not telling Fraser about her mother would keep distance between them. And if she wanted any chance of a future with him, she needed to open herself up to him.

However, she would share information on her terms. "I'll only tell if you let me know what happened to your dad."

Fraser shrugged as he chewed a bit of fried fish. "My dad was flying home from a hunt. The idiot decided to risk flying back in a storm and was struck by lightning. He didn't make it."

Holly frowned. "Did he have a reason for rushing home? I can't see your mum mating an idiot."

"Aye, he had a reason. But still, he should've waited. Faye wasn't born until the following day, once the storm had passed. If Dad had waited for clear skies, he'd probably still be around."

Holly reached across the table and laid a hand on Fraser's arm. "Sometimes parents make less than brilliant decisions, but I'm sure your dad did it out of love."

Fraser sighed. "Aye, I know. I was only five years old at the time, but I still remember bits and pieces of my parents together." He leaned forward. "To be honest, I wish my mum would've found a second chance."

Holly gave a sad smile. "I feel the same way about my dad."

Fraser laid a hand over hers and squeezed. "I fulfilled my end of the bargain. It's time to do yours. What happened to your mum?"

Holly paused a second. Thoughts of her mother always made her sad, and she'd been doing so well to forget her sadness by teasing Fraser. Yet as he looked at her with earnest expectation, she decided he deserved to know the truth. "I was twelve years old when it all started. My mum was a nurse and always had a way with the patients. While some would mistake her kindness for more, none were ever a problem until Gerry.

"I can still remember the day she told my father she thought she was being followed home every day. This was before mobile phone cameras, but she eventually did manage to snap a photo and went to the police.

"But the police were busy at the time with a local gang and said they'd look into it later."

Fraser pointed a chip at her. "But they never did."

Holly shook her head. "No. The bloke even came to the door a few times and had seemed harmless. But one day my mum didn't come home and we reported it to the police." Holly took a deep breath and spit out the rest. "We heard nothing for five days and then they found her."

Holly closed her eyes to keep back the tears. She'd only been thirteen and losing her mother had devastated her.

Fraser lightly touched her arm. "Tell me, lass. Speaking something helps to clear the demons, as my mum always says."

Opening her eyes, she stared into Fraser's blue-eyed gaze, which was full of encouragement.

After a deep inhalation, the words came out in a rush. "She'd been murdered. They eventually tied DNA evidence to the man who had been stalking her. He'd murdered two other nurses over the span of five years. He has a life sentence, but—"

Holly clenched her fingers and released. Fraser finished her sentence, "But it's not nearly enough."

"No. I want him to pay for what he did to my mother and those two nurses. I sometimes wonder if that makes me a bad person."

Fraser took her chin between his thumb and forefinger. "You are the farthest thing from a bad person, Holly. You're caring, open-minded, and determined to help others. We all have moments when we wish to carry out some revenge. But the difference is that you would never do it, not even if the opportunity presented itself." He took one of her hands with his free one and squeezed. "You bring life into the world with your hands. I find it hard to believe you'd be able to end it with them."

Holly merely looked at Fraser. She'd wanted them to eat together so she could get to know him better. But somehow, despite their short time together, Fraser already knew her fairly well. He was right—she couldn't even kill a mouse, let alone another human being.

As she tried to figure out what to say, Fraser released her hand, picked up a piece of fried fish, and he positioned it just before her lips. "Eat something, lass. You'll need the energy."

No one had ever tried to feed her before. Opening her mouth, Fraser moved the fish between her lips and she bit down, never severing eye contact. The act was simple, yet somehow intimate.

Maybe a life with Fraser MacKenzie wouldn't be so bad.

Once she swallowed her food, she asked, "When will I see you again?"

The corner of his mouth ticked up. "That anxious, eh, lass? I expected more of a fight to win you over."

She pointed a finger at him. "I never said you won me over. You'll know when that happens."

He leaned forward. "Aye? And may I have a hint of how to tell?"

Holly ate the last chip and gathered the rubbish from their meal. "You, the master of wooing women, need a hint?"

Her dragonman growled. "Only with you, Holly. Only with you."

"Good. I like to keep you guessing." Standing up, she motioned with her head. "I need to get back." Fraser's pupils flashed to slits and back. She did a quick check, but they were still alone on the far side of the cafe. She whispered, "Tell your beast to cool it, unless you want to be arrested."

Fraser stood and leaned toward her ear. "Then I need to know when I can see you next. I'm not sure I can sneak into the hospital again without being noticed, especially since I'm not here visiting anyone or seeing a doctor. And I need to see you again, Holly." He brushed her cheek. "I need the chance to win you over for good."

Searching his gaze, her desire to tease him further evaporated at the yearning in his eyes. For whatever reason, Fraser wanted her.

He may even love her.

No. She wasn't about to jump to conclusions and have her heart broken.

She debated what to say. Yet as his pupils flashed again, she decided she'd better give him something or his flashing eyes might be spotted by someone walking by. As soon as people knew he was a dragon-shifter, they would take him away from her for good.

And at the thought of never seeing Fraser again, her heart squeezed. She'd dreaded it over the past few weeks, afraid he'd walk on eggshells about the miscarriage and treat her differently. Yet he'd teased her and even stolen her bloody food.

She wanted to keep Fraser MacKenzie.

"My father should be discharged tomorrow. Unfortunately, the DDA will be watching over our temporary housing."

Fraser laid a hand on her lower back. She'd missed his strong, possessive touch.

Her dragonman answered, "I've thought of that." Removing his hand, he took a cheap mobile phone from his pocket and tucked it into hers. "That's an untraceable phone with

207

my secret new number programmed into it. Call me when you're ready, Holly, because what happens next will be in your hands."

She opened her mouth, but Fraser placed a gentle kiss on her lips. Before she could do more than sigh, Fraser was gone.

Holly threw away her rubbish and touched the place where Fraser had slipped the phone. It looked as if Holly would be the one doing the chasing.

And despite everything going on in her life, she looked forward to it. The next step would be contacting Melanie Hall-MacLeod to set things in motion.

Holly might have been debating where her home was the last few weeks, but she finally knew it was on Lochguard.

CHAPTER SIXTEEN

As soon as Fraser pulled the car into its assigned spot near the Protectors' central command building a few hours later, his phone buzzed in his pocket. With a smile, he took it out to read the text message: *Next time, I pick the place. Let you know soon. xxx*

Relief flooded his body. The meal with his human had made Fraser want Holly more than ever. Not just because he was reminded of how beautiful or clever she was. No, just being around her had brightened his day.

While he was pretty sure Holly had enjoyed their time together too, he hadn't gotten his hopes up. But thankfully, it seemed that his human wanted him as well.

And the next time he saw her, he wouldn't settle for kiss marks via text message. He'd claim her kisses for real.

His dragon spoke up. *Good. Holly will be ours soon. I give it three days.*

That's ambitious, dragon. We haven't even found a way to let her father live here, yet.

Someone will. Just make sure not to scare her away again.

Fraser snorted. *Yes, because Holly spooks so easily.*

You never know. The traitors might look for her again.

At his dragon's words, Fraser sobered a bit. *Finn and Grant are doing everything they can to find information on the dragons who attacked us. If Holly was in danger again, they'd tell me.*

Are you sure?

For a second, Fraser hesitated. Based on the conversation he'd heard the day before, Finn hadn't made up his mind about whether to invite Holly back or not. His cousin might not even know that Fraser wanted the lass back more than anything he'd ever wanted in his life.

Glancing at the time, it was only four a.m. As soon as Finn was awake, Fraser would talk with his cousin and convince him to invite Holly back. Then he'd wheedle out any information Finn might be keeping from him. Fraser needed to think of how to protect his mate in the future.

His beast chimed in again. *She hasn't said yes.*

It doesn't matter. She will.

His dragon snorted. *I see you've crossed over to my side. Confidence really does make things happen.*

He was about to scold his dragon when he heard a small rock clang against the side of his car.

Despite what had happened back in Aberdeen a few weeks ago, Lochguard had been safe for months. If a threat had emerged whilst he'd been away, Finn would've called him.

Another small rock hit his car and Fraser's curiosity was piqued.

Opening his car door slowly, Fraser clenched his fingers into a fist, ready to punch if anyone attacked. His dragon was also on standby, in case they needed to shift straight away.

Standing up, he listened for any sounds as he scanned his surroundings. Even in the early hours of the morning, he could see nearly as well as in daylight. But all he saw were rock formations, cottages, and the other clan cars parked nearby.

Inching his way to the back of the car, someone jumped up and clocked Fraser in the jaw. He flew backward and landed on the ground with an oomph.

Before Fraser could do anything, Fergus's voice drifted into the air. "That was for keeping a bloody secret from me."

Fraser's heart skipped a beat. His twin brother was home.

But it was best not to sound too eager just yet. Fraser needed to figure out how upset Fergus was with him first.

Rubbing his jaw, Fraser sat up. "Aye, I reckon I deserved that. Should I brace myself for more?"

Fergus shook his right hand. "I'm tempted, but my hand bloody hurts."

Fraser smiled. "You always said my head was made of stone."

"And it seems I was right." Fergus took a step toward him. "You should've told me Holly was your true mate, brother. I would've stepped aside."

Fraser stood. "Maybe I should have, but she was possibly your last chance at happiness. And I wanted to give you a chance to snare it."

Fergus moved to stand directly in front of Fraser. "But that was my decision to make, Fraser. Not yours."

He shrugged. "I don't know, Fergus. When we drink, you often need me to make your decisions for you. I've never seen such a lightweight before."

Fergus frowned. "I am not a lightweight. Half the time you spike my lager with vodka or some other strong liquor and dare me to drink it."

"Hey, you're the one who accepts the challenge."

"Only because you'll keep daring me until I do."

As Fraser and Fergus stared at one another, they both grinned.

Fraser may not voice it aloud, but he'd missed his twin brother dearly.

Fergus lightly punched him in the arm. "At any rate, for a bloke who likes to talk as much as you do, you seem to keep quiet when it actually matters. You're an idiot. Don't do it again."

A sense of relief washed over him. Fraser knew he and his twin were on good terms again. "I'll work on it, aye? The bigger question is why are you stalking about in the dark?"

"Well, I talked with Finn earlier. He and Arabella knew you'd gone to see Holly. Pulling the car into its parking spot quietly in the wee hours of the morning is your usual trick, so I waited. I wanted to see you before anything else happened. I don't like discord between us."

Fraser blinked. "Wait, Finn and Ara knew I'd gone to Inverness?"

Fergus raised an eyebrow. "Do you know Finn at all?"

"The bastard and his tricks. I'm definitely going to have a talk with him later. He tends to see us as children still, but that needs to change. We're twenty-eight years old, for fuck's sake." Fraser smiled at his twin. "But putting that aside, I'm glad you're home, Fergus. I could dance around the issues and pretend it's nothing, but I've missed you, brother."

"Aye, well, just don't do anything daft to drive me away again."

Fraser winked. "I'll try my best, although I can't make any promises." While he was relieved his twin didn't hate him, there was something else Fraser still needed to address, so he added, "But I hope you can welcome Holly and treat her as part of the family when she comes back."

Fergus raised an eyebrow. "So she is coming back, then? From what I heard, she hasn't contacted you in two weeks. That doesn't sound like a lass who is pining for you."

"She's gone through a lot recently. But let's just say I've convinced her to give me another chance."

"I'm sure Mum will be pleased. She's been secretly wishing for a grandchild for some time."

A flash of sadness coursed through Fraser's body. "She may wait a while yet. Finn must not have told you, but Holly lost the bairn."

Fergus gripped Fraser's shoulder and squeezed. "I'm truly sorry, Fraser." He gave Fraser a little shake. "However, judging by your boasting with the lasses in the past, I'm sure there'll be another one along before much longer."

Fraser and his dragon growled in unison. "Don't bring up other lasses. They don't matter. I only want Holly."

Fergus whistled. "You've fallen hard, brother. Just make sure not to fuck up again."

Fraser opened his mouth to reply when Grant came into sight, pumping his legs as fast as he could carry them. Fraser muttered, "That's not a good sign."

Grant skidded to a halt. "Good, I found you. I need your help, Fraser."

Fraser's stomach dropped. "I'm guessing it's not for a construction emergency, so what's happened?"

Grant motioned toward the Protectors' central command. "Some of the rogue dragons are keeping a hospital and its inhabitants hostage in Inverness."

He drew in a breath. "Which one?"

"I'm not going to beat around the bush. It's the one Holly is staying at with her father," Grant stated.

Fraser's dragon roared. *We must go to her. She needs us.*

Grant grabbed his shoulder. "Don't even think about rushing off. I have something far more important for you to do."

Fraser clenched a fist. "What?"

"I need you to contact Holly and find out what you can about the situation."

Fergus jumped in. "Are they jamming the wireless signals?"

Grant shook his head. "Not yet, which is why we need to act fast. Holly will know your voice and hopefully trust you. I need to know how things are going on inside of the hospital. I have plans in motion, but the more details available, the better plan of attack I can devise." Fraser took out his phone and Grant added, "Not out here. We need her on speakerphone in case Finn or I need to ask questions."

Fraser shoved the phone back in his pocket and strode toward the central command building. "Then hurry up. The longer we dawdle out here, the longer Holly is in danger."

As they made their way inside, a small part of Fraser wondered if his recklessness had yet again put Holly in danger. He'd been careful about leaving the clan, but had someone followed him? Or, had the rogue dragons been lying in wait for days?

Fraser clenched his fingers. Whatever the reason, he would do everything in his power to get Holly back to Lochguard.

Inside, Grant barked orders at the various Protectors and then motioned Fraser over. "Sit here so we can listen in."

Fraser nodded and waited for Emma MacAllister, one of Lochguard's IT experts, to set everything up.

THE DRAGON'S DILEMMA

As he tapped his fingers, he refused to imagine any negative outcome. Holly was alive and Fraser was going to bring her and her father to Lochguard, with or without the DDA's approval.

The trick would be convincing Finn of his plan.

~~~

Holly watched as a large dragon-shaped shadow flew past the window again. The dragon had been doing the same thing for the past twenty minutes.

She refused to imagine what would happen if any of the dragons outside her window started attacking the hospital.

She knew they were being held under siege by a group of dragon-shifters, but no one wanted to divulge any details. The rationale was there might be someone inside the hospital feeding the rogue dragons information.

Whatever the reason, Holly didn't think it was a coincidence the dragons targeted the hospital she was in.

Rubbing her arms, a small part of Holly wished Fraser was still here. Then he could contact Lochguard and ask for help.

She touched the mobile phone in her pocket. Maybe she should call Fraser and see what was going on. It was worth a shot.

Some of the neighboring patients shouted again and she sighed. It wasn't as if that would do any good. Glancing at her father's sleeping form, Holly was glad her dad was a heavy sleeper. The last thing he needed was extra stress.

After taking out her new phone, Holly found Fraser's number and pressed call. The phone rang once before Fraser's voice came on the line. "Holly? Are you okay?"

"I'm fine for the moment. Although, if you could tell me a little bit more about the dragons flying around the hospital and perching on the roofs, that would make my life a little easier."

Fraser's voice was a little less frantic as he replied, "Telling you about it won't do much to solve your problem."

She rolled her eyes even though Fraser couldn't see it. "You know what I mean. All the hospital will tell us is that the dragons delivered a letter with a warning—if anyone tries to step foot outside, the dragons will snatch them and start attacking the buildings."

In the background, she heard some murmurs. Before she could ask who they were, Fraser answered, "Finn is talking with the DDA right now. I should have more information for you in a minute. But while we wait, I need two things from you."

"Yes?"

"First—how are you holding up?"

"Stop being ridiculous. I told you that I'm fine."

Fraser growled. "I won't apologize for being worried about the woman I care more about than any other in the world."

Holly's heart skipped a beat as she blinked at his words. "What?"

Another male voice came over the line, one she instantly recognized. "Holly, this is Fergus. Ignore my brother's daft timing for a second and tell us anything that could help. Everyone here wants you back safe and sound." He paused and added, "Myself included."

Despite the threat outside her window and the possible danger to her life, relief flooded her body. Fergus's words also helped distract her from Fraser's words; she couldn't afford to dwell on them until later. "Good, because Fraser is grumpy when you're not around. He needs you close by."

Fergus barked out a laugh. "Don't I know it."

Fraser spoke up. "Stop talking about me as if I'm not here. Can we focus on the more immediate threat? I need you to tell me everything you can see or hear. How many dragons, where they're located, the works. It'll help us protect you."

Holly brushed a stray strand of hair behind her ear. At least Fraser had recognized the present wasn't the best time for declarations of the heart. "I'm not a trained soldier or anything, but I'll try my best. There are dragons circling the building at regular intervals. I can also see a few perched on the roof of the building across the way. I'm sure they're on all the buildings. I've counted maybe ten different ones so far. Or, at least, I tried to. It's still somewhat dark outside."

"Good job, Holly," Fraser replied. "That will help. Is there anything else?"

She glanced out the window. "I can snap some pictures with the phone and send them to you when we're done."

A string of expletives filled the other side of the phone line. Holly frowned. "Fraser? What's happening?"

As the seconds ticked by without a reply, Holly's heart rate ticked up. Something was wrong.

~~~

Fraser walked away from the console that had Holly on speaker phone and moved into Finn's personal space. "What do you mean those bastard traitor dragons want Holly in exchange for allowing everyone else to go free?"

Finn growled. "Don't take it out on me. I'm just repeating what the DDA told me."

Running a hand through his hair, Fraser turned away and then back again. "Please tell me you're not considering it."

Finn moved closer and punched Fraser in the arm. "I'm going to pretend you didn't just ask me that." Finn motioned toward Grant. "Grant has his own plans on how to handle the rogue dragons. For now, you need to let Holly know what's going on. The lass deserves to hear about their demands."

For a split second, Fraser considered keeping the truth from Holly. Knowing his female as he did, she would offer to give herself up if it meant she could save everyone else, especially her father.

His dragon snarled. *I won't allow her to do that.*

'Allow' isn't exactly the right word.

Ignoring his beast, Fraser met Finn's eyes again. Rather than annoyance or anger, Fraser only saw expectation.

His cousin was counting on him to do his part.

"Right," Fraser muttered and headed back to the speakerphone.

Holly's voice was angry as she ordered, "Fraser Moore MacKenzie, if you can hear me, then tell me what the bloody hell is going on."

Taking a deep breath, Fraser answered her. "We just had some news."

"I gathered that. Although since I don't have supersensitive dragon-shifter hearing, how about you tell me what the hell is going on?" Holly bit out.

Fraser leaned against the desk. "The dragons holding the hospital have demands and Finn just found out what they were."

"And?"

His dragon snarled. *Just tell her.*

Fraser managed to spit it out. "They want you in exchange for allowing everyone else to go free."

"Then—"

"Don't even bloody think it, woman. They damn near killed you in Aberdeen. They'll finish the job this time."

Even though he couldn't see Holly, Fraser could just imagine her narrowing her eyes just by the tone of her voice. "Are all dragonmen so impatient? What I was trying to ask was what is the plan?"

Fraser blinked and Finn answered her. "Holly, lass, it's Finn. Grant has a plan to get you all out of the hospital alive. I don't want to say more on the slim chance someone is listening to your conversation. However, it will be some time yet before they arrive. At the first sign of trouble, you call us back, do you hear?"

Holly's tone was a little less irritated. "Of course. But before I go, can I talk to Fraser in private?"

"Aye." Finn looked to Emma MacAllister. "Sever the bluetooth connection and give Fraser a few minutes." Then Finn gripped Fraser's shoulder and leaned down to whisper, "Calm your lass down, but don't take too long. We need those photos."

Picking up the mobile phone, Fraser nodded and walked out of the room. As soon as he was in one of the small, empty offices off the hall, he cleared his throat. "It's just us now, honey. I just want to say you're handling all of this remarkably well."

Holly's tone was a bit lighter as she replied, "Well, you clearly haven't been around a mother-to-be after thirty-six hours of labor. The dragons are nothing by comparison."

"Aye, and let's hope I never need to witness that. My dragon doesn't do well when our female is in pain."

Silence fell and Fraser wished he had Holly at his side. He'd never been very good at phone conversations; he needed to see a person's face to gauge their emotions.

Still, he was aware of Finn and the others needing the photos from Holly. So he blurted out, "Just be careful, lass. The thought of losing you forever terrifies me."

When Holly didn't respond immediately, he rubbed his hand against the back of his neck. Maybe she meant more to him than Fraser meant to her.

Then Holly's soft voice came on the line again. "You'll have to try a hell of a lot harder to get rid of me, Fraser MacKenzie. I've already made up my mind to be with you."

Both man and beast wanted to shout in happiness and ask Holly to be their mate forever.

But considering the circumstances, he held back. Instead, Fraser gripped the phone tighter. "Now that you've said that, only death will prevent me from bringing you home to Lochguard, Holly Anderson. Take care of yourself."

"I will, Fraser. We'll talk more when I'm home. For now, I'm going to snap those photos."

The line went dead and Fraser stared at his phone.

Despite everything going on, he smiled slowly. Holly was coming home to him and he would do everything in his power to not only keep her safe, but to also make her happy.

CHAPTER SEVENTEEN

Fraser paced the length of the central command's main operation room. Every once in a while he would glance at the news report on the far screen. A hospital held hostage by dragons had been too good of a story to pass up.

Yet every time he saw one of the dragons circling the hospital, Fraser clenched his jaw. They were after his female.

His dragon growled. *If the DDA doesn't punish them, Finn had better do so. Otherwise, our mate will never be safe.*

If only he were a trained Protector, then Fraser could help rescue her. *Believe me, dragon, as soon as Holly is safe in my arms again, I'm going to raise some hell.*

Not right away. We should hold her first and make sure she's okay.

Finn's voice interrupted his thoughts. "Bram is not going to be happy. The fucking rogue traitors are ruining the good image his clan has worked so hard to foster."

Fergus spoke up. "There are dragons on the screen I don't recognize as being from Lochguard. This problem runs deeper than a handful of former Lochguard clan members. I'll look into it as soon as I can. There has to be information floating around somewhere."

Finn grunted. "Even if dragons from other clans are involved, it doesn't matter. For all we know, the Lochguard bunch started it all. I'm just trying to understand why they're targeting Holly."

Fergus answered, "Because she's the first sacrifice we've had under your leadership, Finn. The traitors who abandoned Lochguard never liked humans in our midst. After all, they sided with the old clan leader when he ejected all of the humans and their mates out of the clan ten years ago. That's how the tiny clan of Seahaven was formed."

Fraser stopped pacing and moved to stand in front of Finn. "None of that matters right now, cousin. Holly's life is at stake. Rescue her first and then worry about mending relations."

Finn raised an eyebrow. "Someone's grumpy."

Grabbing Finn's top, he yanked his cousin close. "Imagine Arabella inside that hospital and possibly at the mercy of those bastards. I doubt you'd be calm and collected."

"Probably not." Finn looked to Fraser's hand and he released Finn's shirt. His cousin looked back up at him. "Save your anger for the enemy, lad. We may yet need your help."

Fraser's dragon chimed in. *While we're waiting, tell Finn our demands. There's no reason to wait. That way, we can tell Holly the truth when Grant and the others rescue her.*

Fraser eyed Finn's hard jaw and neutral eyes. *I'm not sure now is the best time.*

Do it, or I will take control and tell him for you.

Unsure if his dragon could pull off the threat or not, Fraser decided to just spit it out. "Of course I'll do anything to help Holly. But there's something I need you to do for me."

"Oh, aye? If it's to do with Holly and her dad living with us, I already have that covered."

Fraser blinked. "How?"

Finn shrugged. "When you snuck out last night, after hearing she'd lost the bairn, I knew you would do anything for the lass. So, I rang Bram and talked things over with him."

Fraser held his breath. "And?"

Before Finn could answer, Faye gave a piercing whistle and all eyes zoomed in on her. She motioned toward the screen. "Both Grant and Kai from Stonefire are arriving at the hospital. You two will have to finish your chat later."

Finn nodded. "She's right, Fraser. We'll talk later."

Fraser swore under his breath, but forced himself to remain silent. He didn't want to risk saying something he would regret later.

Looking to the screen, Fraser watched as Lochguard's and Stonefire's Protectors arrived at the Inverness NHS hospital.

They had better bring his lass back to him safe and sound. Fraser refused to think of the alternative.

~~~

Grant McFarland looked over the green hide of his back and did one final double-check. All of his Protectors were in position for their DDA-approved rescue mission.

And as much as he hated relying on another clan's help, Stonefire's head Protector, Kai Sutherland, also had his dragons at the ready about 200 yards to his right.

Grant's dragon spoke up. *It's okay to ask for help. I wish you would listen to Faye.*

Faye, the female you all but ignored for two years. That one?

His dragon huffed. *I had my reasons. But she is different now. I like her.*

Only because she's lame and you can easily best her in a flying race now.

Not only. I think she's forgiven us for before. But I didn't like her scoffing at us.

Grant regretted hurting Faye two years ago. As much as he didn't like her being hurt, Grant assisting in Faye's recovery had mended relations between them. *She may still do it. I had to nearly tie her to a chair so she wouldn't join the mission.*

She cares about family.

Aye, family. Let's not talk about the mess of ours.

His beast grunted. *It's not your fault.*

Maybe not. But it's never easy being related to a group of traitors.

At that, his beast fell silent and Grant pushed aside all thoughts of Faye or traitors. Inverness should be coming up in a few minutes. Grant couldn't afford to fuck up his first important mission as head Protector. Not just because of his pride, but an entire hospital of humans was also at stake.

Increasing the beat of his wings, Grant finally spotted a few dragons flying and diving around a building. That had to be the hospital where Holly Anderson was being held hostage.

Judging by the numbers, Grant and his rescue team had the advantage.

Yet he'd learned his lesson the hard way about being too cocky, so he approached the hospital with care. The rogue dragons could have others lying in wait with weaponry to knock Grant and his team out of the sky.

A few seconds later he was able to make out a green dragon Grant had known all his life—Roderick McFarland.

His dragon roared. *Roderick is worst of all because he's our uncle. We must destroy him.*

As much as Grant agreed, he was the more level-headed of the two. *We'll see, dragon, we'll see. Saving the humans is our top priority.*

THE DRAGON'S DILEMMA

Before his dragon could say anything else, Grant roared the command to engage. Kai did the same.

Grant's team barreled in opposite directions, the dragons engaging the enemies in pairs. Well, except for Grant and Kai, who would fight on their own.

Kai took on the dragon circling the hospital just as Grant headed for his uncle.

Roderick spotted him and snarled. Even without words, Grant understood his uncle's disdain for him. After all, Grant had stayed with Lochguard rather than join the half of his family who had rejected Finn's leadership. They'd left the clan to forge a new path.

His beast snarled again. *Traitors, the lot of them.*

The only good thing from it all was the fact Grant knew his uncle's weaknesses and strengths.

Grant dove toward Roderick and went for his weaker left wing. But the older dragon dropped out of the sky just in time to avoid the sting of Grant's talons.

His uncle may be thirty years his senior, but Grant had learned most of his tricks from Roderick. Taking down the older dragon would be tricky.

Still, Grant had other training to rely on from his time with the British Army. Beating his wings, he rose several hundred feet in the air and hovered. Roderick stayed closer to the ground and watched him.

Turning away from his uncle, Grant flew toward the hospital for a few seconds before flipping in mid-air and folding his wings and limbs against his body. He dropped quickly through the sky.

His uncle had barely started to move before Grant crashed into his uncle's back.

Pushing off the other dragon's hide, Grant managed to jump back into the sky. Grant's attack plus the extra downward force caused Roderick to spin out of control toward the open space near the hospital car park.

His uncle opened his wings right before he crashed to the ground. In the next heartbeat, Roderick moved. The last second action saved his life.

Grant dove down to keep his uncle restrained, but in the blink of an eye, his uncle shifted into his human form and hobbled toward a nearby copse of trees.

Grant's dragon growled. *Follow him. We can't let him escape.*

He glanced toward the other dragons fighting and noticed a few more traitors had joined the fray. *We must help the others.*

No, we should—

Grant threaded his inner voice with dominance. *Stop it, dragon. We can hunt down Roderick later. He's hurt and won't get far.*

As his beast sulked, Grant moved to help his clan members.

Since most of the traitors were older dragons in their fifties, sixties, and seventies, Grant noticed their reaction times slowing. All they needed to do was keep it up for another ten or fifteen minutes, and their enemies would either surrender or try to flee.

Determined not to allow anyone else to escape, Grant snarled and dove toward his nearest enemy.

~~~

Fraser watched the telly as Grant took on another dragon. Fraser was starting to see why Faye kept supporting the dragonman. He was fierce and skilled. Fraser wished he could pull off all of the split-second maneuvers of Lochguard's head Protector.

Faye motioned toward the screen. "I'd say the tide is turning." She stood and pointed to one of the rogue dragons and then another. "If you watch closely, you can see the other side is growing tired."

While there was nothing Fraser could do about Holly at the moment, he walked up to his sister and lightly squeezed the back of her neck. "You'll be back with them before much longer, Faye. You did a bang up job back in Aberdeen. I'd say your recovery is progressing well."

Faye frowned up at him. "Whenever you're nice to me, you always have some plan. What is it this time, Fraser Moore?"

"No plans, sister. Can't your favorite brother show a little love?"

Fergus snorted. "I'm her favorite, brother. That hasn't changed."

Fraser turned his gaze to Fergus. "Once Holly is safe and sound, you and I might have a little challenge. The winner becomes the favorite?"

Fergus nodded. "You're on."

Faye sighed. "Don't I get a say in this?"

"No," Fergus and Fraser said in unison.

Finn's voice boomed, "Enough. Look. I think the enemy is surrendering."

Looking back to the screen, the camera angle had switched to one on the ground. It showed both Kai and Grant pinning a dragon under each of them. The view switched again and displayed a few moaning dragons covered in scratches and blood.

None of them looked like Lochguard's Protectors. And Fraser would bet his life that none of them were from Stonefire, either.

Finn hugged Arabella close to his side. "As long as there's none of the traitors inside the hospital, we just need to play the waiting game." Finn met Fraser's gaze. "Grant knows to bring Holly and her dad here as soon as it's safe to do so."

Fraser nodded. "Holly's dad was due to be discharged today, so hopefully the hospital will still do so. If that's the case, then they'll be here in a few hours."

Finn kissed Arabella's forehead and then released her to walk over to Fraser. "Come, cousin. We need to chat."

Knowing everyone would be staring at him with questions in their eyes, Fraser quickly followed Finn out of the central command. The second Finn shut the door of a side office, he spoke up again. "While I told you that I talked with Bram about Holly coming to stay, I didn't tell you everything."

Fraser ignored the thundering of his heart. "Just spit it out, Finn."

His cousin crossed his arms over his chest. "The only way the DDA agreed to allow Holly and her father to live here is if you two are officially mated. It needs to be done within seventy-two hours of her stepping foot on Lochguard."

"That seems rather quick."

Finn raised an eyebrow. "Are you having second thoughts?"

"Never," Fraser growled out. "But Holly has had a hell of a few weeks. Between being dropped out of the sky, losing a child, and being held hostage in a hospital surrounded by dragons, the lass needs a breather."

Finn sighed. "I wish I could give it to her, Fraser. But you have three days. The mating just needs to take place in front of me, Arabella, and your family. We can plan a big ceremony later." Finn paused, and then asked, "Do you think you can gain her consent?"

Fraser's dragon roared. *Of course we can. She is our true mate. There's that confidence again.*

Fraser took a step toward Finn. "I can do it, but I'm going to need some help. I can't woo the lass and ease her nerves if she's worried about her father. Do you think you can get my mum and Meg Boyd to look after him for a little while? At least, until we're mated? They're both about his age. I'm sure they can keep each other company."

Mischief filled Finn's eyes. "Aye, I think I can convince Meg and Aunt Lorna. I'm sure the two females will fawn over him. After all, both of their mates died many years ago."

With a growl, Fraser took a step toward his cousin. "On second thought, maybe it's not a brilliant idea after all."

"Which is worse—losing Holly for good or letting Aunt Lorna near a man her own age she might fancy?"

His dragon chimed in. *Who cares if Mum fancies him or not? She's been alone for a long time now. You always mention how you wish she'd found someone else.*

Aye, but not the father of my mate. Besides, what will the DDA say?

Does it matter? They will grant him permission to live on Lochguard if we mate Holly.

His beast was right. But rather than acknowledge it, Fraser sighed. "Holly's dad will be running for the hills before long. I can see it now."

Finn uncrossed his arms and clapped Fraser's shoulder. "Aye, well, let's see how he does first. If they drive him crazy, I can find someone else to look after him."

Fraser's dragon chimed in. *It will be fine. Holly's father needs a break from Holly's worries and fussing, too. Imagine if we had two bonny lasses tending to our wounds. I wouldn't complain.*

I only want Holly, so your dream isn't going to happen.

Of course I want Holly. I hate when you start being literal.

Fraser smiled at his dragon and Finn asked, "I take it your dragon is on my side?"

"You really don't want to know. But yes, we'll try your plan for now."

Finn squeezed Fraser's shoulder. "Good. Then how about you get things ready and I'll let you know when Holly has arrived." Fraser looked toward the door, debating if he should go, but his cousin continued, "I'll tell the others where you've gone, including Fergus and Faye. If anything goes wrong, you'll be the first to know. I promise."

Fraser nodded and his beast spoke up again. *We need to hurry. There is much to do.*

I'm planning her welcome, not you.

His beast huffed. *I want to help. She's my mate as much as yours.*

Fine. But sex is going to have to wait until she's ready. Understand?

When his beast didn't argue, Fraser moved to the door. "Thanks, Finn. For everything."

Finn shooed him with a hand. "Get yourself gone before I change my mind and order you to finish weeding my garden instead. It's only half done."

Fraser grinned. "You can always finish it yourself."

Before Finn could answer, Fraser was out the door and exiting the building. He had a lass to woo and not much time to plan.

He needed to make every second count.

CHAPTER EIGHTEEN

By the end of the day, Holly was in a car on her way to Lochguard.

Her father dozed at her side. His skin had a slightly pink tinge, which was much better than the paleness of last week. By all accounts, her father's health was mending. The hospital had even promised to send someone to continue her father's special cancer treatments on Lochguard.

Just thinking about Lochguard made her stomach flip. Everything she'd wanted was coming true. So much so, her heart pounded inside her chest. Whether out of happiness or nervousness, she didn't know. It was probably a combination of both.

Yes, she wanted Fraser more than any man in her life. And she was confident her father could fit in with some of the older dragon-shifters, too; Aunt Lorna alone would probably chat his ear off.

But while she was fairly sure Fraser would hold her close and try to charm her, she didn't want there to be any awkwardness between them because of the miscarriage.

Holly had had two weeks to come to terms with it. Maybe she was one of the lucky ones since the pregnancy had been so new and she had less time to grow attached or hopeful. But she was ready to have all of Fraser again, both by her side and in her bed. If nothing else, it would help her make new memories to replace the old.

And who knew, they might even have a chance at a child again in the future.

Then Fraser's words came rushing back: *Even if we're never gifted with a child again, I still want you by my side.*

Rubbing her palms against her jeans, Holly decided she wanted Fraser in all ways. She would do whatever it took to convince him of that.

Shay, the young Lochguard Protector assigned as her driver, spoke up. "We're nearly there, miss."

Holly frowned. "I told you before to call me Holly. 'Miss' makes me sound as if I'm your teacher."

"If you say so, Holly. You might want to wake your dad up, though. If Lorna MacKenzie is taking charge of Mr. Anderson's care, she'll be there ten minutes early, tapping her toes and waiting for us."

Holly smiled. "To be honest, I think my dad will enjoy the attention."

Her dad's sleepy voice filled the car. "I can hear you, Holly. Who is Lorna MacKenzie?"

She glanced to her father. Curiosity filled his eyes; the man didn't like being left in the dark. "I told you before, Dad. She's Fraser's mum. Once you meet her children, you'll understand just how strong the dragonwoman is."

"Oh, aye? Well, if she aims to boss me around, she's going to have a surprise coming. I may be ill, but I'm not dead yet."

Holly grinned. "To be honest, I think she likes a challenge. Give it to her as good as you get." Shay merely shook his head in the front seat, but Holly ignored him and focused on her father. "Are you sure you're okay to stay with them a bit? I can delay things with Fraser until you're ready. Just say the word. I won't abandon you, Dad."

Her father smiled. "Don't worry about me, Holly-berry. I'm a strong man. Cancer couldn't kill me. I can handle a wee dragonwoman."

Shay choked in the front seat and Holly bit her lip to keep from laughing. "I'm sure you can, Dad. I'm sure you can."

Her father touched her arm. "I can tell you want to see him, lass. It's all right to take a slice of happiness for yourself, especially since you gave up so much to help me."

"It wasn't that much, Dad. Any child would do the same."

Her dad squeezed her arm. "No, they wouldn't. You are special, Holly. And I want to start repaying you by allowing you some time with your lad." He winked. "Besides, I wouldn't mind a wee bit of attention from a lass my own age."

She chuckled just as Shay made the final turn to Lochguard. "Well, brace yourselves. I spot not only Lorna, but Finn and Meg Boyd as well. Those three are a force to be reckoned with."

Holly ignored the twinge in her heart at Fraser's absence. There had to be a reason why he was late.

To try to fool her father, she made her voice strong. "I inherited my stubbornness from my father. Either one of us can take a challenge."

The gates opened and Shay drove the car just inside them. Once he cut the engine, Finn opened Holly's door at the same time Lorna opened her dad's.

Lorna beat Finn to the punch. "Hello, Mr. Anderson. My name's Lorna MacKenzie. Welcome to Lochguard."

Finn muttered under his breath, "So much for letting me handle things."

Lorna's voice filled the air again. "I can hear you, nephew."

Hoping to prevent a row that would make a poor impression on her father, Holly jumped in. "How about we exit the car first and then finish the introductions?"

Lorna helped Holly's dad out of the car and Finn helped Holly. As Finn guided her around to the other side, he whispered, "Fraser thought it best to let your dad meet the older females first. He'll be along shortly."

While she only half-agreed with the plan, they rounded the back of the car and Holly merely nodded. She could scold Fraser later.

Meg Boyd was already at her dad's side. "My name's Meg Boyd and I'll also be helping to look after you."

Her father grinned. "Two bonny lasses. A man couldn't be happier. You can call me Ross."

Holly resisted groaning at her father's antics. The last thing she wanted to see was her dad flirting with anyone.

Meg giggled. "It's been a fair while since I've been called either bonny or a lass." Meg lightly slapped Ross's chest. "And by a strong man, to boot."

Finn rolled his eyes. "Excuse my Aunt Lorna for not introducing us properly. I'm Finn Stewart, the clan leader here. If either of them gives you trouble, call me and I'll sort it out. I'm one of the few who can get them under control."

Both Meg and Lorna opened their mouths, but Holly's dad turned around and beat them to the punch. "Thanks for the offer, but I think I can handle them." Ross looked back to Lorna and Meg. "I'm still a wee bit tired from my illness. How about you lasses show me where I'm going to stay and help me settle in?"

Holly took a step toward Ross. "Dad—"

Lorna waved a hand in dismissal. "It's no bother, Holly. Fraser should be along shortly and I'm sure you two have much to discuss."

Finn squeezed Holly's shoulder and leaned down to whisper, "I'll chaperone for a bit. It'll be fine."

Lorna raised an eyebrow. "Finlay Stewart, I most certainly don't need chaperoning."

Holly's dad spoke up. "I could do with some tea. How about we all sit down and the three of you can tell me about the clan? Holly's told me a little, but I'm sure the three of you know everything there is to know. Lochguard is surrounded by a fair bit of mythology. I'll need to figure out what is true and what is bollocks." Her dad looked to Lorna, Meg, and finally Finn. "I'm not wrong about you three, am I?"

Holly bit her lip. She'd almost forgotten how Ross Anderson could be quite the charmer.

Finn moved to Ross's side. "No, we can sort it all out for you, Ross. Come. I see Fraser in the distance. I'm sure he and Holly would fancy some privacy for their reunion."

Holly looked into the distance, but didn't see anything. Finn must be using his super-sensitive dragon senses again.

Holly's dad touched her cheek and she met his eyes. Her father murmured, "Don't keep him away too long, Holly-berry. I want to see the man who won over your heart."

She opened her mouth to state it hadn't been long enough for anyone to steal her heart, but Lorna, Meg, and Finn were already steering her father away. Finn looked over his shoulder and winked.

As she tapped her hand against her thigh and looked into the direction Finn had pointed out earlier, a tall, auburn-haired man finally came into sight and her heart skipped a beat.

Fraser had arrived.

Pushing aside her exhaustion, she forgot about wanting to scold the dragonman and she ran toward him. He barely had time to open his arms before she jumped into them. She hugged him closely. "Fraser. You're here."

His strong arms wrapped around her. "Of course I am, honey. I will always be waiting for you."

Blinking her eyes to hold back her tears, she pulled back a fraction to look into Fraser's eyes. "When I first met you, I would've dismissed that as nothing more than pretty words."

He raised an eyebrow. "And now?"

"And now, I couldn't be happier to believe them."

Fraser moved a hand to brush her cheek. "Good, because I'm don't want to waste time arguing. I'm going to kiss you now."

Before she could reply, Fraser's lips descended on hers. As soon as his soft yet firm lips touched hers, she melted against her dragonman.

She'd wondered over the last two weeks what it would feel like to kiss Fraser again. Yet as he nibbled and sucked her lips, his touch was gentle. He was clearly holding back.

Pulling away, she frowned. "Stop coddling me, Fraser Moore MacKenzie. You have a lass wanting a kiss. You'd better do your job properly."

Fraser chuckled. "And people say I'm bold."

"Fraser."

In the next breath, he nipped her lower lip and pushed his tongue into her mouth. At his warm, heady taste, she moaned and pulled Fraser closer.

Kissing Fraser made her forget about the rest of the world. And she could use a little distraction right at that moment.

Just as she clutched his shoulders, Fraser pulled away again. Holly growled out, "I'm in no mood for games, Fraser. Either kiss me or not. Make up your bloody mind."

The corner of his mouth ticked up. "We've gathered quite an audience. I wasn't sure if you were ready to become an exhibitionist or not."

Holly glanced over her shoulder and counted about ten dragon-shifters blatantly staring at her. She wouldn't exactly call herself shy, but the last thing she wanted was to share her reunion with the clan.

Looking back to Fraser, she whispered, "Then take me somewhere private. As much as I love your clan, I want to spend some time alone with my dragonman."

"Your dragonman, eh? I like the sound of that. Maybe I should tattoo 'Holly's dragonman' on my forehead. That will keep the lasses away."

She shook her head. "You're starting to make me question why I came back."

Fraser's grin faded and his pupils flashed to slits and back. "Don't joke about that, Holly. You're staying with me, end of story."

Searching his eyes, there was a mixture of fierceness and something else she couldn't define. Whatever it was, she couldn't bring herself to tease him. "Provided you don't turn into an arsehole, I'll stay."

"Good answer."

Fraser stepped back and swooped under Holly's legs. She squeaked as he held her tight against his chest. "I can walk."

He jostled her against his chest. "Yes, but then I couldn't make the most of my point and do this." He looked past her to the crowd. "Stop gawking. Holly Anderson is my human and I'm not sharing her."

Some of the clan members cheered whilst others shouted obscene suggestions. Holly waited for a flare of indignation, but it never came.

She rather liked Fraser claiming her.

Looping her hands behind his neck, she murmured, "Enough showboating. Take me somewhere private and give me a proper hello."

Fraser glanced down to her gaze and heat flared in his eyes. "Are you sure? I can wait if you need time."

"I had a lot of time to think inside the hospital. A few things kept popping inside my mind. Do you know what one of them was?"

Fraser's voice was husky as he asked, "What?"

She leaned closer and whispered, "That I wanted to make new memories with you to forget the old. I'm healed now and I want you, Fraser, and I want you now. Trouble seems to follow us and I don't want to risk something else stealing you from my side."

~~~

Fraser's heart beat double-time. A noble dragonman would take his female home after a trying day, pamper her, and hold her close whilst they fell asleep.

Yet he wasn't a noble dragonman. Bastard that he was, all he wanted was Holly naked and under him.

His beast spoke up. *She wants to make new memories. Give her what she wants.*

But it's too soon.

His dragon snorted. *You definitely love the lass if you're willing to forego sex when it's offered.*

The Dragon's Dilemma

At the mention of love, Fraser's stomach flipped. *It can't be. We haven't known her very long.*

So? Reckless male that you were, you should know that things don't always happen on a schedule.

Holly's voice was a little less certain when she whispered, "Fraser, we can wait if you're not ready. It's okay."

Fraser searched her eyes and saw concern.

He started jogging toward their cottage. "I'll take you home, at least. Then we'll see what happens from there."

In response, Holly laid her head on his chest and Fraser wondered if he'd said the wrong thing.

His dragon growled. *Tell her we want her and only her. She should never doubt that.*

You're pushy.

It's because you're being an idiot.

Rather than answer his dragon, Fraser said to Holly, "I want you, Holly. Every second of every day whilst we've been apart, I've wanted you with every fiber of my being. But you said you wanted to get to know me better and I'm trying to give you the chance, honey."

Holly tightened her grip on his neck. "I was a fool. I've been targeted twice now by a group of rogue dragon-shifters, Fraser. And in each instance, you did all that you could to help me. And even when you weren't by my side, I wished you were." She leaned back her head and Fraser glanced down for a second. "I want you now, dragonman. If we wait much longer, someone could attack again and I may never have the chance to explore your naked body."

He tightened his grip. "No one is taking you from here. If they try, they'll have to deal with me."

"That's a nice sentiment, but aren't you forgetting about the DDA?"

Fraser reached their cottage and gently set Holly on her feet. He quickly opened the door, rushed them inside, and shut it.

He decided to just tell Holly the truth. After everything that had happened with Fergus, Fraser was done keeping secrets. "I have a way you can stay, Holly. I was going to wait to tell you, but I never want to keep secrets from you. Well, at least the big ones. I plan to have many surprises to give you over the years."

She tilted her head. "Before you start planning our future, how about you tell me how I can stay?"

He traced her brow. "If we perform the mating ceremony within the next seventy-one hours and fifty minutes, you and your father can stay on Lochguard forever." He cupped her cheek. "But you have three days to think about it, Holly. It's a big decision and I'll be blunt—living with us won't be easy. Between the rogue dragon traitors, the dragon hunters, the Dragon Knights, and the general dislike from the vast majority of the human population, your life will become bloody difficult."

Holly placed a hand on his chest and Fraser's heart skipped a beat. He'd missed the soft touch of her fingers.

His female whispered, "I can face anything as long as you're by my side, Fraser MacKenzie. I've been carrying my burdens by myself for three decades. And then your charming self came along and all I can think about is sharing everything—past, present, and future—with you." She paused and then leaned her weight against him. "Not only that, just imagining your arms around me whilst I was in the hospital gave me the strength to be a better person and face the threat." Holly moved her free hand to his cheek and he nuzzled her palm. "I think I love you, Fraser MacKenzie. And I'm not going to ever let you go, so you'd better get used to me being around."

THE DRAGON'S DILEMMA

Fraser stopped breathing. Holly's words sent a possessive rush of tenderness and desire through his body.

Despite his failure to protect her, Holly wanted him.

Both man and beast roared in happiness.

His dragon chimed in. *Stop fighting it and just tell her the truth. She'll want to mate us then.*

Fraser had put off thinking about love because he'd been unsure if Holly felt the same way. He wasn't a dragonman who used the term lightly. Hell, a year ago, just thinking about being in love had given him hives.

Yet as he searched Holly's honey-colored eyes, there was no other female he wanted more. He would give his life to protect her.

He pulled her closer and leaned down until her lips were less than an inch from his. "You *think* you love me? I'm not sure I like that answer."

"Fraser—"

"I love you with my entire being, Holly Anderson. And I think it's about time to show you. Then maybe you'll go from 'think' to 'head-over-heels' in love with me."

Before his female could say anything, Fraser kissed her.

CHAPTER NINETEEN

The instant Fraser's lips touched hers, Holly moaned and accepted his tongue.

Fraser loved her. She could hardly believe it.

She clutched his shoulders but despite Fraser's taste in her mouth and her nails in his skin, it wasn't nearly enough. She needed to feel Fraser's hot skin against hers. She wanted to be claimed properly.

Breaking the kiss, Holly murmured, "Take off your clothes."

Fraser's pupils flashed to slits and back. "I like a lass who knows what she wants."

"Then hurry up because I want you naked and inside me within the next sixty seconds."

With a growl, Fraser stepped back and tore off his shirt. Holly's eyes fell to the muscled planes of his chest. As his hands went to his jeans, she noticed the impressive bulge against his fly.

Remembering Fraser's hard cock inside of her during the mate-claim frenzy sent a rush of wetness between her legs.

Fraser's husky voice interrupted the memories playing inside her head. "Keep looking at me like that, and I won't last long, honey."

She met his eyes again. The flashing pupils didn't scare her; if anything, it increased the pulse between her thighs. "I'm sure if that's the case, I'll just ask your dragon to help with your stamina problem."

With a growl, Fraser walked up and encircled her wrists with his fingers. "I think for that comment, you need a little teasing."

At the heat in his eyes, Holly's heart hammered inside her chest. "It depends on what kind of teasing."

He moved her hands to behind her back and took them both in one hand. He moved the other to her front and lightly traced the swell of her breast. "A little of this."

He rubbed her hard nipple through her shirt in slow circles. Each rough stroke made her knees weak and it became harder to stand.

Fraser removed his finger and Holly opened her mouth, but he beat her to it. "And some of this."

He slowly traced her bottom lip with his thumb. Her lips were already slightly swollen from kissing, but as he brushed back and forth, the friction of his callouses against her soft skin made it even more sensitive.

No man had ever made her body flush with heat by merely stroking her lower lip. Yet Holly couldn't resist moaning.

Approval flashed in Fraser's eyes. "And maybe some of this."

He moved one of his knees between her open legs and rocked against her clit. The pressure sent a thread of pleasure through her body. When he did it again, she leaned forward on his leg for support.

It was on the tip of her tongue to beg him to stop teasing and use his cock, but she didn't want to give him that victory. At least, not yet.

Because if she did, he'd always try to make her beg.

Not as if that were a bad thing, but she wasn't going to feed his ego just yet.

Giving him a heavy-lidded gaze, she murmured, "Is that the best you have, dragonman?"

With a growl, Fraser extended a talon and gently sliced through her top and bra. Before she could do more than squeak, he took hold of her breast and sucked her nipple into his mouth.

Each pull shot straight between her legs. She couldn't help but say, "Fraser."

At his name, he lightly bit her as he pressed against her clit with his thigh. The double sensation nearly made her come; lights already danced behind her eyes. One last rock with his knee would be enough.

Fraser released her nipple and removed his leg. Holly cried out, "No."

Her dragonman flicked open the fly of her trousers and unzipped them. "I think we need to make sure you're wet enough for me, love. Because when you come, I want to feel you around my dick."

"You're being—"

Fraser dove his hand inside her panties and thrust into her with a thick finger. She loved the way he felt inside her pussy.

He leaned down to nuzzle her cheek. "I must be doing a good job. You're drenched for me. Just the way it should be." He moved his finger again. "You're mine and by the end of the night, you'll understand that with every muscle in your body."

He moved back to look into her eyes. Holly should scold him or argue. Otherwise, the dragonman's head would get too big.

But at the desire and love shining in his eyes, she blurted out, "Enough talking, Fraser MacKenzie. Show me just how much you love me with your body. Then I'll believe you truly want me."

Fraser growled out, "I will always want you, Holly. But I'm up for your challenge. I think it's time to show you just how much I love you."

As Fraser's pupils flashed, Holly's heart rate kicked up even more. She'd just taunted a dragonman.

Some might be afraid, but her every nerve tingled in anticipation of what he'd do next.

~ ~ ~

Fraser's dragon wouldn't stop roaring inside his head. *She is wet and all but begging us to fuck her. Why are you stalling?*

Because I want her to remember this day forever. This is the day Holly Anderson becomes mine with both body and heart.

I don't like this romantic side. Fuck her soon or I'll take over.

No.

Before his beast could reply, Fraser built one of the elaborate mazes he'd perfected over the last few weeks. His beast would need at least an hour to find his way out.

Fraser planned to take advantage of every second of that hour.

Removing his hand from Holly's pussy, he tore off the tattered remains of her top and bra. The action sped up Holly's breathing, but rather than touch her, he merely stared at her pale breasts.

Breasts that would never be seen by another male ever again.

"Fraser."

He met Holly's eyes. "Take off your shoes and jeans or I will rip them off, too."

Licking her lips, Holly removed one shoe and then the other. As she slowly wiggled out of her pants, her breasts jiggled as if to entice him further. Only because he clenched his fingers did he not reach out to feel them. He wanted her naked first. Then he would touch her.

And oh how he planned to tease and caress her from breast to arse to thigh.

Holly kicked her last shred of clothing aside and tried to walk away. Fraser grabbed her waist and pinned her up against the wall, her back to his front. He kissed her neck before murmuring against her skin, "Where do you think you're going?"

"I thought dragons liked to chase their prey."

"We do." After nipping her neck, he moved a hand around to one of her breasts and squeezed. "But we can play chase later. For now, I'm going to do this."

Releasing her breasts, he took hold of her hips and drew them back slightly so he could thrust his dick inside of her. Holly moaned and that was all the encouragement he needed to say, "I'm going to take you hard, Holly. I can't have you doubting how much I want you."

Bracing her forearms against the wall, she wiggled her hips against him. "Stop talking and fuck me, already."

Fraser pulled out and slammed back in. "That's my lass."

His dragon banged against the roof of the maze. All of the buildup was killing his beast.

However, even without his dragon, Fraser was done drawing it out.

It was time to brand Holly as his female.

Guiding her hips, he moved in and out in a quick, steady rhythm. With each thrust, his balls slapped against Holly's flesh and the sound drove him to go faster.

THE DRAGON'S DILEMMA

She clutched her inner muscles as he moved and he growled. "Stop it."

"Never."

She moaned as he pounded harder. Then she released and gripped him firmer. Bloody hell. The minx was going to make him come before her and he wasn't going to allow that to happen.

Fraser snaked one hand around her waist and found her clit. Rubbing in rough, quick circles, Holly leaned more against the wall. "Bastard. That's cheating."

Increasing the pressure against her clit, he never stopped moving in and out of her pussy. "I'll do whatever it takes to make my female come first."

Pressing hard against her sensitive bundle of nerves, Holly screamed. As her inner muscles gripped and released his cock, he gritted his teeth. He wasn't ready to come just yet. He still needed to make an impression on his mate.

He never wanted her to doubt how much he wanted her. Hell, how much he loved her.

Holly was his perfect match.

As soon as Holly melted against the wall, Fraser pulled out and spun her around. The dazed expression in her eyes stroked the ego of both man and beast. He smiled.

She frowned. "Why did you stop?"

He nipped her lower lip. "Because I'm just getting started."

Scooping up his female, Fraser moved to the sofa and sat her down on the back of it. Holly blinked. "Is this another frenzy? I thought there was only the one."

As he ran his dick up and down her swollen slit, he murmured, "No, it's not another frenzy." He tapped the head of his cock against her clit. "But I will never get enough of you, Holly. Never."

Then he thrust inside her again and pulled her close. Without a word, Holly wrapped her legs around his waist. "Is that a promise?"

He descended on her lips. As he devoured her mouth, Holly threaded her fingers through his hair and pressed her breasts against his chest. The hard points of her nipples made his dick release a drop of precum.

His dragon gave a frustrated roar inside the maze. *Soon, dragon. I'm nearly done.*

Wrapping his arms around Holly, he continued to stroke his tongue against hers.

Then Holly moved her lower body a fraction and Fraser growled. The human was trying to tease him.

Breaking the kiss, he gripped her hips to keep her still. "I hope you're ready for some more, Holly. Because I'm not holding back this time."

Excitement flashed in her eyes. "Good. Because I always want all of you, Fraser MacKenzie. Remember that."

"You're so fucking perfect. I can't believe you're mine."

Taking her lips again, he kept her hips in place as he created a quick, hard rhythm. Holly dug her nails into his scalp in encouragement and Fraser pounded harder.

Daring to release one hand, he lightly slapped her bum before grabbing it. He couldn't wait to feel her soft arse against his skin as he took her from behind again later.

Holly's hands moved to his arse. She also slapped him before clutching his tight mounds.

He wasn't sure if he should growl or chuckle.

Then Holly circled her hips and he couldn't help but break the kiss and say, "Bloody hell, woman, are you trying to kill me?"

Between her flushed cheeks and kiss-bruised lips, Holly took his breath away. "Maybe later."

Oh, yes. Holly's true self came out when she was naked.

The pressure built at the base of his spine, so Fraser reached between them and circled around her clit.

Holly closed her eyes. "Yes, harder."

He stilled his hand. "Look at me first."

She opened her eyes and the desire and need in them kicked the air out of his lungs.

In the next second, he pinched her clit as he came. Each spurt of semen sent Holly into a fresh orgasm. Her screams of pleasure prolonged his own release.

When he finally spilled his last drop, Fraser hugged Holly close and simply held her.

Both of their breaths were ragged and fast. Yet as Holly's sweet feminine scent filled his nose, a sense of peace came over him. Taking the female in front of him in this cottage just felt right. He couldn't imagine setting up a life or growing old with anyone else.

And not just because of his dragon's instinct. Holly didn't fall for his charm, yet she had a sense of humor to rival his. She was clever, brave, and the most beautiful lass he'd ever laid eyes on.

So it felt natural to say, "I love you, Holly."

Without hesitation, his female snuggled into his chest and answered, "I love you, too, Fraser."

He chuckled. "So you dropped the 'I think' part of it, aye?"

She lightly slapped his back. "Some might say that kind of ruined the moment."

Fraser leaned back to meet her eye. "And what do you think?"

She grinned. "I think it suits it perfectly. Don't ever change who you are, Fraser, because that's the man I fell in love with."

"Good answer, honey. Good answer." He gave her a gentle kiss. "So does that mean you'll be my mate?"

She frowned. "Didn't I answer that already?"

He brushed a piece of damp hair from her face. "You never actually gave me an answer. As much as I appreciate hearing you love me, I need a yes or no."

The corner of her mouth ticked up. "So you're the kind of dragonman who needs everything spelled out to the letter?"

"In this, yes. Because I don't dare hope or start planning the future until I hear a clear 'Yes, I'll be your mate, Fraser' from you."

"Hey, I don't sound like that."

He bopped her nose. "You do, but despite that, I still love you."

"You're exhausting sometimes, Fraser MacKenzie."

He grinned. "That's what my family keeps telling me."

Holly looped her arms behind his neck and tilted her head. "I will mate you."

Joy swelled his heart. He'd been fairly certain she'd say yes, but hearing the words made him the happiest he'd been in his life.

Fraser leaned down to kiss her, but she shook her head. He frowned. "Why are you shaking your head when you just said yes?"

"Because you didn't let me finish. I will mate you, but only on one condition."

He growled out, "What's the bloody condition?"

"I need to meet with your family and make sure everything is okay with them."

"Of course everything is—"

She cut him off. "They're an important part of who you are. In order for you to be happy, you need them. Let's have lunch with them tomorrow and you can meet with my dad at the same time. If everything feels right, then I'll claim you as mine in front of them all."

"I can't see you scooping me up and carrying me away."

She sighed. "Not all of us need to go caveman-like to claim someone."

He lightly tapped her backside. "I'm not sure why you're complaining. I know you like it."

"I'm afraid to confirm or deny that. Your ego is pretty big today already."

Leaning down, he nipped the side of her neck. "Then maybe I need to find other ways of making you answer my question."

There was a warning in her tone. "Fraser."

He chuckled. "Not right now. I'll do it when you least expect. For the moment, I need to feed you. Your stomach keeps rumbling and my dragon doesn't like it."

Holly gently tugged his hair and he moved to look into her eyes. "Do all dragon-shifter males act this way? As if I couldn't take care of myself?"

He frowned. "Of course you can take care of yourself. But a good male keeps his female happy. That way, she won't leave him."

Smiling, she cupped his cheek. "Good answer. But if I say I want to do something, then I'm going to do it. That will make me happy. Understand?"

His dragon growled inside the maze, and Fraser agreed with his beast. However, he would probably need to compromise with his human every day for the rest of their lives. Despite the challenges ahead, he found himself looking forward to it. "For now. But if we ever have a child, I will take care of you whilst you're pregnant. It's a dragonman's duty. I hope you understand that."

Holly searched his eyes. When she finally spoke, her voice was quiet. "If it ever happens, then we'll revisit the idea."

He took her face in his hands and stroked her cheeks. "Even if all we have are ten cats and a hamster, I will be happy. Because, Holly Anderson, all I need is you."

Her eyes shined with wetness. "Fraser."

He gave her a gentle kiss and added, "But I'm drawing the line at ten cats. If you try for number eleven, I'll sleep in the forest by myself. The wee beasties tend to follow me around and the last thing I need is all of those furry bodies trying to squirm into bed between me and my mate."

Mischief danced in Holly's eyes. "Now that you've told me that, I have some plans to make. Maybe your brother and sister will help me see them through."

He sighed. "Bloody fantastic."

Holly laughed and the sound sent a rush of happiness through his body. He could listen to her laugh all day and it would never be enough.

She snuggled into his chest. "Now about that food…"

"Oh, aye? Now you're wanting me to pamper you?" She smacked his bum and Fraser chuckled. "I can't promise anything fancy, but even I can fry up some eggs and bacon."

Nuzzling his skin, she murmured, "You'll do, Fraser. You'll do."

Hugging Holly tight against his body, he closed his eyes and memorized the moment. He was confident everything would go well the next day, but there was always the chance her father wouldn't accept him. After all, Fraser had put Holly's life in danger several times already.

Fraser would treasure every second between now and then. It was a rare gift to find one's mate and earn her love. He wasn't about to do anything to fuck that up ever again.

CHAPTER TWENTY

The next day, Holly stopped about twenty feet from Lorna MacKenzie's cottage and squeezed Fraser's hand in hers.

What happened inside that cottage would determine her future. As much as she loved Fraser, she wouldn't be the one to cause strife in his family. Fergus might have said he wanted her to come back to Lochguard over the phone, but that had been during the heat of the dragon siege.

She only hoped it held true in the present as well. The thought of never seeing Fraser ever again, let alone tease him, was a bleak future indeed.

But if it meant Fraser could mend things with his family, she would do it. For him.

Fraser released her hand and hugged her against his side. As she melted against his heat, he whispered, "You won't believe me no matter how many times I tell you everything will be fine. And here you are, delaying things. If there's one way to upset my mum, it's to be tardy."

She frowned up at him. "That isn't helping, Fraser."

"Hey, it's the truth." He squeezed her again. "If I know my family at all, and I do, then they won't hate you, honey. If anything, they're going to try to draw you into the madness. Faye, in particular, has been looking for an ally against me and Fergus her whole life."

"It's not Faye I'm worried about."

Before Fraser could reply, the door opened to reveal the tall, auburn-haired form of Fergus MacKenzie.

Holly held her breath and waited for the hatred or worse, indifference, to flash in the dragonman's eyes. But Fergus merely shouted, "Oi, hurry up you two. Faye and Arabella are starving and their whining is driving me crazy."

She released her breath as Fraser answered, "Maybe we should stay out here a bit longer, Fergus. Then you can be the focus of their irritation a wee bit longer."

Fergus shook his head. "If I have to carry you inside this house myself, I will, brother." Fergus then grinned at Holly. "And then I'll be back for you."

Fraser growled. "You'll not touch her, Fergus. Holly is my female."

Fergus raised his brows. "She's about to become my sister-in-law and if you think I'm going to never hug the lass or poke her side, then you clearly don't know me, let alone our family, very well."

Fraser's grip tightened around Holly's waist. "Then don't touch her skin. I'm going to implement a gloves and jumper rule. If you wear both of them and don't touch your cheek to hers, then I'll allow you to hug Holly."

Holly was about to protest about Fraser allowing anything, but Fergus was in front of them in the blink of an eye. Before she could utter a word, Fergus growled out, "Are you trying to order me around?"

Fraser leaned closer to his twin. "Aye, I am."

Something sparked in Fergus's eyes. He then grinned slowly and reached out a finger to poke Holly's cheek. Fraser roared as he released his grip on Holly and tackled his brother to the ground.

Holly sighed as the two brothers wrestled in the grass. She needed to figure out how the hell she could tear the two of them apart. Given that both of them were at least 200 pounds of muscle each, it was going to be quite the feat.

So distracted by Fraser and Fergus, Holly didn't noticed Lorna MacKenzie show up next to her. Holly jumped when the dragonwoman muttered, "The idiots."

Holly glanced over and saw that Lorna was carrying a wooden spoon. "They're fighting because of me."

Lorna shook her head. "Bollocks. They've found something to wrestle about nearly every day of their lives. It's when they're not picking on each other that I start to worry."

Holly blinked. "This is normal?"

Lorna grinned. "Aye, it is. Does it want to send you running for the hills?"

Holly straightened her shoulders. "Of course not."

Lorna reached out her free hand and lightly patted her cheek. "You'll do, Holly." Lorna looked back at the men. "Leave this to me."

In the next instant, Lorna smacked the closest male bum with her wooden spoon. One of the twins yelped. Only when he shouted, did Holly recognize Fraser's voice. "Mum, stop it. We're not children any more."

Lorna waved her spoon. "You could've fooled me." She looked to Fergus. "You, in particular, I'm disappointed about, Fergus Roger. You know what's waiting inside the cottage."

Holly dared to ask, "What's waiting inside the cottage?"

Lorna looked at her with mischief in her eyes. "You'll just have to come inside and see, child."

The Dragon's Dilemma

Holly didn't detect any worry or nervousness in Lorna's voice or eyes. She only hoped that meant it was a good surprise; Holly had had far too many of the other kind of late.

The twins stood up and brushed the dirt and grass from their clothes. Fergus was the first to speak up. "Aye, well, shall we go inside, then? I think Fraser learned his lesson."

Fraser shoved Fergus. "More like you learned yours."

Holly sighed again. She started to see Lorna MacKenzie in a whole new light; the dragonwoman was a saint for raising the three MacKenzie siblings.

Just as they started walking toward the cottage, the front door banged open. It was Faye MacKenzie.

Faye scowled and clapped her hands. "Are you two clowns quite finished? I'm starving. The sooner you get your arses in here, the sooner I can eat."

Fraser scowled. "Thanks for the greeting, sister."

Faye shrugged. "Do I ever greet you when I'm hungry? It's not like I'm going to start now." Faye turned. "Now, come on before I send Finn out here. He'll get you inside asap, especially as Arabella isn't feeling well."

Holly's curiosity piqued. "What's wrong with her? Maybe I can help?"

Lorna jumped in. "I doubt you can, lass. Arabella is having triplets and she's still in a bit of a shock."

Fraser frowned. "When the bloody hell did they find that out?"

Lorna answered, "Yesterday evening. So I'd recommend we all head inside as soon as possible. Finn and Ara came to support you and Holly, but Arabella isn't feeling all that social."

Holly moved to Fraser's side. After taking his hand, she tugged. "Come. I want to see if there's anything I can do to help her. Expectant mothers who find out they're having multiple births need to be watched closely. As much as I hate to say it, they often go into bouts of depression."

Lorna chimed in. "I was hoping you could help her. But don't let on that you know about the triplets yet. It'll ruin the surprise we have for you."

Holly looked askance at Lorna. "Okay. But can I at least introduce Fraser to my dad first?"

Lorna nodded. "Aye, but let's get a move on."

As Lorna herded them all inside, Fraser squeezed her hand. His touch helped to ground her.

There might not be rogue dragons dropping her out of the sky or holding her hostage inside a hospital, but it looked as if there would never be a dull moment on Lochguard.

~ ~ ~

As Fraser walked down the hall with his mate's hand in his and his brother right behind him, his tension eased away. Things looked to be going right with his family.

His dragon spoke up. *Of course they are. You and Holly worry too much.*

Not everything is as simple as you like to think.

Holly is our mate, which makes her a MacKenzie. You love her, so the others will, too. It's not complicated.

Fraser wanted to sigh, but knew it'd cause Holly and his mother to worry. Instead, he looked to Fergus and whispered, "What's the surprise?"

Fergus shook his head. "A thousand horses couldn't drag it out of me."

"I thought we weren't keeping secrets?"

"This is different—it's a surprise." Fergus mimicked zipping his lips closed and throwing away the key.

The next second, they walked into the dining room and Fraser blinked.

Not only was the table decorated with a table cloth, candles, and fancy china, a giant cake sat on a table off to the side, next to a large black box. There was also a few sheets of silver fabric draping from the ceiling, tied around the middle with cord. Sprigs of heather draped from each cord.

The room was decorated for a mating ceremony.

Fraser met Finn's eyes. Despite the circles under his cousin's eyes, they were also filled with humor and happiness. Finn waved a hand. "Surprise."

Holly frowned. "What's going on?"

Ross Anderson walked up to Holly. After kissing his daughter's cheek, Ross murmured, "They seem to think you're going to marry your dragon-shifter today."

Holly looked to Fraser. "Did you know about this?"

Fraser shook his head. "I swear I had no idea. But I guess this means I need an answer."

Faye growled out, "Well, she'd better give one because if there's not going to be a mating ceremony today, then I'm going to start eating."

Fraser ignored his sister and kept his attention on Holly. "What do you say, honey? If my family went to the trouble of throwing us a surprise mating ceremony, then I think it's safe to say they want you to be part of the family."

Lorna chimed in. "Why wouldn't we? It'll get you out of the house."

Everyone chuckled. Even Arabella smiled.

Fraser brushed Holly's cheek. "Will you agree, lass? Please?"

Holly opened her mouth, but then shut it again. Fraser's dragon snarled, but he managed to keep his beast in check.

His human looked away from him to her father. "I guess I should introduce my dragon-to-be, then. Dad, this is Fraser MacKenzie. Fraser, this is my dad, Ross Anderson."

Ross put out a hand and Fraser shook it. He met Ross's eyes. "Nice to meet you, sir."

Ross waved a hand. "Call me Ross. If I'm ever knighted, then you can call me Sir Ross. Not before."

Holly lightly hit her dad's arm. "Dad, not now."

Fraser grinned. "I think you're going to fit in just fine here, Ross. Just fine indeed."

Ross winked. "I reckon so, too. But I think my daughter has waited long enough to marry the lad of her heart. Take good care of her, son."

Fraser straightened his shoulder. "Aye, I will."

Holly raised an eyebrow. "Are you two quite done? I'd like to give Fraser my answer now."

Ross kissed his daughter's cheek again and then moved to take a seat. As soon as he did, Holly looked back up at him. "Yes, Fraser, I'll be your mate."

Fergus whistled as Lorna shouted, "Thank goodness."

Fraser ignored all of that to place his hands on Holly's waist. "Normally I'd offer you a silver band engraved with my name in the old dragon language, Mersae. But we'll just have to exchange the arm bands later."

Holly nodded, but then Fergus snapped his fingers. "Wait a minute."

Fraser scowled at his twin, who was picking up the large black box. "Can't you wait two bloody minutes, Fergus?"

Fergus raced over with a twinkle in his eye. "No, I can't." He opened the box to reveal two traditional mating bands. "I had these made for you, brother. Just in case."

Fraser touched the smaller one, engraved with his name. "You did this?"

Fergus nodded. "Aye. I didn't want there to be any doubt of my support for your mating."

Holly whispered, "Oh, Fergus."

Fergus moved his gaze to Holly. "I meant what I said yesterday, about wanting you to come home safe and sound. I can see how you make my brother happy, and that makes me happy. Just take care of him, aye?"

Holly nodded. "Of course."

Fergus winked at Holly before handing the box over to Fraser. Just this once, he'd let the wink slide.

Fraser's dragon growled. *As long as he doesn't wink at our female again.*

Next time, I'll let you out and you can tell him.

Content, his beast settled down. That was Fraser's cue to take the smaller silver band out of the box and hold it out. "With this band, I take you as my mate, Holly Anderson. With your stubborn, clever self at my side, I can face anything and anyone. I love you, Holly. Will you accept my claim?"

She smiled and took the band. "Yes, I do. Although I'm not sure I can wear it right now over my jumper."

He leaned close and whispered, "Just promise me you'll wear it later, when we're alone. That's my name in the old dragon language engraved on its surface and I want to see my name on your naked arm."

He watched her trace the symbols. "I should be offended, but I'm assuming the other band has my name on it, aye?" Fraser nodded. "Then I want to see my name on your arm, too."

"Good." He kissed her gently. "But first, you need to claim me in front of my family to complete the mating ceremony."

Holly lifted the larger silver arm band from the box and looked into his eyes again. "With this band, I take you as my mate, Fraser Moore MacKenzie. Aye, you're attractive, but the reason I love you is for your humor, dedication to those you love, and stubbornness. Life will never be boring with you and I look forward to whatever adventures may lay ahead."

He raised an eyebrow. "Anything else you'd like to add? Maybe about love?"

Holly rolled her eyes. "Of course I love you, you bloody man. Though I sometimes wonder why."

Fraser tossed the box aside and plucked the band from Holly's fingers before drawing her close. "Just ask me if I accept your claim and then I can kiss you properly."

Holly tilted her head. "Not sure I want my dad to watch that."

Fraser growled. "Holly."

She laughed. "Okay, okay. Fraser MacKenzie, will you accept my claim?"

After saying, "Yes," he descended on Holly's lips. As he held his female close, his family cheered and clapped. What had started out as a disaster had turned into a happy ending for not just Fraser, but Holly and her father as well.

Dear Reader:

I hope you enjoyed Fraser and Holly's story. I love all of my dragons, but I really enjoyed writing theirs. There are a lot more Lochguard books coming in the future, so I hope you stay along for the ride. Finn is going to have his hands full in more ways than one...you can turn the page for an excerpt from the next book, about Fergus, and see what I mean!

Also, if you haven't yet read my other dragons series, about the Stonefire Dragons, then what are you waiting for? You can check out the first book, *Sacrificed to the Dragon*, which is available in paperback.

Oh, and if you have a chance, would you leave a review? It would help me out a lot.

Thanks so much for reading!

With Gratitude,
Jessie Donovan

The Dragon Guardian
(Lochguard Highland Dragons #2)

Gina MacDonald may be pregnant and on the run, but she will do anything to protect her unborn child—even go up against a dragon-shifter. While hiding in the wilds of the Scottish Highlands, she soon notices the black dragon perched on the nearby hills. She debates if he is related to her past or not, but then a pain overcomes her and the dragon finally swoops down to help. Despite her determination to stay clear of all dragon-shifter males, his touch not only helps ease her tension, it sets her skin on fire.

Fergus MacKenzie protects his clan by collecting information and warning them of threats. When a redheaded American shows up out of the blue along a nearby lake, he watches her to find out more. However, when he sees her bend over in pain, he flies down to help her. Afterward, he should walk away. But he can't stop thinking about her green eyes and addictive touch. Both man and beast want her more than anything in their lives.

As Fergus learns more of Gina's past, he knows she will bring danger to his clan. Torn between protecting his family and following his heart, will Gina and Fergus be able to find a happy ending? Or, will danger force Fergus to choose between love and clan?

Excerpt from *The Dragon Guardian*:

CHAPTER ONE

Fergus MacKenzie sat on top of one of the hills surrounding Loch Shin in his dragon form and adjusted his grip with his talons. Despite waiting for the last hour to see the redheaded human female, she had yet to step outside.

That shouldn't surprise him given that it was January in the Scottish Highlands. The wind and chill in the north wasn't for the fragile. While everything he'd learned about Gina MacDonald over the last few weeks spoke of her strength, she was also heavily pregnant. For all he knew, she could be giving birth right that second.

Fergus's inner dragon spoke up. *Look. Her door is opening. Maybe we can actually talk to her today.*

Fergus watched as Gina stepped outside and headed for the chicken coop. The wind whipped her long, curly red hair behind her and the human pulled her jacket closer around her body.

His beast spoke up again. *Today might be our last chance for a while. We should speak with her.*

Fergus wanted to talk with the human more than he would ever admit to anyone. Not even his twin brother knew how Gina had invaded Fergus's dreams since the very first day he'd seen her. Dreams that more often than not had both of them naked and tangled in the sheets.

Pushing away those thoughts, Fergus answered his dragon. *We have no claim on her. I can't risk a confrontation with the father of her child.*

His dragon huffed. *We haven't been able to find out anything about him. If he's unwilling to protect his female, then he has no claim on her.*

Not true. What if he's in the armed forces and currently stationed overseas?

That is a very small possibility.

It could still be true.

Fergus debated returning to his home on Clan Lochguard when the female gripped her belly and hunched over. Without thinking, Fergus glided down to Gina's house. The sheep ran to the far side of one of the pens and he landed. Imagining his wings shrinking into his back, his talons changing into fingers, and his snout taking the shape of a human face, Fergus stood in his human form five seconds later. Uncaring about his nakedness, he rushed over to the female and shouted, "Are you all right, lass?"

The woman glanced over. Her eyes widened before quickly darting down to his cock and back up to his face. Taking a deep breath, she stood up and frowned. "You're the dragon who's been watching me for weeks."

He took a step closer. "That doesn't matter right now. If you need help, then tell me. I can ring a doctor or your husband."

"I don't have a husband." Gina rubbed her belly and then let out a sigh. "But the damn spell has passed, so care to tell me why you're standing in my yard buck naked?"

Just like the first time he'd heard her speak, he found her American accent foreign yet endearing. "Aren't you in labor?"

"No. I was trying to keep my food down. The smell of chicken scat makes me want to puke."

His dragon chimed in. *Get her inside. I don't like her out in the cold.*

Fergus had asked the same question a million times before, but decided to try once more. *Why do you care so much?*

Just get her inside first.

Fergus motioned with a hand toward the door. "Let's get you out of the cold, get me a blanket or a towel so I can cover some of my nakedness, and I'll answer whatever questions you might have."

The corner of Gina's mouth ticked up. "Oh, really? Whatever I want? I can't wait to make the big, bad dragonman squirm."

Ignoring her tease, he moved to her side and placed a hand on her lower back. Despite the layers of clothing between her skin and his, a small jolt shot up his arm. He couldn't remember the last time that had happened with a female. "I assure you I don't squirm. Now, let's get inside. It's bloody freezing out here."

Gina started walking and humor danced in her eyes. "Are you going to use that as an excuse for the size of your penis?"

He blinked. "What?"

"Well, just about every guy I've ever met says the cold makes him shrivel." She paused and leaned over. "But in your case, that makes me wonder just how big you are when it's warm."

Fergus cleared his throat. He wasn't about to allow the lass to disarm him. "The first time I met you, whilst in dragon form, you said you knew the dragon clan in Virginia back in America. I'm fairly confident the rumors about dragon-shifters and their cocks are the same there as here."

"Maybe. But I like the idea of making you uncomfortable."

He frowned. "Care to tell me why?"

Gina laid a hand on her stomach. "It's fun. And believe me, it's been months since I've had any fun."

~~~

Gina MacDonald wasn't sure what had come over her. The black dragon constantly watching from the hills had irritated her over the passing weeks. Who was he to spy on her? Not only that, but he never had the balls to talk with her so she could find out why he was there. She didn't think Travis had sent him.

No. She refused to think of that bastard.

And yet she was spilling her guts to the Scottish dragonman. Sure, it was true she hadn't had any fun since her mother had shipped her off to Scotland, but it was hardly something you told a stranger.

The dragonman pushed lightly against her back and Gina nearly moaned at his touch. She would give her left arm for a massage.

The mysterious dragonman spoke up, his yummy Scottish accent making her want to shiver. "Aye, well, sometimes fun has to wait. You're about to have a child, so get used to it."

She glanced over at the tall Scot at her side. "What, do you have a brood of five kids at home and are speaking from experience?"

"I don't have any children."

His tone was a little too controlled. The smart thing would be to drop it, but Gina didn't like unanswered questions. "But you do want them someday."

The dragonman faltered in his step. His dark blue eyes met hers and she drew in a breath. It seemed dragon-shifters were attractive on both sides of the pond.

THE DRAGON'S DILEMMA

Clenching her fingers, Gina pushed aside her attraction. After all, that was what had landed her in the current situation.

They reached the door and the dragonman turned the knob. Gina debated the negatives of inviting a strange man into her house. But then the wind gusted. Longing for warmth, she decided to trust her gut that the man wouldn't hurt her, and she stepped inside. "Come in, then, Mister...?"

"MacKenzie. Fergus MacKenzie."

Gina snorted. "You can't get much more Scottish than that."

Fergus clicked the door closed. "Fergus is a strong name. It means man of strength or man of force."

She put on a mock Scottish accent. "Aye, and it's a verra bonny name, too."

She didn't think it was possible, but Fergus frowned deeper than before. "We're doing accents then, aye?" His voice turned into a high-pitched Valley Girl accent. "I'm, like, so super cool. And, like, you're hella crazy."

She managed to keep it together until Fergus waggled his eyebrows and Gina barked out a laugh. "You should talk like that all of the time. It suits you."

His voice returned to normal. "But Americans love it when I roll my 'r's."

Not wanting to acknowledge it was true, Gina turned, picked up a blanket and tossed it at Fergus. "Cover yourself and I'll pour some juice."

From the corner of her eye, she watched Fergus wrap the blanket around his lean hips. The tattoo on one of his upper arms bunched and flexed as he did it.

Dragon-shifters really were too attractive for their own good.

Not now, Gina. We learned our lesson, remember? Keep it together.

271

Clearing her throat, she went into the kitchen. Just as she was about to lean against the counter and take a breather, Fergus waltzed into the room as if he owned it. Spotting her against the counter, he muttered, "Bloody stubborn female."

Before Gina could reply, he was next to her. Picking her up as if she weighed nothing, she cried out, "Put me down."

Fergus adjusted his grip. "No."

She slapped his chest. "As I told you when we first met, I have ways to defend myself against dragon-shifters."

"Aye? Well, if carrying you to a chair offends you, I wonder how any male came close enough to get you with child."

"Are you trying to insult me?"

Fergus gently rested her on the kitchen chair and remained bent over so his eyes were level with hers. His pupils flashed to slits and back before the corner of his mouth ticked up. "Lass, I have a younger sister and a twin brother. Believe me, when I insult you, you'll know it."

She opened her mouth and Fergus pressed her lips together with his warm, rough fingers—fingers that no doubt could do wicked things to her body.

Gina blinked. She needed to get Fergus MacKenzie away from her or she would most definitely do something stupid. Given her track record over the last year, she really didn't need to add any other mistakes to her list.

And spending time with Fergus would be a mistake she couldn't afford to make. Not with a child on the way she needed to protect.

Unable to speak, she raised her eyebrows. Fergus grinned and she stopped breathing. She loved how his eyes crinkled at the corners.

THE DRAGON'S DILEMMA

Fergus finally spoke up. "I'm going to release your lips on one condition—you promise to sit here whilst I fetch you some juice and a snack. Nod if you agree."

She should just nod and be polite. She really should.

Yet Gina didn't like Fergus's commanding tone. It was almost as if he expected her to follow his every word without complaint.

He may be taller and with a lot more muscle, but she hadn't come this far in life only to have someone try to take control.

Drawing on her high school years of drama club, Gina closed her eyes and moaned as if she were in pain. Fergus instantly released her lips. "What's wrong, Gina?"

Rather than think about how he knew her name, she hooked her leg against the back of his knee and yanked him forward. Fergus fell to the ground. Before he could make a move, she pinned his head between her legs. "Okay, dragonman. Let's get a few things straight right now. One, it's not nice to invade someone's personal space without their permission. Do it again, and I won't be so lenient."

Despite her best effort to sound badass, amusement danced in Fergus's eyes. "And I assume there's a number two?"

She growled. "You're going to tell me why you've been watching me and how you know my name."

"Actually, that's three things in total."

"Are you always this annoying?"

"There's nothing annoying about pointing out the details. I do it every day for my job."

For some reason, she wanted to ask what his job was. Fergus was a lot different from Travis, who had been a Protector.

Then she remembered Fergus shushing her lips like a child and Gina leaned closer to Fergus's face. "That's nice and all, but how about you answer my questions? The longer you take, the greater the chance I could go into labor. You probably don't want to be under me when my water breaks."

––––––––––––––––––

Want to read the rest?
The Dragon Guardian is available in paperback.

For exclusive content and updates, sign up for my newsletter at:

http://www.jessiedonovan.com

Author's Note

I hope you enjoyed Fraser and Holly's story. I fell in love with Clan Lochguard while writing *Healed by the Dragon* and writing about them in *The Dragon's Dilemma* was so much fun. The Scottish clan is a little crazy and over the top; they are pretty much the opposite of Stonefire. I love all of my dragon-shifters, but as a writer, it's always fun to tackle something a little different from time to time.

If you're wondering about the next book, it's about Fergus MacKenzie and a certain pregnant redhead. I'm still trying to decide the title, but the opening has already popped into my head and writing it should be easy. I don't have an exact release date, but it will be out in early 2016. Make sure to sign-up for my newsletter for the latest information.

As always, I have some people to thank. I don't know what I would do with my editor, Becky Johnson of Hot Tree Editing, or my cover artist, Clarissa Yeo of Yocla Designs. Both of these ladies have had a huge impact on my writing career. Becky has made me a stronger writer and Clarissa has helped to create the brand that is Jessie Donovan. I am extremely grateful to work with them both.

I also wish to thank my beta readers—Donna, Iliana, and Alyson. They give my stories the final polish. The small things these ladies point out are amazing and I love that they tell me the truth. It's rare to find such dedicated and helpful people and I hope they know how much I appreciate them.

Lastly, I wish to thank all of my readers. You make writing full-time possible. Not only that, many of you help brighten my day with pictures, comments, or just talking about my characters with me. Make sure to join my fan group on Facebook. The members of that group helped to pick the title of this story and I love to share the writing process with them.

Thanks again for reading and spreading the word about my books. Until the next book, happy reading!

ABOUT THE AUTHOR

Jessie Donovan wrote her first story at age five, and after discovering *The Dragonriders of Pern* series by Anne McCaffrey in junior high, she realized people actually wanted to read stories like those floating around inside her head. From there on out, she was determined to tap into her over-active imagination and write a book someday.

After living abroad for five years and earning degrees in Japanese, Anthropology, and Secondary Education, she buckled down and finally wrote her first full-length book. While that story will never see the light of day, it laid the world-building groundwork of what would become her debut paranormal romance, *Blaze of Secrets*. In late 2014, she became a *New York Times* bestseller.

Jessie loves to interact with readers, and when not traipsing around some foreign country on a shoestring, can often be found on Facebook. Check out her pages below:

http://www.facebook.com/JessieDonovanAuthor

And don't forget to sign-up for her newsletter to receive sneak peeks and inside information. You can sign-up on her website:

http://www.jessiedonovan.com